Johan Padan
and the Discovery
of the Americas

Johan Padan and the Discovery of the Americas

DARIO FO

Translated from the Italian by
Ron Jenkins

with the assistance of
Stefania Taviano

Grove Press
New York

Originally published in Italian and Italian-dialect bilingual
edition by Giunti Publishers as *Johan Padan a la Descoverta de le
Americhe*

Published simultaneously in Canada
Printed in the United States of America

FIRST EDITION

Library of Congress Cataloging-in-Publication Data

Fo, Dario.
    [Johan Padan a la descoverta de le Americhe. English]
    Johan Padan and the discovery of the Americas / Dario Fo;
translated from the Italian by Ron Jenkins with the assistance
of Stefania Taviano.
        p. cm.
    ISBN 0-8021-3777-6
    1. America—Discovery and exploration—Fiction.
2. Indians of North America—First contact with Europeans—
Fiction.   3. Indians of North America—Florida—Fiction.
4. Florida—History—To 1565—Fiction.   I. Jenkins, Ronald Scott.
II. Taviano, Stefania.
PQ4866.O2 J64313 2001
853'.914—dc21   00-048377

Grove Press
841 Broadway
New York, NY 10003

01 02 03 04   10 9 8 7 6 5 4 3 2 1

Johan Padan
and the Discovery
of the Americas

Translator's Preface

"Dario Fo and the Memory of the Body"

"Memory . . . everything begins from there. Not only for remembering things, but for learning the significance, the place, and the time that is inside and behind every word. I'm an actor . . . for me memory has to enter through the mouth . . . to listen means to move your lips, your feet, articulate your face, stretch your throat, learn to speak . . . to become the instrument of your own memory, as if you're looking for a piece of music on a guitar. . . . Then your imagination takes you a step farther. It enables you to remember more."

—Dario Fo

Dario Fo's monologues are drenched in memory, not the passive verbal memory of intellectual detachment but the active muscular memory of a man who sees the world in constant motion. The language of Fo's texts is born of memories that entered his mouth and found form in his body. Fo's identity as a writer is inseparable from his identity as a physical actor. Fo moves when he writes, playing his body like a guitar, coaxing syntax from his muscles the way a musician coaxes chords from vibrating strings.

The opening lines of *Johan Padan and the Discovery of the Americas* are typical of Fo's kinetic style. They are shaped by his idiosyncratic research into sixteenth-century explorations of the Americas. Fo's memory has distilled dozens of history books, diaries, letters, and memoirs into a cinematic montage of physical action. Sailors are shouting as they prepare to set sail. "Faster! Faster! Let go the moorings! Haul up the yardarm! Hoist the mainsail! Weigh anchor! Heave away!" The mariners are hoisting, heaving, and hauling as their ship is moving out to the open sea. Fo's narrator plays all the parts, giving voice to each of the sailor's cries with a different rhythm and tone. There is urgency. There are vivid visual details. And, above all, there is action. Officers give orders. The crew throw their bodies

into the work. The sails are unfurled. The ship crashes through the waves.

When Fo or any other actor performs this opening sequence, the action is embodied in gestures performed by one man playing all the parts. On stage this creates the illusion of a ship full of bustling mariners, but an astute reader can see the movements encoded in Fo's text even without the help of an actor. The words themselves are a blueprint for action, action that is rooted in the sources of Fo's physical memory.

The first thing Fo did after reading about the exploration of the Americas was to draw pictures of it, transforming the words of history into dozens of drawings. These visual sketches became the repository of Fo's memory and he used them on stage as cue cards when he first began to perform the story of Johan Padan in public. At that point the written narrative was in a state of flux. The paintings triggered memories that inspired the physical and verbal improvisations Fo presented to his first audiences. Eventually Fo, with the help of his wife and collaborator Franca Rame, began to write and edit the text in a language full of action. Fo's drawings abound in swirling movement. The bodies he depicts are captured in an astonishing array of dynamic positions, so it is not surprising that the memories triggered by these drawings would be expressed by Fo in words that pulsate with a physical drive of their own.

Although Fo's play seems to be written in the form of a monologue, it is actually constructed as a series of overlapping and interlocking dialogues. Fo makes this clear from the start when he steps out of the story to directly address the audience with comments on how difficult it may be to understand the nautical terms in the opening sequence. This device enables Fo to establish a dialogue with the audience that makes them aware of his presence as a modern actor, which overlaps with his presence as Johan Padan, the sixteenth-century narrator of the story. The dialogue between Fo, the actor/writer, and Padan, the character, is one of many submerged conversations that gives this play a layered resonance. Like Fo, Padan is a storyteller and a clown. In one episode Padan recounts an apocryphal version of the Gospels that recalls Fo's epic retelling of the Bible in his 1969 masterpiece *Mistero Buffo.* The self-referential dialogue between Fo and his central character is enriched by the dialogue between Fo's words and his drawings, and by the dialogue between the text and the body of the actor who performs the play (or who is imagined to be performing the play by the reader).

The most controversial dialogue embedded in Fo's monologue is the dialogue between history and the imagination, between Fo's version of the encounter between Indians and Europeans and the official version taught in history classes. Fo's sly notion that imagination "enables you to remember more" suggests that imagination is a necessary element in historical memory, allowing us to remember things that might not have actually happened but that are a necessary component of historical truth. Fo invents outrageous scenes to make history vivid to the senses: a lesson on how the American Indians cooked iguanas; an acrobatic account of making love on a hammock; a battle chronicle in which the Conquistadors are vanquished by fireworks. Fo's variations on history are like musical riffs in a jazz improvisation. The notes don't exist until the musician makes them up, but once he plays them it becomes clear that they were inevitable.

Ultimately Dario Fo is a jazz artist of memory. He composes his texts on stage, while his body is engaged in an impromptu act of physical remembering. Sculpted into the syntax of each phrase is a memory of the improvised gestures and rhythms that first brought it to life.

While making my first rough translation of *Johan Padan* I spent a few weeks with Fo and Rame at their summer home in Cesenatico, Italy. Fo performed much of the text for me as we worked together, demonstrating in miniature the gestures that accompanied the monologue on stage. This encounter brought back memories of my first experience working with Fo in 1986 as the onstage simultaneous transla-

tor of his American tour of *Mistero Buffo.* Working with Fo in the theater and in his living room I have learned that the music of his language is inextricably linked to the actions it elicits in an actor's body. While I translated Fo's texts into English in front of a live audience I watched him translate the words into the kinetic language of his body, and I was compelled to come up with phrases that matched the flow of his physical action. The choreography of the text's performance was embedded in the rhythmic structure of the language.

By inviting me to serve as his simultaneous interpreter on the stage, Fo introduced me to the techniques that are essential to translating his language on the page. By inviting me to his home to translate *Johan Padan,* Fo gave me a refresher course. I had already assimilated the rhythms of his voice during our work together on stage, but watching him read small portions of the text at his home reaffirmed the intricacy of its physical details. In the intimacy of his living room Fo had no need to act out the narrative with his body, but he could not stop himself from accompanying his readings with tiny gestures, subliminal traces of actions that were encoded into the language when it was first conceived. The sounds of the words were charged with a physical memory that he acknowledged with delicate hand gestures of which he was probably not aware. His fingers became the sails of ships or the path of fireworks across the sky. Each phrase was a pictograph, and his muscles responded by constructing a sequence of miniature hieroglyphs to match the action. Fo was remembering the text the way he had written it, with his body. I have tried to translate it the same way, with sensitivity to the kinetic and pictorial origins of the story, and with hopes that readers may occasionally have the urge to dance out a few passages with their fingers.

—Ron Jenkins, 2000

(Ron Jenkins, a former circus clown and graduate of the Ringling Brothers Clown College, is chair and artistic director of the theater department at Wesleyan University. He began his work with Dario Fo in 1985 with the support of a Sheldon postdoctoral fellowship from Harvard University. This translation was completed with the support of a Guggenheim Fellowship.)

Author's Preface

First of all, you should know that this is not a woeful tale of Indian massacres perpetrated by the Conquistadors. And it is not the usual story of a defeated race. On the contrary, it is an epic chronicle of Indians who were victorious.

There are two basic types of narratives about the discovery and conquest of the Americas: those written by scribes who followed the explorers and Conquistadors and on the other hand, the stories of the unknown co-protagonists, who didn't really count, the "no-tagonists," the lowliest of the troops, who recounted adventures they had experienced when they found themselves right in the middle of the conquests . . . in the role of prisoners, or even slaves.

One of these unfortunate adventurers was Johan Padan, a kind of zany scoundrel who was on intimate terms with the gallows. He lived in the 1500s and found himself, in spite of himself, taking part in the discovery of the Americas.

There really was a Johan Padan. Perhaps his name wasn't actually Johan Padan, but his actions are authentic. In fact they are based on dozens of true stories told in the first person by low-level supporting players from all the countries of Europe.

When all the desperate people, who didn't count for anything in the official history of the discoveries, arrived in the Indies and made contact with the equally desperate locals, they discovered that they could count for something. In fact, they counted for a lot.

Johan Padan, a man of the mountains, doesn't like sailing, but he finds himself, in spite of himself, forced to take a long voyage. He ends up as a prisoner of cannibals who fatten him up with the intention of eating him. He is saved by a stroke of fortune, and becomes a shaman, chief wizard, healer . . . and is named "the son of the rising sun." And on top of it all, he is compelled to teach Catechism and the Gospels to thousands of Indians. Terribly apocryphal Gospels, of course.

The malcontent members of the sailing crews who went over to the side of the conquered are more numerous than we can imagine. And keep in mind that they did not settle for simply surviving. They made themselves into strategists and military leaders who helped the Indians hold out a little longer against the invasions of the Christians.

Sia ben chiaro che questo, innanzitutto, non è il racconto lamentoso sulle stragi perpetrate dai conquistatori sugli indios. Non è la storia dei soliti perdenti. E', anzi, l'epopea di un popolo di idios vincenti.

Esistono due tipi fondamentali di cronache sulla scoperta e conquista delle Americhe: quelle stese da scrivani al seguito degli scopritori e dei conquistatori e, dall'altra parte, il racconto dei co-protagonisti che non contano, i "nullagonisti", gli zozzoni di truppa, che ci vengono a raccontare le loro avventure vissute da molto vicino, spesso, addirittura, ritrovandosi nel bel mezzo dei conquistati, nel ruolo di prigionieri . . . , e magari, schiavi.

Uno di questi avventurieri sventurati è Johan Padan, una specie di zanni scellerato, pendaglio da forca, vissuto nel '500 . . . che, suo malgrado, s'è trovato dentro la scoperta delle Americhe.

Johan Padan è veramente vissuto, forse il suo nome non è proprio quello di Johan Padan, ma le sue gesta sono autentiche, infatti sono tratte da decine di storie vere raccontate in prima persona dai comprimari di bassa forza provenienti da tutti i paesi d'Europa.

Tutta gente disperata che non conta niente nella storia ufficiale delle scoperte, ma che, giunta nelle Indie, al contatto con i disperati locali, scopre di poter contare qualcosa, anzi, moltissimo!

Johan Padan, uomo delle montagne, non ama navigare ma si trova, suo malgrado, costretto al grande viaggio. Si ritrova prigioniero dei cannibali che lo allevano all'ingrasso con l'intento di mangiarselo. Si salva per un colpo di fortuna e diventa sciamano, capo stregone, medico e vien nominato 'figlio del sole che nasce'. E' costretto, oltretutto, ad insegnare la dottrina e le storie dei vangeli a migliaia di Indios.

Vangeli terribilmente apocrifi, naturalmente.

Più numerosi di quanto non ci si immagini furono i marinai dì ciurma, le mezze tacche di truppa, che si trovarono a passare dalla parte dei conquistati. E sia chiaro, non si accontentarono di tirare a campare, ma si adoperarono come strateghi e ammaestratori militari affinché gli indios riuscissero a resistere più o meno lungamente all'invasione dei cristiani.

We know the names of a few of these men, most notably Guerriero, Altavilla, Cabeza de Vaca, Hans Staten.

But today you will have the extraordinary opportunity of meeting one such man in person, and hearing from his own mouth the story of the most mythical of all these renegade lowlifes: Johan Padan, "the son of the rising sun."

—Dario Fo

Noi conosciamo i nomi di alcuni di loro, i più noti sono Guerriero, Altavilla, Cabeza de Vaca, Han Staden.

Ma oggi vi diamo la straordinaria possibilità di conoscere di persona e dalla sua viva voce il racconto del più mitico fra tutti gli zozzoni rinnegati: **Johan Padan "fiol del sol che nase":** Johan Padan "figlio del sole che nasce".

Dario Fo

Prologue

Johan Padan is a character we also find in the commedia dell'arte, called by other names: Giovan, Giani, Zanni. This Johan is a kind of Ruzzante, more precisely a Zany, the prototype of the mask of Harlequin, who, as we will see, was born in the valleys of Brescia and Bergamo, and finds himself literally propelled to the Indies when he is engaged on a ship that is part of Columbus's fourth expedition.

To tell the truth, I had not even thought of writing this text, let alone encountering a character of such complexity, until the summer of 1991 when I was invited to Spain, Seville to be exact, with Franca, to make a presentation for a theater full of critics, theater writers, actors, and cultural experts about the structure of *Isabella, Three Tall Ships, and a Con Man,* the play I was supposed to present in the spring of 1992 at the exposition in honor of Columbus. It was a play that I had staged with Franca about twenty-nine years earlier (1963), for the opening of the theatrical season at the Odeon in Milan. At its debut and for the duration of its tour, the play aroused scandals, consensus, sensation, and polemics, especially on the part of reactionaries.

Today the behavior of theater audiences has changed a great deal. People participate with tranquillity and serenity, sitting in their chairs without living the situation. Their listening is passive, digestive . . . like televison.

On that occasion in Seville, I talked about our debut in Genoa, the native city of Columbus, where the press published harsh criticisms of the play in defense of the famous explorer, whom I had treated severely, presenting him as a cunning swindler, cynic, and even a thief who wasn't beyond a little robbery.

There was a great uproar. We had been warned that many spectators were coming to the theater armed with a variety of vegetables—oversized cabbages, tomatoes, and zucchinis—to throw at us. We began the play tensely, waiting for the insults, the raspberries, and . . . the vegetables. But instead we were thrown off balance: after a few minutes of perplexity, the audience began smiling and then letting themselves go in fits of laughter, with lots of belly laughs and guffaws. Applauding, they shouted: "Yes, he's *one of us*!!"

The people of Genoa had a great sense of humor, and they still do. The fascists did not demonstrate such good humor at the premiere in Rome. At the Valle theater they even tried to climb up on the stage and attack us, but the response of our actors, supported by the stage technicians and a good part of the audience, was enough to chase them away.

But let's get back to the incident in Seville. I recounted the plot of the play to that audience of Spanish critics and cultural experts, and I reminded them that almost twenty years earlier, under the Franco regime, a company called "Els Joglars" had tried to stage the show in Barcelona, but they never made it to opening night. The entire company was arrested at the end of the dress rehearsal. The actors ended up in prison, together with the director, the stage technicians, and even the prompter . . . that will teach him!

That audience froze when they heard my punch line. Not a laugh. On the contrary, they looked at me like I was some kind of imperti-nent provocateur. Unperturbed, I continued talking about the diaspora of the Jews who were thrown out of Spain at the time when Colum-bus was getting ready to depart for his discovery of the Americas. I told how at the end of the 1400s Isabella had organized a veritable plun-dering of the possessions of the Jews. There were a great many Jews in Spain at that time, about two hundred and fifty thousand. Before being thrown out they were stripped of all their possessions, furniture, and real estate, and then sent away, literally naked, to various countries throughout Europe, including Italy. Livorno, for the record, was born as a result of this tragic event. The deportation of two hundred and fifty thousand Jews brought millions of gold Maravedis to the Queen and the state treasury. It was a staggering sum . . . something like the entire public debt of the Italian government.

At this point I realized that I was facing a genuine wall of hostility. Then I discovered why. Like a true pilgrim I didn't know that precisely during those days a campaign had begun in Spain to convince the Vatican to sanctify Queen Isabella, known as La Cattolica ("The Catholic").

It was a gaffe of epic proportions.

Someone passed by my shoulder and whispered, "Be careful, they still have the fires stoked up under the stakes." I made an im-promptu attempt to recapture control of the situation and said, "This is only one of the ideas I had in mind. The truth is that I would actually enjoy much more . . . staging for you . . . something else. It's a story about the adventurous voyages of a poor devil, a sailor in rags, a kind of Ruzzante who ends up in the Indies in spite of himself. He travels with Columbus and extraordinary things happen to him. It is the story of the discovery of the Americas, not as it was seen from the castle, but from the under deck, that is from the viewpoint of a lowlife who is one step away from the gallows." I spoke of this character with great enthusiasm . . . improvising. All of a sudden the climate in the room was turned around. There was an unexpected burst of applause, accompanied by a collective sigh of relief: "Beautiful! We like that! It's a truly thrilling story!"

When I returned to Italy I threw myself into researching texts about the discovery of the Americas written by protagonists who were almost unknown. That was how I discovered the account—practically a ship's journal—of a sailor who had the slightly grotesque name of Cabeza de Vaca. His peripatetic adventures seemed to be almost exact duplicates of those that I had recounted in Seville. I found another autobiographical chronicle, very similar to that of Cabeza de Vaca, written by Hans Staten, a German sailor who had also found himself in the Indies and lived the life of Robinson Crusoe. He was imprisoned by Indians, who fed him, caressed him, and fattened him up with the intention of eating him. Researching adventures narrated by sailors of the lower ranks I came across Sigala, a Genoan who had sailed with Columbus, arrived in Florida, and become head of a tribe of Maciuco Indians. I also met a sailor from Palos: Gonzalo Guerriero, who deserted from the expedition of Tristan do Cabaco and ended up as a prisoner of the Incas, who after having condemned him to death had second thoughts and elected him their sacred wizard. And finally I discovered the tales of Michele da Cuneo, who was the right-hand man and confidant of Columbus. This sailor was an unbiased witness to events that were terrifying, especially given the pitiless realism with which they are expressed.

What struck me most about da Cuneo's account was the invention of a language that availed itself of all the idioms of the Romance languages, a kind of lexical pastiche used at that time by all the sailors of the Mediterranean, a mixture of numerous languages and dialects: Lombardian, Venetian, Catalanian, Castiglian, Provençal, Portuguese . . . and also a little Arabic, just for the fun of it!

I said to myself; "This is my man! I'll call him Johan Padan and I'll make him speak this grammelot of the seaports."

Naturally the lexically unbiased spectators gifted with exceptional imaginations will have the advantage of understanding the punch lines even before I finish speaking them. The rest of you, the normal ones, will laugh a little later . . . at the end of the wave.

The story begins at the moment in which our Johan Padan is fleeing Venice and the persecution of the Tribunal of the Inquisition. He is on a ship, a brigantine that is pulling out of the port of Serenissima, heading for open seas. We hear the shouts of the sailors as they encourage one another to set the sails.

Part One

Faster! Faster! Let go the moorings! Haul up the yardarm! Hoist the mainsail! Weigh anchor! Heave away! All sails full! Heave away! Crank the winch! We're moving. We're moving. Away from Giudecca! Away from the lagoon. Away from Venice. Faster! Unfurl the jib!

(A woman once stopped me at this point and said: "Oh God, is the whole story going to be in this kind of language?" But after all, this is the way sailors talked in the port of Venice in the sixteenth century. You want it to make sense! I'm the one performing it and I don't understand, so how can you expect to?)

Oh, how the wind rips and billows the sails . . . we're moving . . . we're moooooving . . . ! Out! We're out! Out on the open sea. I'm saved! Saved! I, Johan Padan, am saved!

Saved from what?

From the Inquisition! From the gallows . . . from being burned alive! The agents of the Most Holy Tribunal got it into their heads that I was the one who was mixed up with that witch.

I'm talking about the girl that the guards took away in chains . . . Yes, the one they say casts spells and enchantments . . . has her own pitchforks . . . sticks pins into puppets . . . strangles cats and scrutinizes their intestines to foretell the future . . . speaks to the devil . . . speaks also with the dead . . . with the spirits . . .

What exaggeration! Ha! Talking to the dead! . . . To the devil . . . well, maybe now and then . . . just for fun.

It's not true that I was mixed up with her . . . I just stayed close to her because I was in love. Well, yes, I was a sort of assistant to the girl, but only as a pretext, so that I could stay with her.

If you only knew how much she made me languish with jealousy . . . because she, that beautiful witch, always had so many doting lovers under her petticoats! And they courted her with countless gifts. Princes! Monsignors! Senators of Serenissima. There were ten of them from Serenissima courting her! . . . Not all ten! . . . Two or three of the ten . . . but she wasn't a whore!

Vaji! Vaji! Vàlsa l'ormégg! Arma la rànda! Su ol trinchètt! Jléva l'àncora! Sü! Aìssa! Slarga tüto! Aìssa! Va col paranèll! Se va, se va! Via de la Giudecca! Via della Lagüna! Via de Venéssia . . . Vaji! Vaji col fiòco! . . .

A questo punto, qualche giorno fa una signora ha esclamato: "Oddio, non sarà tutto in questa lingua qua?!". Ma d'altra parte, questo è il linguaggio dei marinai del porto di Venezia nel '500, volete capirlo? . . . Non lo capisco io che lo recito e pretendete di capirlo voi?!

Oh, che ol vénto ol lira e sgiónfia le véle . . . se va . . . se vaahaa! Föra! Sémo föra! Föra all'avèrto. Són salvo! Salvo! Mi, Johan Padan son salvo!

"Salvo de chi?"

"De l'Inquisisiün! De la fórca . . . de vèss brüsàt! Quèi del Tribünàl Santìssirno i s'éra metüd in mént che mi fuèssi quèl che ghé tegnéva man a 'sta stròlega. Sunt 'dré a dì de la stròlega che le gùàrdie avéva portàt via in cadéne . . . Ma sì, quèla che i dise che la fa le factüre, i incantesimi! Che la gh'ha i furcùn, che enfrìca i spilóni deréntro i pupàss, che i stròsa i gati e po' ghe scrüta le vessìche per endovinàrghe le futuràrie . . . che ghé parla col demonio, che ghé parla anca coi mòrti . . . coi spìriti . . .

Esageràt! Ah, ah, ah! Parlare co' i morti! . . . Col diàvolo . . . quàlche vòlta . . . così per dire.

No' è véra che mi ghé tegnìvi man . . . mi ghé stàvi apprèso soltànto perchè so' innamoràt. Beh sì, ghé févi anca un pòco de assistént a 'sta fiòla, ma solo pór ol pretèsto de stàrghe insèma a lée.

Savèsse come la mé faséva deslenguìre de gialusìa, che lée, 'sta bèla stròliga, gh'avéva intórno a le sotàne, tanti de quèli servénti amorós! E tüti ghé faséva un fraco de cortisanerìe e de regali. Prènse, adiritüra! Monsignori! Senatori dè la Serenissima. A gh'era i dièse de la Serenissima che ghé fasévan la curt! . . . No' tüte e dièse! . . . Dóe o trè de i dièse . . . ma no' era pütàna!

1

It's just that when she was near me, she looked only at me . . . she talked to me with words that would intoxicate you, the kind you invent while making love.

But oh, what love!

She taught me all the tricks about foretelling the future by reading the stars . . . the moon! I remember once, we were stretched out on the sands of Paranello island . . . it was night . . . it was summer . . . we were naked and making love . . . when all of a sudden she said:
"Stop!!"
"What is it?"
"Look at the moon!"

Sojaménte che quando a l'era tacàda a mi, no' la vedéa altro che mi . . . me parlava a mi co' quèi paròli d'enciochìrte che s'envénta fando l'amóre. Ma ohi, che amóre!
La m'ha insegnà tüti i truchi per endovenàr quèl che capita aprèso lezzéndo i stèll . . . la lüna!
Mé regòrdo, stévemo stravacàdi sü la réna a l'isola de Paranèl . . . l'era nòce . . . e l'era estàte . . . s'éremo desnüdi a far l'amóre . . . de bòta me fa: "Ferma! !"
"Se gh'è?" "Varda la lüna!"

"Why? . . . What's wrong? . . . Are you embarrassed to be seen by the moon?"
"No. Don't you see that the moon is shining clear and large, with those little clouds circling round and round it."
"So what?"
"It's a sure sign that a storm's coming soon! Winds will ravage everything from here to San Marco."
"Come on, cut the crap, girl! There's no sign of it . . . not a cloud . . . the sea is tranquil . . . and the lagoon is placid as piss. There's not even a bird in the sky . . ."
"No birds is another sign that a storm is on its way! Quick! Jump in the boat!"
And off we went, rowing like crazy.
"But where are we going?"
"Row! Rooooooow! We're going to Saint Mark's!"
We arrived at Saint Mark's just in time, got rid of the boat and started running. We made it across the field and around the corner . . . and as soon as we got under cover we heard the thrashing of the hurricane: BRAAM! . . . Rip-roaring winds! The waves coming across the lagoon tore up the shoreline, ripped the ships from their moorings, and uprooted the docks as well. Two huge slow breakers lifted up a ship and carried it all the way to the field at Saint Mark's in front of the church. Then another breaker came and swept it into the church. The navy was in the nave! There was a priest on the pulpit. "STOOOOOOOOOOP!" he shouted (*makes a gesture of benediction*).
BUAAMM! . . . He was swept away still hugging the prow!

She was a phenomenon, that witch . . . she could foresee everything!

"Perchè? . . . Se gh'è? . . . Ti gh'ha vergognànza de la lüna?"
"No . . . No' ti védet che la lüna l'è ciàra, granda, con tüte le nuvulète tóndo tóndo d'intorno?" 'E alóra?"
"L'è un ségn treméndo che tra pòco ghé sarà tempèsta! Ghe sarà un vénto che ghe strassa de tüto fino al campo de san Marco!" "No' di' strunsàde, fiöla, andémo!, ma se non gh'è neànche un ségn . . . una nìvora intórno . . . ol mare l'è tranquìlo . . . la laguna l'è piàtta che la pare una pisàda. No' gh'è 'gnaca un usèlo che vola . . ."
"Proprio parchè no' ghè usèli a l'è un àlter sègn che l'è adré a 'egnìr la tempesta! Via! Salta sü la barca!" e via, a remàre 'mé mati.
"Ma dove andémo?"
"Vòga! Vògaaa! Andémo a san Marco!"
Sémo 'rivà giusto a San Marco, 'emo bütàd la barca coréndo, 'emo traversà tüto el campo, sémo 'rivàt de drìo al cantón . . . quando érimo al covèrto s'è sentì un uragàn che tiràva: BRAAM! . . . Uno squaracia-ménto! Le ónde che 'rivàvan deréntro la lagüna, i raspàva la lagüna, tiravàn sü le barche da l'ormég, le stcionconàva co' tüti palón . . . I so' 'rivàt dòi cavalón, grandi, lénti che han catà 'na nave e l'han purtàida in del campo de San Marco devànti alla gésa . . . L'è 'rivà un altro cavalón che l'ha inforsügnàda deréntro la gésa . . . una nave nella navàta!!
A gh'era el prévete sul transètto "FERMAA !" grida (*fa il gesto di benedire*): BUAMM! . . . L'ha scurazà embrassàd a la prua!
L'era un fenòmeno 'sta stròlega . . . la indovinàva tüto

4

It's a pity she didn't foresee what happened to her the day the guards barged in and put her in chains by order of the Holy Inquisition.

They brought her to be judged by the Tribunal . . . I was there when she passed by . . . and I was a coward! The official pointed his finger at me and asked: "Aren't you mixed up with her?"

"Her?" (*Pause*) "Never saw her before!"

I was shitting my pants like crazy! Just the idea of being carried to the Tribunal of the Inquisition with the judge pointing his finger at me and saying: "Now tell me all about your trafficking with the devil and those goats of the anti-Christ" . . . it gave me the creeps.
"But I don't know anything!"

Pecàt che no' ha indovinàt quèl che gh'è capità a lée ol ziórno che són piombà i guàrdi e l'han incadenàda sü l'òrden de la Santìssima Inquisisiün. L'han portàda sótto judìsio al Tribuàl . . . Intànto che pasàva, mi éro lì presente . . . E lì sunt stà un vigliàch! Chè l'ofiziàl me pónta el dit a mi e e! me dise:"Ti no' té se de la congrega de quèsta?".
"De quèsta? (*Pausa*) Mai vedùta!"
Me catà 'no' scagàsso de no' dire! Mi, a l'idéa de vèss portà in Tribunàl de l'Inquisisiün col giùdese che me puntà el dido e me disé: "Adèso, ti mé racónte tüti gli imbrogliaménti che ghi fàit viàlter coi diàvoi, coi cavrùn de l'antecrìsto!" me sentevo mal.
"Ma mi no' so niénte!"

"Put him on the wheel, right away!" Just the idea of being tied to the wheel with all those spikes . . . it's very uncomfortable! And in the end I was sure they were going to burn my ass! So, with a fire under my butt I went running to the main docks . . . there was a brig setting sail . . . I said: "Do you need a caulker . . . someone to patch the sails? Ready to go! I'm your man!" And in a flash I was onboard.

"Métélo sùbit a la róda!" Mi, a l'idéa de vèss ligà sü la róda con tüti i spintorlón . . . che i me dà un fastìdi! . . . e po' finìva de següro che i mé brüsàva el culo! Alóra mi, col fòco drìo a le ciàpe sunt 'ndài coréndo dove che gh'era el mòlo grande . . . a gh'era un brigantìn che l'era dré a salpà . . . Gh'ho ditt: "A gh'é besògn d'un calafadòr . . . un che ratòpa véle? . . . Pronto! Son chi!" e via che sunt muntàt.

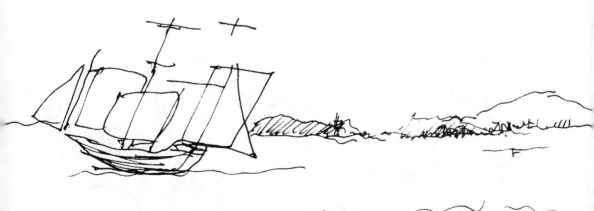

I took cover under some rigging and crouched down like a rat . . . and then when we were out at sea I stuck my head out and said to myself: They're just taking a trip around the block . . . no farther than Chioggia!
"Where are we going?" I asked.
"Seville!"
Some trip around the block!!
I asked: "Are you going to stop for a rest somewhere along the way?"
"Yes."
"Where?"
"In Tunis!!!"

I was stuck out at sea. Twenty-five days on a boat!!
Me, a born landlubber . . . I came into the world in the mountains between Brescia and Bergamo.
Me, who gets terrified just looking at water . . . The first and only time I was ever in water was when I was two days old . . . for my baptism! It still gives me nightmares.

We arrived in Tunis and from Tunis we went to Málaga and from Málaga we went down to Seville. But Seville isn't on the sea!!! I thought it was on the sea, but . . . No! Seville is on a vast plain with a canal, dug by the Arabs, that goes all the way to the sea. You arrive with your ship. You wait. Some horses show up. Some mules arrive. You get attached to them like a wagon and dragged like a big barge. And that's how you slide your way into the city's port on the river.
Seville . . . what a marvelous city. You have to see it! All those red and gold cupolas with the high bell towers that climb up to the sky. There are all these houses with fountains everywhere, so that when you walk down the street sprinkles of water rinse over you.

Me son infilàit sotacovèrta . . . son sta' schìscio 'me un rat . . . das po', quando éremo a slàrgo, sun vegnì föra cunt la crapa e me son dit: bòn, se anderà giüsto drìo el cantón . . . maximaménte a Chiòggia. "Dóe se va?" dimando. "Sivìglia!" "Proprio drìo el cantón!!"
Digo: "Per strada ghé se fermerà a catà un respìro?" "Sì" "Dove?" "A Tünese!!!"
Mi, sbatü per mare! Venticìnque ziórni de nave!!
Mi, che sunt nasüo de tèra . . . sunt 'egnüdo al mondo fra Brèssia e Bèrghem . . . mì, che l'acqua mé fa impressiün sojaménte a vardàla . . . che me ricòrdo la prima e üneca vòlta che m'han butà in de l'acqua gh'avevo dòe ziórni . . . per el batésimo . . . A gh'ho ancóra gl'ìncubi!!
Sémo 'rivàt a Tünese e da Tünese sémo andàit a Màlaga e da Màlaga sémo deséndui a Sevìglia. Ma Sevìglia no' è sul mare!!! Mi credéa che fuèsse sul mare . . . No! Sevìglia l'è in un pianün treméndo con un canale, scavàt anmò de i àrabi, ch'el végn giò fin al mare. Ti te 'rìvet con la tòa nave, te spècet, arìven i cavàli, arìven i müli, te tàchen come un carèto e te trasìneno cumpàgn de un barcón . . . cossì ti va slissigàndo fino al porto de la cità dentro 'sto rio.
Sevìglia . . . che sità meravegiósa, besógna vedérla! A gh'è tüte 'ste cùpole ròsse e d'òro cunt 'sti spintorlón de campanìle che se ràmpiga in ziélo . . . A gh'è tüte 'ste case cunt le fontane dapertüto, te vé per la strada co' 'sti spìntorli che te anàfiano . . .
Mi éro incantàd a 'miràr 'sta sità . . . e come desbàrgo, me retròvo davànti de bòto un catastón de légna con quàtro sentàdi in sima, còmodi . . . che i brüsa tranquìli!

I was dumbstruck with admiration for this city . . . then as soon as I got off the boat, I found myself right in front of a huge stack of wood, and comfortably sitting on top of it were four people . . . calmly burning.

"But who's that burning?"
"Heretics!"
"And who condemned them?"
"The Tribunal of the Inquisition."
"Holy blood of God! I escape from Venice with a fire at my ass . . . and as soon as I get to Seville there's another one in front of my balls!!"

These fanatics were always setting people on fire: heretics who didn't want to repent, wizards who didn't want to renounce witchcraft, Moors who didn't want to convert . . . and Jews . . . for any reason at all!

They don't do it just for spite . . . they burn the body to free the soul. The body turns to ashes and the happy soul goes off to heaven. What hearts they have!

"Ma chi è che brüsa?" "Erétici!" "E chi l'è che li gh'ha cundanà?" "El tribünàl de l'Inquisisiün!!" . . .
Sangre de diòs! Scapo de Venésia col fòco drìo a! culo . . . arìvo a Sevéglia me lo retròvo denànzi le bale!
'Sti fanàteghi dàva fògo a la zénte in continuasiün: ai erétici che no' voléva abiürà, ai stregón che no' vorséva condanà la stregonerìa, ai mòri che no' vorséva la conversiòn, ai güdìi ebràichi . . . per qualsìasi resòn!
Lòro no' i faséva per cativéria, ghé brüsàva el corpo per liberàrghe l'ànema . . .

The stench of burning flesh!

But these people of Seville were not sad. No, on the contrary, as soon as they finished their acts of collective roasting . . . they ripped off the black vestments they were wearing, and all of them, men, women, and children, threw themselves into a joyous frenzy of singing and dancing . . . I remember they had castanets, that's what they called them . . . these wooden things that came from the Arabs . . . they beat them against one another to make music . . . TRATATATATA TA. (*He sings while miming a dance of castanets.*)

El còrpo de carbonèla e l'ànema felìs che l'andàva in ciel! Pensa che còre!
Una spüssa de carne brüsàda!!
Ma 'sta zénte de Sevéglia no' era triste, no' anze, apéna fornìt 'sta funziün d'aròsto colectivo . . . bütàva via ogne vestiménto négri che gh'havéa adòss e se lanzàva tüti, dòne e òmeni, in una grande alegrèssa e i cantàva e i balàva . . . e me recòrdo che gh'havéano delle snàchere, se ciàmen cossì . . . ròbe de àrabi . . . tòchi de lègn, che lóro i picàvan e i faséven de le cansón . . . tratatatata ta. (*Canta mimando di danzare usando le nacchere*)

"Ah, sweet lassy . . .
We were so hot
TRA TATATATA
That we bathed in the stream
TRATATATATA
And to dry you . . .
I lent you my shirt.
And you never even realized
That in it was hidden my heart!"
TRATATATAT

And then . . . PIM-PAM! Fireworks . . . that burst into the luminous sky!

"Ahi! Ahi, dòlze fiòla . . .
pèl gran calóre
TRATATA TATA
derénto la fònte se sémo bagnà
TRATATATA
e per sugàrte . . .
la mia camìsa mi t'ho emprestà
e nemànco ti sét encorgiüda che deréntro
gh'éra nascondüo ol mé còre!"
TRATATAT

E via! Pim-pam . . . pam!, i föghi d'artifìz . . . che vegnìva sü in del ciél tüto un luminón!

They finished everything off with fireworks. And it was there, in fire, that I found my calling, because I could make fireworks like the world had never seen. I made fireworks of intoxicating luminosity. I took a big hollow reed, filled it with saltpeter, put in some sulfur and then some coal. Then I lined up eight reeds linked to each other, then twelve reeds, then all the fuses: a long one, then a little longer one, then a shorter one . . . then I lit them all: PIAMM . . . BAAM . . .

I was a master of pyrotechnics.

Lóro i finìva tüto coi fòghi d'artifìzio. E proprio lì, nei fuochi ho trovà sùbit de laurà, chè mi so' un artifiziér che no' gh'è al mondo . . . Mi fasévi dei stciopóni 'luminànti de imbriagàrli. Ciapàvi un tubón grand, lo impicàvo de salnitro, ghé metévo deréntro ol sòlforo e po' la carbonèla, po' ghé fasèvo òto cane v'üna contro l'altra embragàde, po' dódese cane, pò tüte le micce: una lònga, una un po' pü longhìna, un po' pü curtìna . . . po' ghe davo fògo al tüto: PIAMM . . . BAAM!
Artifizér de òro, mi éro!

Just for the record I should remind you that right around that time Columbus of Genoa had just returned from the Indies. He was a man of imagination . . . having made the entire journey in less than a month, not by heading there directly but by going to the Indies in reverse. What an imagination. He got there by going backwards!

Tanto per la crònica, débio recordàrve che pròprio in quèl tempo a l'era tornàt apéna de l'Indie ol Colombo genovés, òmo de tèsta . . . ché lü l'éva fàit tüta la traversàda in gnanca un més, però no' andàndoghe per ol driz, ma arivàndoghe a le Ìndie pòr ol de drìo!

Because in those days when you went to the Indies directly, you had to go across the Mediterranean to Tunis, and when you got to Tunis there was a desert, so you had to take a camel (*executes a few dance steps miming the uneven walk of the camel*): camel, camel, camel, camel, camel. Then you go over the mountains on a mule or a donkey: donkey, donkey, donkey, donkey. You get off and there's a river, a boat, you cross to the other side, then there's a desert: desert, desert, desert, camel, camel, camel, camel, then there's more mountains, a mule, a horse, another mule . . . then you get to the sea . . . Finally the sea! A boat, a ship . . . Ohhhh . . . camel, camel, another camel . . . It took a while!!!

There were people who left when they were babies, and came back old men.

The incredible thing was that you could recognize people who came back from the Indies right away . . . by the way they walked . . . watch how they walked (*demonstrates a shaky bowlegged walk*). Remember that camel?

Anyway, this Christopher Columbus had quite an imagination. He went by sea for thirty-five days "the wrong way" and got to the New World by the back door.

But I have to say that he himself was shown the back door, because after he returned from all those big discoveries, nobody gave a shit.

He said: "I went to the Canary Islands in thirty-five days!" "Yes, that's nice. That's nice . . ."

No one cared because he didn't bring anything back. Gold, he didn't bring any. Precious stones, he didn't bring any. Coral, he didn't bring any . . . all he brought back was four rotten pearls, ten muzzled savages with tattered feathers . . . a few terrified parrots, with their feathers standing up on end, and bulging eyes that seemed to be shouting "Help!" But the monkeys he brought back were beautiful. They had shaved asses . . . flaming red . . . and they masturbated from morning to night.

"But Christopher Columbus, what kind of junk did you bring back?"
"I took what I found."
I knew him and he said to me: "Johan Padan, have faith . . . I know for certain that there are buckets full of gold in that new world . . . If you come with me, I'll cover you with gold. I'll make you rich!"

Pénsa che tèsta! Gh'era arivàit per rovèrso! . . .
Ché alóra quànd se andàva per le Indie par al derìto, in travèrso il Mediteràneo, se arivàva a Tünese, a Tünese gh'era el desèrto . . . se ciapàva el camèlo: (*accenna passi di danza mimando la camminata sbilenca del cammello*) camèlo, camèlo, camèlo, camèlo, camèlo. Po' se arivàva a le montàgne cunt un mulo o l'àseno: àseno, àseno, àseno, àseno. Se desendéva, gh'era al fiume, gh'era una barca, se traversàva, po' gh'era el desèrto: desèrto, desèrto, desèrto, camèlo, camèlo, camèlo, camèlo, po' gh'eran le montàgne de nòvo, un mulo, un cavàlo, un mulo de nòvo . . . po' se arivàva al mare . . . Finalmente al mare! Barca, nave . . . Ohhhh . . . camèlo, camèlo, camèlo de nòvo . . .
A l'era un po' longa!!
A jéra quèi che partìven che i era bambìn, i turnéven dei vegèti.
La ròba tremènda è che se recognoséva sübit quèi che vegnìven de l'Indie . . . per come i caminàva . . . guardate come camminavano . . . (*Esegue una camminata tutti sussulti e sbrirolamenti*) Gh'avìt in mènte ol camèlo? . . .
Bòn, varda che tèsta 'sto Colombo Cristòforo! L'è andàito per mare in trentasìnque ziórni catàndo el rovèrso mondo per el de drìo!
E bisógna dì, che per ol de drìo l'ha catà anca lü, parchè, con tütta 'sta gran descovèrta, nesciün ol cagàva.
Lü diséva: "Ghe sunt andàit travèrso le Canàrie in trentasìnque ziórni!". "Sì, sta bòn, sta bòn . . ."
No' interessàva perchè no' avéa portàt niénte! Ori, no' ghé ne avéa portàt, piétre sbarluscénte no' ghé ne avéa portàt, coràli no' ghé ne avéa portàt . . . gh'avéva' portàito quattro pèrle smargiùte, smarsìde, diézi selvàzz, tüti smusugnénti cunt le plüme tüte smargagnàde . . . dei papagàli spaventàt, stremìt . . . cunt le pltime tüte drisàte . . . coi ògi tóndi che fasévan: "Aiuto!" . . .
Invece le scìmie bèle . . . col cül pelà . . . rósso infiamàt . . . che se smasturbàvan de matìna a séra.
"Ma Colombo Cristòforo che rasa de sciavatàd te ghé purtàit?" "Mi ho catàt quèl che ho truvàt."
Mi o! cognosséva e lü el me diséa: "Johan Padàn dame confiénsa . . . mi sabi de següro che in 'sto mondo nòvo gh'è oro a càntere. Se ti végnet con mite còvro de òro, te fago siòr!"

Do you understand? He was trying to convince me to sail with him on his ship.

And why not? I'm a phenomenon! I know how to read an astrolabe. I'm a scribe. I have beautiful handwriting. I'm a marvelous calligrapher. I'm a caulker. I can sew up the sails . . . I can man the cannons. I know the winds. I'm good at languages. There's not an idiom in the world that I don't speak. I can converse in all tongues and dialects: dead languages, living languages, and everything in between.

And I am the kind of person who, when he hears a stranger speaking intricate and incomprehensible phrases, I listen for a week . . . and TACH, in the end I speak just like he does!

I don't understand what he's saying, but I speak!

He asked me again if I wanted to go with him on his third voyage . . . And I said to him: "Dear Discoverer, if you find a road to the Indies by foot . . . I'll follow you even if I have to ride on the back of a pig!"

Never say things in vain, because after vainly speaking in vain, you might find yourself really riding on the back of a pig. You'll see what I mean later on in the story.

To begin with, it happened that there arose a horrible persecution against the Jews. An elaborate deception was devised by the Holiest Catholic Queen and her dear husband to throw them out and take away all their goods, money, and houses.

Te capìt? Lü me tampenàva parchè me montàsse su la sòa barca. Bèla fòrsa, mi sunt un fenòmeno! L'astrolàbio mi el légi . . . mi sunt scrivàn, mi scrivo in bèla grafia, mi sunt gerogrìfico meravegióso. Mi sunt calafadòr. Mi cuso le véle . . . mi pòdo andàre ai canóni. Mi cognòsso i vénti. Mi cognòsso le léngue . . . no' gh'è idiòma al mondo che mi no' parlo. Mi converso in tute le lèngue, i dialèti, le léngue morte, quèle vive, quèle che stan così e così . . .

E po' mi sunt un che quando ascòlta un forèsto che parla tüt ingrignàt, che no' se capìs . . . l'ascòlto pe' 'na setimàna . . . tach, a la fin parlo come lü! No' capìsso quèl che digo, ma parlo!

Ancóra ol mé domànda se gh'ho in ménte de andàr con lü per ol tèrzo viàggio . . . e mi ghé dìghi: "Caro descovridùr, se trovì 'na strada de andàrghe a pe' in 'ste Ìndie.., ve végno a drìo anca in grópa a un porsèl!"

Mai parlàre a svànvera, che svànvera svànvera, dopo te arìva de bòn de retrovàrte a cavalcà un pürscèl. Vedarì in avànti de la stòria.

Tanto per encomenzàre càpita che stciòpa 'n'altra treménda batüda de persecusión adòsso ai giüdìi. üna gran tràpola enventà da la Santìsima Rejna, catòlica e del so' caro marìo per descasàrli e portàrghe via tüti i so' béni, i denàri, e le case.

12

In Seville there were some shrewd Italian bankers from Florence and Genoa who profited from the situation by turning it into a big business. They secretly repossessed the houses of the Jews before they were confiscated . . . and in exchange gave them houses of equal value in Livorno or Naples . . . sealing the deal with letters of credit.

I knew all about the trick, for the simple reason that at the time I was working for one of the bankers. Doing what? Transcribing! Yes, I told you, I was an excellent scribe and calligrapher, I wrote out these letters of credit by hand . . . with a script that was . . . ah! Then the Jews arrived in Tuscany and Lombardy and found what had been left for them in the bank. It was an ingenious ruse!!

A gh'éra lì a Sevéglia dei italiàn de Florénza e Génoa, dei gran balòs, banchér che, 'profitàndo de l'ocasün, i féva dei gran afàri. Lóro ghe ritiràva de nascondùo le case ai güdìi prima che fuèsse confiscà . . . e in scàmbio ghe dàva 'n'altra casa a Livorno o a Napoli del mèsmo valore . . . sü la paròla . . . scrita sü üna lètera de crédit.

Mi cognosévi bén tüto l'intrapolaménto, per la sémplice resòn che del témpo me s'éri metüo al servìssi de vün de 'sti banchér. A far cos'è? A desténder le scritüre. Sì, ve l'ho dit, mi s'éro un scrivàn gerogrìfego provètt. Mi le scrivévo *de mia man* 'ste "lètere de crédito" . . . d'una scritüra ah!, lór po', 'sti judü, arivàvan in Toscània e Lombardéa e se ritrovàveno quèl che i gh'avéa lassàto lì al banco. L'era un marchingègn 'genióso!

The only problem was that the Queen began to suspect that there was some skullduggery going on . . . her crown was spinning like crazy . . . she arrested ten Jews, gave them a little roasting . . . they talked. Then she arrested some of the Genoese and Florentine bankers and gave them a roasting.

Sojaménte gh'è capitàt che a la Rejna, gh'è vegnüt un gran dùbeto che ghe fuèsse un trucaménto de entralàsso . . . ghe son giràt le corone a vòrtise, l'ha catà diéze giudìi, gh'ha dàito 'na brusatàta, quèi han parlà, po' han catà i genovési e i banchiéri fiurentìn, gh'han dàit un'altra brusatàta.

And then the judge of the Inquisition got ahold of the letters of credit . . . the ones that I wrote . . . What rotten luck! He reads them and says: "Beautiful . . . I'd like to meet the man who wrote these!"
And what am I supposed to do? Wait for them to come get me? I make a run for it!

With the usual fire up my ass, I head fast as lightning to the port and jump like a mountain goat onto one of the ships from the fleet that Columbus of Genoa was taking on his fourth voyage. It was already untied from the dock. "Stoooooop!" I walked on water!

E po' e! jùdice de l'Inquisisiün gh'é capità in man le lètere de crédito . . . quèle che gh'avevo scrivüdo mi . . . Varda un po' la ny rògna! Le lége e e! dis: "Bèle! . . . Me piaserìa cognósser quèlo che le ha scripto!" . . .
E mi che fago? Aspèto che me branca? Via! Sémper col mè solito fògo drio al cül, 'me ün fülmin me son presentà al porto e monto saltando 'mé un stambèch sü una de le nàvi de la flòta del genovés Colombo, che l'è adrée a salpà per ol quàrto viàgg.
L'era già destacàda del molo: "Fermaaa!" Gh'ho caminàt su le acque!

When we got out to the open sea I introduced mself: "I can do any job. I make fireworks. I can sew. I can read an astrolabe. I can man the cannons . . ."

"No! We don't need anyone for those jobs. They're taken! The only job still open is the keeper of the pigs, cows, donkeys, and horses down in the ship's hold."

These beasts were packed in below deck because in this new world they didn't have the kinds of animals we did: horses, mules, donkeys, cows, and pigs had never been seen there. So all the ships that landed there had holds full of these animals for repopulation! And that's how I ended up making the voyage under a blanket surrounded by these animals, who shit from morning to night. They weren't used to the movement of the waves, so every time there was a breaker (*referring to the defecating animals*): PARAPUM one, PARAPUN two, PAA!

Ah, now I know why the French wish you luck by shouting, "Lots of shit!"
I was in luck up to my neck!

One night there was a tremendous storm. The waves pounded against the side of the ship. It rose up and they battered it from all sides. The beasts down below were thrashing all over the place. The horses were kicking their hooves at the cattle. The cattle were goring the donkeys with their horns. The donkeys were mauling the pigs. And the pigs were in the middle of it shouting: "That's enoooooough!!" In the end they were all ripped to pieces in a bloody mess.

Somebody shouted to me: "You know how to sew. Here's a needle . . . start sewing!"

I sewed up the cows, the pigs . . . all their wounds . . . I saved those beasts . . . and they really loved me for it!

Quando che sémo stàit allo slàrgo me sunt presentàt: "Mi sunt bòn de fa tüti i mestér, mi sunt artifiziér, mi pòdo cusìre, mi sunt bòn a lézere l'Astrolàbio, mi pòdo andàre ai canóni . . ." "No! No' gh'é de bisògn de sti mestér, i è tüti covèrt! L'ünego trabàco vacante l'è quèl de guardiano de porscèli, vache, àsini e cavàj in fóndo a la stiva!"
De 'ste bèstie gh'éra stipàt el sotobordo per via che in 'st'altro mondo, de 'ste rasse nostràne no' ghe n'è: cavàj, muli, àseni, vache e porscèli no' se son gimài vedùi. E alóra tüte le nàvi che i desendéva jéra riempìt in dè la stiva de 'ste bèstie per farghe tüto el reempòpolo! Così a mi m'è tocà viazzàre in sotocovèrta in mèzo a 'sti animàj, che i cagàva de matìna a séra! No' jéra abituàd ai sciacquón de le onde . . . come gh'era un refròn: (*allude al defecare delle bestie*) PARAPÙN v'ün, PARAPÙN dòi . . . PAA!
Ah, gh'ho capìt parchè i franzósi per dirte bòna fortüna i te vòsa: "Tanta merda!"
Mi a s'éri pròprio deréntro a la fortüna fina al col!
Che una nòte gh'è stàit 'na tempesta tremènda, gh'era i onde che sgracogiàva adòso a la nave . . . la valzàveno e la sbatusciàva de qua e de là . . . e 'ste bèstie de sòta che sbalanzàvan . . . A gh'era i cavàli che tiràvan zocolàde a le vache, le vache che incornàvan i àsini, i àsini che sgargagnàva i porscèli, i porscèli in mèzo: "Bastaaa!!" i vusàva. A la fin éren tüti sbragà e sanguignénti.
Mhan ciamàt a mi: "Cüsidòr! La gügia . . . cusìse!"
Ho cüsìt le vache, i porscèli . . . tüte le ferìde . . . Le gh'ho salvàde tüte 'ste bèstie . . . che po' mé vorséveno un bén!

Finally we arrived at the isle of Santo Domingo!
What splendor!
I had never seen such clear water! You could see to the
bottom: the coral, the colored fish . . . there were plants
that reached up to the sky, flying monkeys, and singing
birds.
As soon as we threw out the anchor, the savage Indians
came out to meet us in the little boats they call canoes.

A la fin, sèm 'rivà a l'ìsola del Santo Doménigo!
Che splendòr!
No' gh'avevo gimài vidùo un'acqua così ciàra! Se
scozéva el fóndo, i corài, i pèssi coloràdi . . . a gh'era
'ste piante che se rampegàvan in ziélo, le scìmie che
volàvan, 'i üsèi che i cantàva.
Apéna pogiàda l'àncora, ghé son vegnüti incòntra i
selvàtigh indiàn sü 'ste lóro barchète che i e ciàma
canoe.

They came singing, laughing . . . they were all colored and
naked . . . only a feather to cover them, and that was it . . .
their little spinnakers dangling in the wind.
They rowed with short oars, paddles, that propelled them
rapidly from here to there.
Beautiful people . . . well formed . . . clean . . . because at
every opportunity they'd throw themselves into the water to
wash themselves with great joy, and they swam like fish, even
in the deep sea. They dove for pearls and coral and then put
them in their mouths . . . like this: "Would you like a pearl?
Take it!" (*He mimes the act of spitting out the pearl.*)
"Thank you!"
Very beautiful people!
Especially the girls . . . naked the way they were born . . .
without shame . . . they weren't embarrassed at all: tits in
the wind . . . bellies in the wind . . . buttocks in the
wind . . . everything in the wind! God what a wind!

They were so kind, these savages! Almost too kind!

I venìvan cantando, ridendo . . . éran tüti coluràdi,
sbiòti . . . desnüdi, con una piuma e basta!
E el bindorlón che andàva!
I remava coi rémi curti, pagaie, che fa' andàr rapide
de chi e de là.
Bèla génte . . . bén formà . . . polìdi . . . che loro, in
ògni ocasiün se büta in acqua a netàrse con gran
plasér, e i nòda 'mé i péssi anca in profondo al mare!
I catàva le pèrle e i coràj e po' i metévan in bóca . . .
così: "Ti vòl una perla? Cata! (*Mima l'atto di sputare*)
"Gràsie!"
Pròprio bèla gente!
Insòvratüto le fiòle . . . biòte come i son nasciüde . . .
sanza pudóre . . . no' i gh'ha vergógna miga: zinne
al vénto . . . vénter al vénto . . . ciàpe al vénto . . .
tüto al vénto! Dio che ventàda!
A i era così zentìli 'sti selvàtighi! Un'esagerasión!

Especially the women.

You didn't have to perform a whole song and dance for them . . . no! You just had to do a little pantomime to make it understood that you liked one of them, and suddenly she was embracing you! These lasses have a magnificent ritual: they come to you, smile, lower their eyes, take you by the hand, and bring you into the forest! They jump on your neck: you lie down, with her on top of you, and make enchanted love with moans and laughter!
But not on the ground! On the leaves . . . on huge leaves that they call leaves of love . . . the size of a bed . . . a double bed . . . they even had queen-sized!

And when you started making love there were the songs of the birds . . . in four-part harmony . . . and the singing butterflies . . . there were the monkeys that flew from tree to tree . . . "UHUUUUUHHH. AHHAAAA . . . keep it up!!" they shouted. "Keep it up!"

And when it came to eating, they would give you the food out of their own mouths to make you happy.

And we Christian Catholics . . . good men . . . started out ceremoniously offering them little bells, and glass trinkets . . . and then we began to plunder everything they had: to carry off their women and children onto ships to be used as slaves in our sacred world of Christianity.

Soprattutto le femmine, No' gh'era miga de besògn de fare tüte le menfrìne de 'sto mondo . . . no! Bastàva che te févi un po' de pantomima per farte capìr che te piaséva v'üna, che sübit quèla t'embrassàva! Ste fiòle gh'avevàn un rituàl mannìfico: i venìvan . . . i soridévan, sbasàvan i òci, te ciapàvan per una man e te portàvan in de la foresta! Te saltàveno al colo: ti rovèrso . . . lée rovèrsa e stciopàva un amor strancantào de lamenti e ridàde!
Ma no' per tèra! Sü le fòje . . . de le fòje grande che se ciàman fòje-d'amore . . . 'na piàssa, 'na piàssa e mèsa . . . dóe piàsse . . .
E quàndo se comensàva l'amóre, gh'era el canto e el controcànto dei usèi, de le parpàie che cantàvan . . . gh'era le scìmie che volàva de àlbero in àlbero . . . "Uhuuhh . . . AHAAH . . . Fòrzaaa!!—le criàva—Forzaaa!"
Per ol magnàre po', se tiràva via de bóca lorn i bocón, per favorìrte a ti!
E noja!tri, cristiàn catòlici . . . brava zénte . . . prima a fa' tüti i cerimoniósi . . . a offerìrghe campanelìn, vétri de fufàia . . . e po' s'è comenzà a sgaràrghe via tüto quèl che gh'han: a stràparghe via dòne, fiòl e caricài in sü la nave, per traghetàrli stciàvi in del nostro santo mündo dei cristiàn.

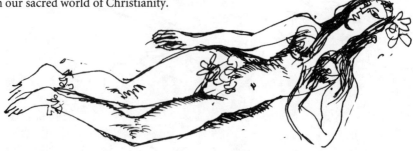

Until the time came when they lost their tempers. Thousands and thousands of them arrive streaming from all directions, armed with bows and arrows, livid with rage, shouting: "Give us back our people or we'll attack!"

And our captains were stupefied: "But why are you so angry?! We never thought of carrying off your relatives as slaves . . . we just wanted to take them for a little ride . . . introduce them to a few nice people . . . some nice cities . . . teach them the doctrine of the only God and the heavenly Trinity! And then present them to the King and our Holy Catholic Queen, who is as goodly and sweet as pie!"

And they responded: "No thank you. We've had enough little rides . . . the ones that you took away on the first and second voyages never came back. Come on, give them back to us . . . right now . . . or we'll start throwing spears and arrows!"

As soon as they said "spears and arrows" dozens of cannons were rolled out onto the decks of the ships and then began firing a broadside. TA-TA-A-BOOM!

Tanto che, 'riva un mumént che' a quèi gh'è gira i bòcoi. I 'riva in mila e mila strarepàndo da òmnia parte, armà de archi e saètte incasàt neghér e i vusa: "Déghe in drìo sübit la nostra zénte o ve saltémo adòso!"

E i nostri capitàni, tüti stupefàtcti: "Ma parchè fèt tanto i inrabìt?! Nojàltri no' se pensàva miga de portàrvei via come stciàvi 'sti vòstri parénti . . . se vorséva sojaménte farghe fare un girètt . . . farghe cognósere un po' de bèla zénte . . . bèi ciutàd . . . insegnàrghe la dutrìna del déo ünego e trino che sta nel ziél! E po' presentàrghei al Re e a la Rejna nostra catòlica, che l'è bòna e dólze 'mé ol pan!"

E quèi ghe respónde: "No' grazie, basta con i girèt . . . imperchè quèi che avìt portàt via al primo e al segóndo viàgg . . . nesciün l'è più returnàt. Avànti, déghe indrée quèsti chi . . . e sübit!, se no' comenzémo a lanzàr frèze e lanze!"

No' i avéva dito "frèze e lanze" . . . che dal bordón da le nàvi i son spuntàdi 'na mügia de canóni e hann comenzià a sparare bordegón: TA-TA-A-BOOM!

And you could see the mutilated warriors catapulted into the air . . . and then the horses came out with the cavalry, instilling great fear . . . because the Indians didn't know what horses were. They had never seen them before and believed that the horse and cavalryman were a single beast . . .

e se vedéva 'sti gueriér che i saltàva per ària sgaragnàdi . . . e i vegnìva föra i cavàj co' i cavajér . . . che lori i cavài no' i cognoséva miga, no' i ghe aveva gimài vedùe e i credeva che cavàgio e cavjér fuèsse 'na bèstia sola . . .

20

a horrendous oddity of nature: "Monster," they shouted, "monster!" And they turned white with terror and ran away. And the cavalrymen shouted, laughed, stabbed, skewered, and sliced them in two . . . heads were flying. Senseless butchery!

'na stramberìa orénda de natüra: "El mostro!—i criàva—El mostro!—e se"Feva sbiancài de terór e i scapàva. E quei, i cavajér criàva, i ridéa, i sponzonàva, i sbusàva, i li tajàva in dòe . . . teste che volàvan . . . Üna matànza proprio d'embesìl!

You should know that I'm no sissy. I'm no choirboy either. When I was eighteen I was in the infantry of Lanzichenecchi. I did my share of slaughtering in battle . . . and even after . . . but I slaughtered people who wanted to slaughter me! This was a massacre for no reason.

Annihilation for the sake of annihilation.

These Christians cut the limbs off of children and bashed them against trees . . . flattened them! They cut women in half and eviscerated them. It was sickening.

The chaplain said: "Johan Padan, that's enough of this whining . . . What are they doing in the end? Are they killing Christians? No, they're killing people who have no souls, no hearts, no religion . . . they don't have the spirit of God. When you kill one of them it's like slaughtering a dog! Don't make it a tragedy."

I won't make it a tragedy, but I don't like it!

It turned my stomach, so much so that I wanted to go home! I kept looking to see if I could spot a ship that was going back. But there were no ships leaving. They just kept arriving. Four or five ships landed every week, unloaded the animals they had in their holds, and then after replenishing their supplies of water and vegetables they set sail for the west: "Where are you going?"
"To look for El Dorado," they answered, cursing . . . unfurled their sails and went off.

Sia ciàro che mi no' so' 'na feminèta! No' so anfànte de còre, che mi a desdòto anni s'éro in de le fanterìe dei Lanzechenéch . . . e ne gh'ho fàite de scanaménti in batàja . . . e anco aprèso . . . ma scanàvo zénte che voléva scanàrme a mi! Ma èsta l'era üna becarìa sénsa cognisiön. Masà, tanto per masà.

'Sü cristiàn che catàveno i fiulìt e i sbatéva contra i arberi: stciepàt! I tajàva in do' le fèmine, squarzàde. De vomegàre!!

Ol capelàn ol m'ha dit: "Johan Padàn, basta co' 'sto mogügn . . . cossa i fa a la fin? I masa de' cristiàn? No, i masa zente che no' gh'ha spirto, no' gh'ha core, no' gh'ha relizión . . . no' gh'hanno né anema né deo . . . Quando te màsset ün de quèi l'è iguàl che copàr un can! No' far traghédie!".

No' farò traghédia, ma no' me piàse!

Gh'avevo el stòmaco seràdo, tanto che vorséo tornàr a casa! Miràvo de contìnuo se scorzévo quarche nave che tornàse in drìo . . . Ma no' i partivàn . . . dessendévan solo! Gh'évan nàvi che dessendévan ògni settimàna, quàtro o zìnque, scaregàvan i animali che i stéva in de la stiva, po' se empegnìveno de acqua e de verzüre e féva rotta in vèrso ponénte: "Dove andìt?" "A la rezérca de l'Eldoràdo." i rispondéa e biastemàndo, isàveno tüte le vele e via che andéveno.

For me it was no fun at all to stay with my comrades, who were only good at getting drunk, playing cards and dice, stabbing one another in scuffles; and then for a sideshow watch them get aroused and throw themselves on the women. Was that a life? The only thing I really enjoyed was trying to communicate with people . . . you must have guessed by now: I have an obsession for languages, idioms . . . finding out how people speak . . . what they think, what they say . . . trying odd words and discovering ways to say things. But it was difficult to get near the Indians. They were afraid, they were always terrified that afterward, all of a sudden, a horse monster would show up.

To put them at ease, I played the clown. When I met them I pretended that I was the one who was scared, before they had a chance to be: "Oh! A savage! . . . A monster!" And they laughed.
Sometimes.
So I asked them: "Indians, how do you say sun?"
And they answered: "Aleghe."
"And the name of the sea?"
"Criaba."
"And how do you say man?"
"Opplaca."
"And how do you say woman?"
"Feila."
"And how do you say child?"
"Icme!"
"And what do you call a woman who makes love?"
"There are many ways of saying it, because there are many ways of doing it . . . and so there are many words for love."
I asked about everything, stealing their words . . . and I took notes. Then I showed up one day when five or six savages were having a quarrel . . . I went up to them and said: "Able esset atere prialf ti io mastico . . . (*He improvises a speech in grammelot-gibberish, with gestures to indicate he is interrupting arguments between two different groups. He listens, take sides, laughs, and does a mocking dance.*) They looked at me dumbstruck: "A white Indian!" I spoke their language.

A mi no' me piaséva neànca star con èsti mèi compari bòni so! de imbriagàrse, ziogàre a carte e a dadi, scanàrse l'un l'ólter in barùfa e po' per contorno vidèi arasà, sbàterse adòso a le fèmene. Ma l'era vita? L'ünega roba che me piaséva de bon l'era zercàr de enténderme co' la zent . . . che viàlter l'avrèt capìt: mi gh'ho 'na fisa de l'idioma, del linguàz . . . de cognóser come i parlà la zénte . . . quèlo che i pensa, che i dise . . . infilàrghe parole strambe e descovrìre tüto un descórso. Ma l'era defizil andàrghe arénta visìn . . . i se spaventàva, i gh'avéva sémpre ol teròr che aprèso, de bòto, saltàse föra un mostro cavàjo.
Mi, per convìnserli a pórse tranchìbi, fasévo el paiàsso. Quando i incontràva fasévo mostra da avérghe spavento mi, prima che loro: "Oh! Un selvàzz . . . un mostro!". E loro i rideva . . .
Qualche volta.
Così mi ghe domandava: "Indios, come se dise el! sole?". E loro: "Abeghé". "E el nome del mare?" "Criaba" "E come se dise òmo?" "Opplaca" "E come se dise dona?" "Feila" "E come se dis bambìn?" "Icme! E come se dise dona che fa all'amore?" "Gh'è tante manére de dirlo, parchè gh'è tante manére de farlo.., e alóra gh'è tante manére de dir l'amore."
Mi ghe domandàva tüto. Mi ghe robàvo le parole . . . e me 'segnàvo . . . e so' arivàt un ziórno . . . gh'era zìnque o sis selvàzz che i féva barùfa . . . sunt andàit lì visìn, gh'ho fàit: "Able esset ateré prialí ti io masticó . . . (*improvvisa uno sproloquio in gramelotte: con gesti fa immaginare di interrompere la discussione tra due gruppi diversi, ascolta, polemizza, ride e accenna una danza a sfotto*) . . . me vardén stüpìt: "Un Indios blanco!" Parlàvo ìndios!

I was almost disappointed when the orders came: "We're going back home!"

But I was so happy to be heading back that I loaded twice as much onto the ships as everyone else: I loaded water, I loaded vegetables . . . I even loaded five fat pigs that we had to take to Santo Domingo. Meanwhile the others loaded throngs of Indians onto the ship, enslaved prisoners . . . a hundred and twenty-five of them locked up in the hold, below deck, in place of the ballast . . . and to stop them from screaming they stuffed their mouths and throats with chaff.

We left. It was burning hot. Not much to eat . . . not much to drink. The poor Indians started dying. The sailors took the corpses and threw them into the sea.

After a few days, behind the stern in the ships's wake, we caught sight of a bunch of big fish following us: they were waiting for their meal of Indians.

They liked Indians.

So the sailors said: "Why don't we fish with these savages?" They took some dead Indians, fresh from that morning, stuck them on hooks, threw them into the sea, and went fishing.

M'é quasi despiasüd quando gh'han dàito l'órden: "Se torna a casa!".

Ma era tanta la felizitàd che gh'avevo de returnàr da via, che mi ho caregà el dópio de tüti i àlter: mi caregàvo l'acqua, caregàvo le verzure . . . ho caregàto anca sinco porseli grasi, gròsi che dovévemo scaregàre a Santo Domingo. Intànto 'i àlter i spignéva su la nave 'na mugia de Indios, pnisonér stciàvi . . . centoventisìnco incanceràt in de la stiva, in del fóndo, al posto de la zavòra . . . e per no' farghe criàr gh'avéan metüo de la stòpia in boca fina nel gargòz.

Se parte. Gran caldo, magnàr pòco . . . poco de bévar. 'Sti poveràzz de ìndios i coménza a crepàre. I cadàvri de quèi, li ciapàven e bütàvan a mare.

Qualche ziórno a prèss, drée a la poppa, lungo la scia, scorgèm 'na mùgia de pèss grandi che i ghe següta: i aspècia el pasto dei indiàn.

Ghe piasévan gli indios!

Alóra i marinàni han dit: "Perchè no' peschémo co' 'sti selvàz?". Han catà dei ìndios morti, freschi de ziornàda, gh'han infricàt dei ami in de la pele, i bütàvain del mare e pescàvan.

But it just so happens that there is a God in heaven who every once in a while gets so mad that his halo starts spinning, and he sent a storm with a wind so strong that you could see it scoop the waves out of the rolling sea. Our sails were ripped to shreds, and we were all staggering around like drunkards.

We heard a tremendous crash. We had smashed into a rock! "We're sinking! We're going to sink! Bring out the rowboats!"

Solamente che gh'è stàit el Déo padre eterno che ògni tanto ghe zira il triangolo, che gh'ha mandà giò 'na tempesta con un tal vénto, che se vedéva il mare a rotolón che sbracagnàva le onde. Se sémo retrovàit con tüte le vele strasciàde e andèimo balàndo come tanti ciùch.

Se sénte un "crasch" treméndo, émo sbatü cóntra a uno scòi!

"Pico! Andémo a pico! Giò le barche!"

There were only three. I asked the captain: "Where should I go?"
"No, there's no room for you five animal keepers. Go sink with the Indians and the pigs!"

I don't know what got into me, maybe it was anger . . . maybe it was pity: I threw open the door to the hold and all the Indians leapt out on top of me . . . I was trampled under their feet and they threw themselves into the sea!

Luckily my four fellow animal keepers were around to help me up.
"Get moving! Quick, the ship is going under!"
Down in the hold the pigs were still squealing desperately.
"Save the pigs!"
"Why?"
"One should never go into the sea without a pig!"
Because these animals have an unrivaled sense of direction. They can orient themselves in the sea even during a storm. You throw them in the water and: TAK! They immediately point their snouts in the direction of the closest shore . . . When they go "OINK, OINK, OINK, OINK!" four times, you're headed to land, and they're never wrong!

And that's why the Genoese people say: "On every ship you should always bring aboard an authentic pig . . . besides the captain . . . who's just an ordinary pig."

My companions and I went down and grabbed five pigs.
One by one we strapped ourselves to
the pigs with ropes tied around our
waists . . . and then, all together,
each one of us embracing
his own pig:
"Bon voyage! . . .
OHOHOHHHHHH . . .
BOOOM!"

Domandi al capitano: "Dove me sistemo, mi?".
Gh'era tre barche: "No, per vojàltri sinco guardiàn de animàl, no' gh'è pòsto, andé a pico coi Indios e coi porsèi!"
No' so de dove m'è vegnüd . . . forse per inrabiménto . . . forse per pità: ho dervìt a spalancà ol bocapòrt, salta föra tüti i indiàn, che mé végne adòsso . . . i mé schìscia sóta ai pie e se büta a mare! Per fortüna gh'è lì i àlter quàtro mèi compàgn guardiàni, che mé tira in pé'.
"Svelti! Ràpido, che la nave la và sóto!"
Giò, ne la stiva, gh'è ancamò i porsèi che sgrìffian disperàt.
"Salvémo i ponsèi!" "Perchè?" "No' se va a mare sénsa i porsèi!" Che 'sti animài i gh'ha un sénso ünego, che no' gh'è iguàle, de orisontàrse anco en tempèsta derénto al mare. Ti te i büti en acqua, e lori: TACH!, i punta sübeto el muso següro vèrso la còsta più pròxima . . . quando fa quàtro volte: "üho, uho, uho!" là, gh'è la costa e no' i se confonde mai!
E a l'è anca per quèst che i genovés i dise: "Bisógna portà sémpre, sü ògni nave, un porsèi veràz . . . óltra al capitàni che l'è un porco normale!".
Mi e i me compàgn andèm de sotto e catémo sinco porsèi, un per un ghe se imbraghémo ai porsèi co' le còrde ligàde intorno a la vita . . . po', tüti insèma, ognùn ambrassà al so' pròpnio porsèi: "Andémo a mare . . . OHOHHH . . . BOOM!"

It's not that I was possessed by a sudden Christian passion for pigs.

It was just that I knew about a story by Homer, the poet . . . where he talked about shipwrecked Greeks who were saved by embracing pigs, because a pig is so round and fat that he'll never sink!

He goes under for a while, but then: GLUB, GLUB, GLUB! (*mimes a pig floating up to the surface*) he always comes floating back up. It's a buoy made of fat! And he has that little curly tail that's made just right for you to hold on to without slipping loose. You grab on to that tail, and he's off. (*Mimes the swift swimming of a pig.*) . . . SSCITTSS . . . TRITRI TRI . . . It's a buoy with hooves!

Te védet la profesìa de cavalcà i porsèi!

No' è che m'era stciupà ün'emprovìsa passiòn cnistiàna per i porsèi.

E' che mi savévi de una racónta che ol fa Omero e! poéta . . . quando el dise dei nàufraghi grèch che s'èn salvà embrasàdi ai porsèi, perchè il porsèlo così graso, tóndo, no' va a picco! Ol va sóta un po' . . . das po': BLO, BLO, BLO . . . PLUF!, (*mima il maiale che torna a galla*) el torna a galezzàre! L'è una boa de grasa! El gh'ha quèl cuìn tüto rìsulo apòsta che ti te lo brànchi e no' slìssega mai . . . te se tàchet a 'sto cuìn, lü va . . . (*mima la nuotata veloce del maiale*) sscitss . . . : tritritri . . . l'è una boa cun le szapètt!

We were holding on to our pigs like this when the waves came: "No, we're not going under!" (*Mimes kissing the pig as soon as he resurfaces.*) SMACK . . . a big wet kiss! Another wave and "OHOOOO . . ." SMACK! Another wet kiss . . . After a while the pigs started liking it . . . they went under even when there weren't any waves! So the five of us, each embracing his own life-saving animal, and smooching it too . . . traversed the thrashing waves that ripped off our shirts and trousers, and we made it to land . . . naked! If the Tribunal of the Inquisition had discovered us, they would have burned us alive!

We made it to shore! The pigs had saved us . . . and now there we were, on the sand of the bay, naked, embracing our pigs . . . who were also naked.

Éremo embrasàdi a 'sti porscèi che quando 'rivàvan le ónde: "E no', de sóto non andàmo!" (*Mima, appena risalito, di baciare il maiale*) SMACK . . . un basìn! Un'altra onda e . . . "OHOOOO . . ." SMACK! un'àlter basìn! É che gh'é comensà a piasérghe anca al pursèl . . . andàva a pico anche senza ónde!

Dònca, nojàltri sinco, imbrassà ognùno al so' anìmàl de salvatàgg, sbasotàndolo . . . sémo anivàti, travèrso ónde scaracolànte che ghe sbrandelàva braghe e camìsa a la còsta, nudi! Che, se ghe catàva ol Tribünàl de l'Inquisisiün, ghe brüsàva vivi!

E sémo arivàt a la costa! I porsèi gh'avéva portàit a salvaménto . . . e adèso éremo lì su la 'rena de la marina, desnüdi, co' nostri porsèi . . . sbiòti anca lori.

Ohhhh! We were cold! I looked at my skin . . . it was pastel blue. My companions were turning blue too. The pigs were shocking pink!

The only one in good shape was the Catalan, who was so fat we called him Jellybelly. With that gut he didn't need a pig . . . in fact he was the one who saved his pig! Then there was another one who had red hair and we called him Red. Then there was a Negro, a Muslim from Tripoli. We called him Negro. And there was the skinny one that we called Skinny . . . because we men of the sea have a great imagination when it comes to nicknames!

I said: "It doesn't matter that we were saved, because now we're going to freeze to death."

So much for miracles.

I look at the hills along the shore and there are people! Savages come running down.

Bòja!, che frìo gh'è vegnü adòsso! . . . Vardo la mia pèle . . . a l'era bluètt, i me compagni tüti bluètt . . . i porsèi ziclamìn.
L'ünego che stàva ben a l'era el catalàn . . . che l'era così grasso ch'el ciamàvemo Trentatrìpe. 'Sto panzon gh'aveva minga de bisógn del porsèl . . . infàcti l'era stàito lü a pütà a salvamént el so' purscèl! Po' ghe n'era ün àlter che o l'era rosso de cavèi e ol ciamàvimo Rosso, po' gh'era un negro, che l'era musulmàn de Tripoli, ol ciamàvimo Négher, gh'era un magro col ciamàvemo Magro . . . perchè noialtni zénte de mare, gh'avémo una fantasia per i sovranòmi!
Mi ho dit: "E' inütil che ghe sémo salvàit, che tanto, tra poc, co 'sto frìo, sémo tüti morti gelàt!".
Varda quando se dise el miracolo!
Vardo la costa, miro la colìna . . . a gh'è de la zénte!
A gh'è dei selvàzi che desénde coréndo.

A hundred of them, two hundred, all armed with bows and arrows. "Uh-oh," I say. "If they've met Christians before, we're screwed. They'll cut us to pieces."
I gathered my courage . . . and started shouting words from their language that I had learned:
"Aghiudu, en li sala . . . chiome saridde aabasjia Jaspania . . . " They understood everything! "Mujacia cocecajo mobaputio Christian!"
"Eheee?"
The only word they didn't understand was "Christian."
We were saved. (*He begins a dialogue in grammelot-gibberish in which he translates for his companions the things he has just said.*)
"Give us something to cover ourselves with, because this cold is going to turn us to ice, stone-cold dead!"
"But what can we give you to cover yourselves when we're just as naked as you are?"

But listen to how intelligent those savages were: They took some chaff and burned it. They made a bonfire and then circled around us to protect us from the wind . . .

Ma zénto, dosénto, tüti armà co' i archi e i frèzze. "Bòja—disi—se quèi han cogniosüdo i cristiàn, sémo fotüdi, ghe fan a tòchi!"
Me fo' coràjo . . . e me bütti a criàr paròle ne la sòa lèngua che gh'ho imparà: "Aghiu du, en lì salà . . . chiomé saridde aabasjia Jaspania . . .—I capìvan tüto!—Mujacia cocecajo mobaputio cristiàn."
"Eheee?" L'ünica parola che no' avévan capìt era cristiani. Érimo salvi! (*Inizia un dialogo in grammelot, quindi traduce per i compagni quello che ha appena detto*) "Déghe quarcòsa de covrìrghe che chi gh'è un frìo che andémo tüti in giàsa, morti stechìt!"
"Ma cosa ve demo de covrìrve che sémo più sbiòti de voi altri?"
Ma varda l'inteligénzia de 'sti selvàzz: han catà de le stòpie e le han brüsàde, han fàit un falò e poi i sè metü tüti in zìrcul intorno e ghe covrìva per nascònder-ghe del vento . . .

Then, since their village was far away, they made lots of bonfires . . . every hundred feet there was a bonfire . . . then they took us in their arms . . . there were two hundred of them . . . and carried us to the next bonfire . . . a little toasting and then we were off again . . . a little toasting and off we go . . . a little toasting . . . and they did the same thing for the pigs . . . toasting, toasting . . . oink oink!

Because they had never seen pigs before and thought that they were another race of Christians . . . just a little fatter.

We arrived at a village with well-made huts and we were installed in a big hut with a brazier in the middle. There was lots to eat and drink.

"I think this treatment is a little too affectionate," said Red, "for us and for the pigs. I smell something rotten. I'd hate to find out these savages are cannibals and that they're treating us so well because they want to eat us."

"Don't be ridiculous," yelled Jellybelly. "This is the third voyage I've made to the Indies and I've never met Indians with pieces of arms and legs hung up to dry in their huts, like those charlatans Amerigo Vespucci and Alfonso Gamberan talked about . . . They just told those stories to have an excuse for treating the Indians like animals: 'They're cannibals, so we can make them slaves.'"

po', sicome el vilàzo l'era lontàn, han fàit tanti falò . . . ògni zénto pasi gh'era un falò . . . po' ghe catàva embràso, che lóro éran dosénto e ghe portàva dóe gh'era un altro falò . . . 'na brüsadìna e via de corsa, brtisadìna e via . . . brtisadìna . . . e anche coi porsèi . . . brusadìna, brüsadìna . . . ahi ahi!

Chè loro no' i cognoséva i pursèi e i credéan che i fuèss cristìan de un'altra rasa . . . un po' plu ingrasà. Arìvom al vilàzz co' le capàne ben costruìde e i ghe sistema dénter una gran capàna con ol brazér in dól mèzz. E gh'era ròba de magnar e de bévar.

"A mi—ol dis ol Ross—'sto tratamént tròpo afetuóso, tanto per nüngh che per i porsèi, mé spüssa niénte de bòn. No' vorarìa descovrìr che quèst i sont selvàzz canìbal e che i ghe trata bén soltànto per magnàrghe." "Di' no' dei stronsài!—ol sbòta ol Trentatrìpe—Mi l'è ol tèrzo viàzz che fo' in 'ste Indie e no' gh'ho gimài incontrà indiàn che gh'avèss deréntro a le bn capàne tòchi de giàmbe o de brasa pendùi a secà o sotto ol sale, come te van a racontàr quèi caciabàle del 'Merìgo Vespucci e de l'Alfónso Gamberàn . . . ché, 'ste storie, lori le racònta per avérghe po' el bòn pretèst de. tratàrli compàgn d'animàl: son canìbali, se pòl farli stciàvi."

All other discussions aside, I have to say that these savages were certainly the sweetest and kindest Indians I had ever met.

For sleeping, they didn't make us lie down on straw mats, maybe full of fleas, no! We were suspended in the air on hammocks . . . maybe you don't know about hammocks. It's a net suspended between two wooden poles, with ropes that hold it stretched out from here to there. Then there's a little fire underneath to give you some heat when you lie down. But it's difficult to get up onto it. If you're not experienced, you may try sitting with your butt first and (*mimes a hammock turning upside down and a fall to the ground*) PATAPUM! A whack in the ass! No! You have to do it with your knees! (*mimes mounting the hammock with a bent leg*) . . . You stretch out this one (*mimes opening the hammock*), then you stretch out the other one (*mimes extending his other leg*), and then . . . PATAPUNFETE! (*Mimes falling to the ground.*) Because it's not just a question of the knees. It's a question of balance . . . equilibrium . . . dynamics, because when you get on, you have to position your knee like this, but then give it a good strong kick! (*Mimes making the hammock swing like a swing.*) Then you turn this one and that one, then you go JOM, you stretch out, you wait, one, two, three . . . one pulls you, one goes down, the knee for support, twist here, turn there!!! (*Mimes a long and regular oscillation.*) It's all in the dynamics.

I was so good at it that in four beats I was stretched out as cozy as could be . . . With my little fire below to heat me up I slept like a baby.

Varda, óltra ògni descórso, débbio dire che quèsti selvàteghi i era de següro i indiàn più dólzi e gentìl che gh'avèssi gimmài incontràt.

Per farghe dormire . . . no' ghe faséva stravacàr sui paión, magari co' le pürese, no'! Sospandùe par l'àire, ne le amache . . . che voi no' cognossè miga le amache! A l'è una rete soapendùa tra dó palunìn de lègn, co' de le corde che la tégne slongàda de qua e de là. Po' gh'è ün scaldìn de sotavìa per darte el calór quando te se stravàchi. Però l'è difìzil montàrghe de soravìa! Chi no' lo sàbie miga se sèta de culo, e: (*mima che l'amaca si rovesci e di cadere per terra*) PATAPUM! 'Na cülàda! No! Bisogna andàrghe de genöcio! (*Mima di montare sull'amaca, con una gamba ripiegata*) . . . Po' se slàrga questa (*mima di allargare l'amaca*), po' si slàrga quest'óltra (*mima di stendere l'altra gamba*), poi . . . PATAPUNFETE! . . . (*Mima di cadere a terra*) Perchè no' l'è nemànca questión de genöcio, l'è question de balànza, de dèsechilìbrio, l'è question de la denàmica, che ti quando te monti, te dévi sestemàr ol genöcio cossì, ma po' darghe un spintorlón pu' che ben! (*Mima di far oscillare l'amaca come fosse un'altalena*) Po' te ziri de quèsto e de quest'altro, po' te fé Jom, te slàrghet, te spècet, un, doe, tri . . . V'un che te tira, v'un che va giò, genöcio de seconda, vòlta de qui, gira de là!! (*Mima un'oscillazione lunga e regolare*) L'è la fòrsa de la dinamica! Mi eri così bravo che in quàter temp éro belo che destendùo . . . el mè scaldìn de sóta me mandava calór e mi me endormivo come un bambìn.

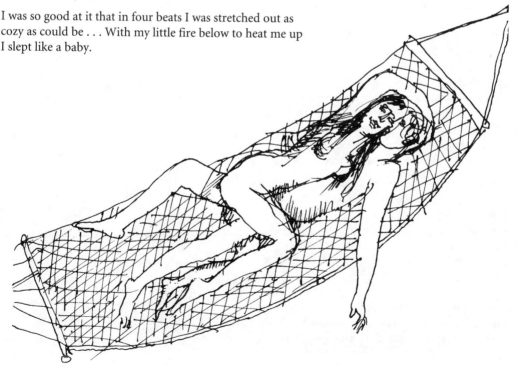

One night I feel a tender sweetness pressed against my face, then two marvelous round things . . . I go down with my hands, I feel two more round things . . . it was a girl . . . a nude girl who came into the hammock to embrace me, to give me a little tenderness! And all my other companions, they too each had a girl in their hammocks embracing them. Think of the tenderness. But it was already difficult enough for one person to stay put in a hammock. Imagine two!! I tried to wrap my arms around her waist and straddle her with my legs . . . OHHH AH . . . PAA! . . . I flipped the whole thing over!

My ass landed on the brazier. AHHH! (*Mimes jumping back up like a spring.*) PAAAA! I was back on the hammock in a flash. It's all in the dynamics!

But I wanted to make love with this girl. Fortunately she taught me how: "Pay close attention . . . first of all: the trick is to grab a hook-hold with your big toe and the toe next to it . . . then open your legs so that the hammock stretches out . . . nice and wide . . . then put your arm under my waist TACCHETA . . . slide on top of me switching the position of your legs and the toeholds and . . ." PAA!!

I fell with my head pointed down vertically toward the ground . . . but I didn't hit the ground! My testicles were tangled up in the netting: "AHHHH!!!"

And she, the girl, was lying on the hammock, swinging and laughing contentedly! But I'm bullheaded stubborn. While my companions were lying under the trees at siesta time, I secretly tiptoed into the hut with the hammock and practiced equilibrium exercises . . . I tried it with one foot, with one hand. I tried it upside down, standing on my head. I became a hammock dancer like the world had never seen. I could make love hanging from my fingernails, from my feet, from my ears, my teeth . . . my buttocks . . . And when I was possessed by a twinge of folly . . . one, two, three (*mimes a full spinning circle on the hammock*) IHHEHHOHHAHH, a spinning wheel of love!!

It was wonderful staying in that place. There was only one thing that really disturbed me . . . It was the way they treated their beasts. They had animals that you don't know about . . . the turkey, they called it a gobbler, which is a big disgusting chicken . . . that thinks of itself as a peacock! It has a neck that looks like an ostrich with leprosy, and two eyes full of cataracts! The only thing it has that is truly beautiful is its feathers, beautiful feathers of turquoise and black . . . so when he wants to make himself feel important BRUUM . . . he unfurls his fan (*spreads out his arms and mimes the regal gait of the turkey*). He walks all lopsided as if to say: "Look at the beautiful feathers I have coming out of my ass."

Una nòte me sento un dolzór tenero chi atacà a la fàcia, pò dóe tóndi meravegiósi . . . vago giò con le man, sento altri dóe tondi . . . A l'era una fiòla . . . una fiòla desnüda che era vegnüda derénto l'amaca per embrasàrme, per farme tenerèsa. E a gh'era tüti i àlter mè compàri, anca lóro in ògni amaca co' una fiòla che l'embrasàva. Ti pénsa la tendrèsa che i gh'avévan . . . Ma l'era già difízil starghe in uno solo in de l'amaca, figuràrse in dóe!! Mi gh'ho fàito per andàrghe a zìnzer la vita e co' la giàmba zérco de ambrasàrla a scavalcóni . . . OHHI- IH AH . . . PAA! Me se ribalta tüto!

Sunt andà col cül in del zendariér. AHHH! (*Mima uno scatto a risalire come una molla*) PAAA! Éro già ridestendüo sü l'amaca! . . . La fòrsa de la dinamica! Ma mi ghe volevo far l'amor co' 'sta fiòia. Meno mal che lée m'ha insegnàt: . "Sta aténto . . . prima ròba: el truco è che te deve fare la forzèla col didóne del piè . . . e l'altro dido . . . po' te slarghi le giambe en manera che l'amaca la sta bela destandùa . . . slarga . . . po' te me pàsset el braso sòta a la vita . . . TACCHETA . . . me te slìseghi de soravìa destciambiàndo la posi- ión de le giàmbe e de le forsèle e . . . PAA! ! Sunt andàito giò co' la tèsta vertegàl contro el terén . . . No' so' 'rivàt ~ al terén! . . . I coión me son restàit imbragài in de la rete: "Ahhh!".

E lée, la fiòla, destendüa sü l'amaca, che la sbandolàva e la rideva contenta! Ma mi sunt un caparbio tremendo! . . . Intànto che i mè compagn i stàvan stravacàdi sóto le piante a l'ora de la siesta, mi de nascondón, gatón gatóni, entràvo derénto dove gh'era la capanóna co' l'amaca, e fasévo dei esersìs de deseschilìbrio . . . andàvo con un pìe, andàvo co' una man, andàvo derèsa cun la crapa de revèrso . . . Son diventà un balanzadór de amaca che no' gh'è al mondo! . . . Fasévo l'amor, me atacàvo con tüto, coi ungi, coi didi dei pie, co' le orège, i dénci . . . le ciàpe . . . E quando me catàva el sghiribizzo de folìa, vun, dòi (*mimq~una giravolta completa dell'amaca*) :IHHEHHOHHAHH, el ziro de la muèrte!!

A L'era una meravégia stare in quèl logo; soltànto gh'era una ròba che me dàva veraménte un sciacrón treméndo . . . A l'era co' i tratàva le bèstie. Lóro i gh'ha dei animàli, che vi àlter no' i cognossé miga . . . ol tachìn, ch'el ciàmen dindón, che l'è un galinàsso schifoso . . . el crede d'èsere un pavón! Al gh'ha un colo che pare un struso co' la lébra, doe ògi de cataratta! . . . L'ünega ròba che gh'ha bèla pro- prio so' le plume, de le bèle plüme bluètte, negre . . . che lü, quando se da' un po' d'emportànza BRUUM . . . slarga 'sto ventàio (*spalanca le braccia e mima l'incedere regale dei tacchino*), ol camìna tüto sforbanzóso che par ch'el diga: "Varda che bèle plüme che me son sorte dal cül!"

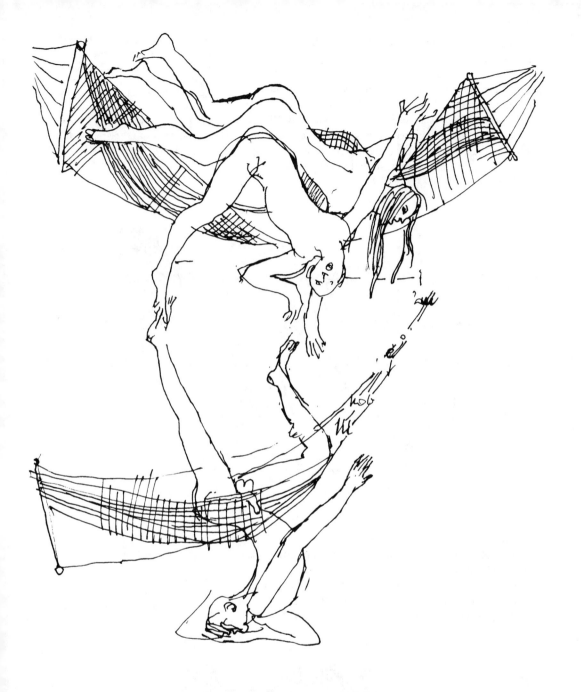

And that's just when these savages grab him and pluck out all his feathers . . . while he's still alive! (*Mimes the Indians plucking feathers from the animals.*) GNIAK-GNIAK! "Ahiaahaahaa!" . . . all the squawking! GNIAK-GNIAK . . . and this turkey was jumping all over the place: GNIAK-GNIAK-GNIAK . . . What cruelty!

Bòn, a quèl momento gh'è 'sti selvàzi che ghe salta adòso, ghe strapa tüte le pène . . . da vivo! (*Mima l'indios che strappa le piume all'animale*) GNIAKGNIAK! "Ahiaahaahaa!" . . . dei sbordón! GNIAK-GNIAK . . . e 'sto tachìn ch'ei salta de qua e de là: GNIAK- GNIAK- GNIAK! . . . Ma che cruèl!

"We are not cruel," they responded. "That's how the meal is supposed to be prepared . . . because if you pull out the feathers after you kill the turkey, the skin comes off with the feathers, along with little bits of meat! All the flesh underneath gets gristly and stringy. It's tasteless! But if you take a turkey while it's alive: SGNIAK-SGNIAK-SGNIAK, and pluck the feathers, it creates movement, the blood circulates, the nerves are stimulated, as if you were giving it a massage . . . the flesh softens, so that when you eat it, it's sweet, like butter!"

"No' è cruèl—me disévan—a l'è perchè noialtri preparémo el magnàr . . . chè se ti te ciàpet ol tachìn, te lo massi e po' te ghe stràpet le plüme, le plüme te végnen via co' la pèle e co' la pèle anca tochi de carne! E tüta la polpa che gh'è sóta a l'è slégna, sbragna, no' sa de niénte! Invece, se te brànchet ol tachìn de vivo: SGNIAK- SGNIAK-SGNIAk, te strapi le plüme, se fa tüto uno svirgolaménto, ol sang svirgola, o' gh'è tüti i nervi che sgòca . . . l'è come farghe un masàg . . . la carne la devénta una moresìna che quand ti te màgnet a l'è un dolzór, l'è un botìro!

And they give the same treatment to the wild pigs they have that are all full of bristles. They pull them out of the skin in tufts: PIO PIO PIO TRALLA! . . . But they don't do it out of meanness or cruelty. Their religion tells them: "To eat is to live!" For these savages eating is like a religion.

E i faséva lo stesso mestér anca coi porsèli seivàteghi che gh'han loro, che son pién de setole. Ghe strapàvan tüti i peli a sgionfón: PIO' PIO' PIO' TRALLA . . . ! Ma noi faśévan per cativéria cruèl, lóro i gh'han 'sta relizión che dise: "El magnàre è la vita!". Far de magnàre per quèi selvàzz a l'era una come una re1izión.

We're the crude ones. We're the ones who are uncivilized. We take a piece of meat, throw it in the fire, and that's it! A crab . . . boil it, and that's it!

They put all the feeling of a ritual into their cooking. For example, when they cook an iguana . . .

What's an iguana? It's an animal, a gigantic lizard, that you don't know about. It's disgusting. It's a dragon dwarf! It has crests like a dragon dwarf, and a mouth that, if it gets ahold of you . . . it can eviscerate you with its teeth . . . it has bulging eyes, and at the end of its tail is a stinger and if it nicks you: GNIAC . . . you're immobilized! It moves on legs with taloned feet. There's no place you can hold on to it . . . the only thing you can do is grab it by the crest on its back, a huge crest, a big bone . . . TAC, you grab it (*mimes lifting the crest, while the iguana thrashes its legs, tail, and head*), he's going: GNA GNA! Stop! (*Extends his arm to avoid being scratched by the animal.*) Keep still there! Then you take a pot, a big pot of boiling water, you throw in a little salt . . . and then you throw in the lizard, in all his writhing glory, and put the cover on . . . because that's the way he likes it. BIDUBUDON! He makes a racket inside: PATAPAPAA! The mouth comes off: TAPATAPAA! The eyes come off: TROPETITOTOO! The crest: TOM PIM TOM! The bones: TOM TOM! The legs: PEM PEM! The tail: PAA! (*He makes the gesture of digging into the pot to show the iguana to his audience, expressing amazement.*) A chicken!

You eat this iguana . . . Me, the first time I ate it, I swear, VLAAM, I threw up right away!
Because I wasn't used to the taste. You have to develop a taste for it . . . in fact when I had developed a taste for it . . . after a few weeks . . . I still threw up!
These people were happy people, cheerful. Every occasion was an excuse for a party.

One time some savages arrived from the other coast.

Noialtri sémo grosóni, sémo rùsteghi, noialtri un tòco de carne . . . ghe démo üna sprecagnàda de fògo e via. La granzéola . . . una buìda . . . e via! Loro in del cüsinà ghe méte tüto el sentimento d'ün rituàl. Par esempio quando i cüsìna l'iguana . . .
Cos'è l'iguana? L'è un animal, un lusertolón treméndo, che viàlter no' cognossé miga. L'è schifoso . . . a l'è un drago nano! A gh'ha tüti i crestón propri come un drago nano, a gh'ha üna boca che se te cata!, . . . ghe spunta dei dénci che te sgniàccan . . . dei ògi a spintorlón e in fondo a la cóa gh'ha un spinùn che se te bèca: GNIAK! . . . te s'è ingessà! Se mòve su dei giàmbi con ai pìe dei óngi treméndi! No' te lo poi brancare in nesciùn lòco . . . l'unico l'è catàrlo su la cresta de la stcèna . . . un gran creston, l'ultimo dei crestón, un oso grande . . . TAC, t'ol cati (*mima di sollevare la gran cresta, l'iguana che si divincola sbattendo gambe, coda e testa*), lü: GNA' GNA'! Fermo! (*Stende il braccio per evitare le graffiate dell'animale*) Stà fermo là! Poi te càtet un buiùn, una gran pentola de acqua che buie, te sbati derentro el sale . . . e lü, el iusertolón, te lo sbàtet dentro tüto bèlo vispo 'me l'è, el quercio de soravìa . . . che a lü ghe piàse! BIDUBUDON! Deréntro fa un rebelòto: PATAPAPAA! Ghe parte la boca: TAPATAPAA! Ghe parte i ògi: TROPETITOTOO, tüta la cresta: TOM PIM TOM, i òsi: TOM TOM, i giàmbi: PEM PEM . . . la cua: PAA . . . (*fa il gesto di cavarlo dalla pentola e di mostrarlo al pubblico esprimendo meraviglia*) Un pulàstro!
Te màgnet 'sto iguana . . . Mi le prime volte che lo magnàvo, giuro, VLAAM, vomegàvo sübeto! Perchè no' gh'avevo ol gusto, che lì gh'ha importànsa farghe el tasto, el gusto . . . infàti quando gh'ho fàito ol gusto . . . ma anche dòpo una setemàna . . . VOMEGÀVO lo stèso!
Quèsta zénte l'è zénte alégra, felìz, ogni ocasiün a l'era bòna per far festa. Una volta sunt arivàit dei selvàzi che vegnìven da un'altra costa . . .

They were amazing giants! Narrow waists . . . buttocks tight as Saint Sebastian, legs long as acrobats, slender fingers, lustrous eyes . . . And the women they had with them: creatures like you've never seen! They had long necks, these round faces, and what eyes! Hair that came down to their knees. Nipples pointing up. Their buttocks were like balconies . . . if you took a vase of water full to the brim and put it on their buttocks . . . they could walk without spilling even a drop.
They were queens!

And when you got them all together, they went wild! They danced, they sang, they laughed, they ate, they got drunk on beer, because they had so many different kinds . . . what happiness!

The only thing was, when the party ended, without warning, they jumped on us Christians, tied up all five of us like pigs, and dumped us into their boats: slaves!

Our kind saviors had sold us for a song!

I was thrown in at half price. A door prize!

They were all splitting their sides with laughter.

Eran dei zigànti meravegiósi! Gh'avevan dei vidìn, ciàpe stagne da san Sebastian, giàmbe lònghe da zompainmbànca, mani lónghe, ògi sbarluscénti . . . Le done che gh'avéan insèmblia: fèmine giamai vedùe! Gh'avéan un colo alto, 'sta facìna tonda, con dei ògi! I caveli che i arivàvan fino ai ginögci, le zinne che se rampegàvan . . . Le mostrava de le ciàpe a balcón . . . che se te catàve un vasèto de acqua repién raso e te ghe lo pogiàvi su le ciàpe . . . loro i caminàva . . . ma neanca una lacrima spantegava! De le regine!

E tüti insèmia i féva un gran rebelòt! I balàva, i cantava, i ridéva, i magnàva, i se imbriagàva de bira, che loro ghe n'ha de gran güstì . . . una felizitàd!

Soltanto che a la fin de la fèsta, sénza né un né dòi, ghe salta adòss a noialtri zinque cristian, ghe liga su tüti e sinco come porsèli e ghe sbate dentro le loro barche: stciavi!

I nostri zentìl salvadór gh'avéva vendùi per 'na cialàda.

A mi me gh'avéan dato de sovraprèsso. De regalia. Tüti i ridéva a sganàssa.

The only ones not laughing were the girls who had embraced us in our hammocks. They had streams of tears coming down from their eyes . . . They wept without sobs or sighs.

Our masters began to row, still singing and dancing: they were having quite a party those savages! And we were thrown down to the bottom of the boats.

After two days and a night we arrived at their shore. It was amazing . . . a shoreline like you've never seen before! The water was clear, placid, deep. You could see all the fish as if they were swimming in air. It was so clean that you couldn't see the surface of the water. You didn't know where the water ended and the sky began . . . There were fish with fins that jumped up out of the water and flew into the sky . . . and there were birds that dove down to the bottom of the sea and swam underwater.

How confusing!

And there were these marvelous trees full of flowers . . . but so many flowers! The land was so florid . . . in fact it was Florida!

L'Uneghe che no' rideva miga éreno le fiòle che stéveno embrassàde co' noi àlter ne l'amaca, quèle le gh'aveva lacrimoni longhi che i dissendéva dai ògi . . . le piagnéva sénsa sengùlti ne lamenti.

I nostri patrón han comenzà a remàr cantando, balàndo: faséven gran festa 'sti selvàzi! E noàltri sbatü sul fondo de le barche!

Dopo dò ziórni e una note sémo 'rivàt a la costa lóro. Gh'è aparùt una meravégia . . . una costa gimài vedüa! Gh'era l'acqua ciàra, lìmpia, profonda, se vedéva tüti i pèssi come nodàssero int el'aria, a l'era cussì pulìda che ol pel de l'acqua no' se vedéva, no' se capiva doe comenzàva ol ziélo e doe el mare . . . A gh'era dei pèssi con de le alette che saltàvan föra del mare, volàvan in del ziélo . . . e in del ziélo gh'éran dei üsèi che se ficàva in fóndo al mare e i nodàva. Una confusiün! . . .

E gh'éran 'sti àlberi meravegiósi pién de flòres . . . ma quanti flòres! Tüta florìda l'era 'sta tèra . . . A l'era appunto la Florida! . . .

It was paradise for these savages. For us it was hell. We were forced to work in the water from morning to night gathering crabs and cracking them, digging for cassava roots, mangoes, burning, cutting . . . and by evening we were exhausted, dead tired. We threw ourselves into the hammocks: alone! There was no one to embrace us. Not a girl in sight.

L'era un paradiso per 'sti selvàzi . . . per noiàftri l'inferno. Ghe tocàva trabagàr de matìna a sera deréntro l'acqua a catàr granzéole, stciepàrle, sgrafàre manioca, el mango, brüsàre, tajàr . . . e a la séra érimo scansàdi, strachi d'embrogàr, ghe se bütàva in de l'amaca . . . e soli! No' gh'era nisciùn che ghe ambrasàsse . . . no' una fiòla.

My companions were seized by unspeakable melancholy and I told them: "Don't let them see how sad you are. Don't make long faces. They don't like it. It annoys our masters to have sad slaves. We're slaves . . . but we're happy!" So when I met those masters, I played the clown: "Oh . . . I like being a slave! What a beautiful life! Nobody better try to free me . . . or I'll murder him!"

Then came the day the moon changed . . . it became full . . . I always pay attention to the moon, ever since my witch taught me how to read it . . . I looked at it and noticed how round and clear it was . . . without a halo! Suddenly I said to myself: It's a sign! My whole life is going to change. That night I was lying in my hammock, when two girls came and took me away. They brought me to one of the prince's huts . . . there were fur mats. They threw me into a big hammock adorned with fluffs of cotton, clean and perfumed. And then both of these girls lay down to embrace me, kissed me all over, and caressed me . . . in ways I can't tell you . . .

I me' compagni gh'avévan una melanconia che no' se pòl dire e mi ghe diséva: "No' féve vedée intristìdi. No' fe' i musoni, che a quèsti no' ghe piàse. A 'sti nostri padrón ghe dà fastidio i stciàvi tristi. Stciàvi . . . ma alégri! Tanto che mi, quando incontrava 'sti paron, fasévi el bufón: "Eh . . . a mi me piàse far lo stciàvo! Bela vita! Guai a chi me libera . . . lo masso!!" gridavo.

Po' el ziórno de lo scambio de lüna . . . che la devègn intréga, che mi ghe fago sémper atensiòn a la lüna de quando mé l'avéva imparàt la mia stròlegha . . . la vardo e scòvro che l'é rónda e tüta ciàra . . . senza alón! De bòto me son dit: "Questo l'è un segnàl! Chi, se cambia tüta la mea vita!". La mèisma nòce mi éro in de l'amaca stravacà-longo, son vegnüde doe fiòle, m'han catà, m'han portà in un'altra capàna de prènze . . . gh'era deréntro de le stole, dei pelàmi. M'han butà sü un amaca larga co' dei fiòchi de codón, tüta ciàra e parfumàda, e po', lóro, tüte e dòe 'ste fiòle, se son destendùe embrassàide a mi e han comensà a sbasotàrme, a farme carèse . . . de le ròbe che no' pòdo racontàre.

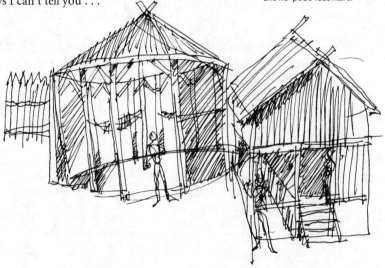

36

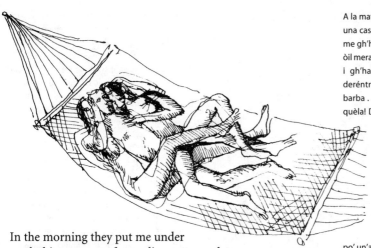

In the morning they put me under
a splashing stream of cascading water and
washed me. They spread perfumed oil all over me, a
marvelous oil! I had very long hair and they began to put it
in little braids with coral inside. I had a long beard too . . .
and they began to braid that as well! And they also put
flowers all around my neck and shoulders, and two flowers
in my ears! . . . (*pause*) A floozy!

To top it off, they put me up on a tree stump . . . and they
both began to paint me. They made signs with paint-
brushes . . . a circle on my back, in yellow . . . then another
woman came and drew a stripe all around my buttocks, in
light green . . . then someone else drew an orange circle on
my belly . . .
They painted my penis blue!
Aha . . . a pretty birdie in the sky!
My comrades were looking at me in astonishment,
bewildered: "What kind of game is this?
What are they doing to you?"
I couldn't figure out a reason for this
eccentric ritual either. It must be
because they like me, I told myself.

A la matìna m'han metüo sòta un d'acquón, gh'era
una cascàda d'acqua a spindorlón, me han lavàito,
me gh'han tüto imborgognà d'un olio profumà, un
òil meravegióso! Mi gh'avéva dei cavèi masà lònghi,
i gh'han commenzà a farme de le trezìne co'
deréntro de li coràli; gh'avevo lònga anche la
barba . . . han comenzà a farme trezìne anche a
quèla! De giùnta m'han metü dei flòres intorno al
còlo e anca sü le spale e dòe fiorón sü
le orège! . . . (*Pausa*) Una bagàssa!
Por fornìr i m'han fàit montàr sü un
ciòch de tronco . . . e tüti intórno han
comensà a pituràrme. Mé féveno dei
segni co' un penèlo a tóndo sü la
stcèna, de colór giàldo . . . po' arivàva
n'altra dòna e mé féva un rigòn
intórno a le ciàpe, de un verdulìn . . .
po' un'altro mé desegnàva un zércio colór d'arànzo
sü la panza . . .
E ol pisèlo azùrro!
Aha, aha . . . ol bèl üselìn del ziélo!
I mè compàgn i mé guardàva luchìt e disturnàt: "Ma
che ziògo l'è quèst? Cosa te fan cos'è?"
Anca mi no' reusìvo a trarghe una resòn da tüto 'sto
stciònco rituàle. Sarà perchè ghe sunt simpàtich—
mé disévi.

But then all of a sudden they began subjecting me to a treatment that gave me the chills: women, children, and even men began to pluck out hairs from all over me . . . from my stomach . . . from my legs . . . they pulled out the hairs from my beard, from my armpits . . . and from down below too . . . under the belly button . . . oh how it hurt!

"That's enough, you wretches! What do you take me for, a turkey?"
"Yes!"
"You want to eat me?"
"Yes!"
I fainted!
As soon as I woke up, I understood what the whole song and dance was about, with the colored circles on my butt, chest, and legs. They were reserving their favorite pieces of meat!!!

I felt like my soul had left me and I collapsed on the floor like a rag from the fear. But they were scared too . . . they were afraid I would die right there on the spot . . . Because they don't eat meat that dies on its own. They have to kill you themselves . . . to be sure that it's fresh. Otherwise they throw up!

Ma ohi, de bòto han metùo in pie un trataménto a mi che m'ha fa' vegnì i sgrìsui de teròr: fèmene, fiolìt e anca i òmeni han comenzàtt a strapàrme péli un po' depertüto . . . da sòra ol stòmego, da le giàmbe . . . péli de la barba i mé strapàva, de le asèle . . . anca più sotto . . . sotto ai bombonìgo . . . che l'è un dolóre!
"Basta desgrassià! Mé gh'avìt ciapàt per un tachìn?"
"Sì!"
"Me vorsìt magnàre?!" "Sì!"
Sunt svegnüdo!

Apena me son desvegiàt, ho capìt còssa l'era tüta 'sta manfrina de farme i zérchi culuràdi sü le ciàpe, el petorón e sü le giàmbe . . . a l'era la prenotasión dei quarti de carne che ghe piaséva!!
Mé son sentìt andà via l'ànema e son crodà per tèra come uno strasc per ol dolòr-spavénto.
Ma anco lóro se sunt spaventàt . . . gh'é ciapàt ol teròr per la pagüra che ghe crepàssi lì. Che lori . . . la carne morta de per lée, no' la magna migha. I te déve masàr lóro . . . frèsco de giornàta! Se no', vòmegano!

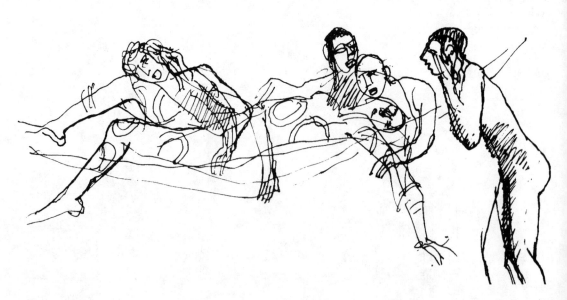

38

With a thin voice I asked the shaman, chief of the wizards . . . he was nice . . . he had big horns: "Tell me why out of all the Christian slaves you picked me? Me, who's all skin and bones. You could have just as easily chosen one of my companions, who are fatter and firmer. There's Jellybelly . . . you would have had food for a week!"

"Because you are friendly . . . The meat of one who laughs is good for you. It's easy to digest. It gives you good dreams. While the meat of long-faced sad sacks like them gets stuck in your throat. It ferments in your stomach. It makes you burp. And in the end it gives you bad breath!"

Meanwhile the sun was setting and I understood that the next day they were going to slit my throat and hang me by my feet from a hook to let my blood flow out . . . like they do with pigs.

Con un fil de vóse gh'ho dimandàt ai Sciamàn capo dei stregón . . . l'era simpàtego . . . gh'avéva i cornóni: "Diséme perchè fra tüti nojàltri cristiàn stciàvi, avìt scernìt de magnàrme pròprio a mi? A mi, che so' tüto pel e osa. Podéve bén catàrve un de mé cumpàgn che ghe n'è de pì bèli grassi e stagni. Gh'è quèl Trentatrìpe . . . te magnàvet tüta una setemàna!".
"Perchè ti te sét simpàtego . . . Carne de un che ride l'è carne bòna, se diserìsse ben, la te fa far dei bei sogni! Invece de contra, la carna de' musoni come quèli, la te se stròsa in dei gargòzz, la te fermenta in del stòmego, la te fa far de' ruti tremendi, e po', a la fin, te spüssa sémper ol fiat!"
Intanto dessendéva el sol e mi ho capìt che dimàn m'avéviano 'tacà sü a un gansón per farme colare ol sango . . . come un porsèlo.

No, I'm not going to let you butcher me.

During the night I used my teeth and nails to cut up the ropes and free myself.

Ma mi non sto chi a farme scanà!
Coi öngi e co' dénci ho stcepàt la còrda e mé sunt liberà.

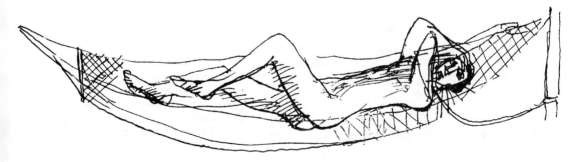

I had the desperate idea of escaping into the forest by climbing the fence. I knew very well it was a preposterous idea, because there was no hope of staying alive in the forest for even two days, with all the wild animals and snakes you'd meet there. Above all there was the jaguar. The jaguar is a spotted beast . . . a lion without a mane! It jumps on you . . . with claws that rip off your skin from head to foot.

I didn't care. It's better to be eaten by a jaguar, or a puma, or a crocodile, than to end up as a roast.

M'éra 'gnüda l'idéa desespérada de scapàr par la forèsta, scavarcàndo la stecionàda. Mi savévo bén che l'era pròprio un'idéa stcervelàda, che no' gh'éra esperànsa de restàrghe vivo nemànco per do' ziórni in la forèsta, con tüte 'ste bèstie e i serpént che s'incontràva. O gh'era sovratüto el giaguàr. El giaguaro l'è una bèstia tüta macculàda . . . un león senza cavèi! Te salta adòso . . . a gh'ha dei öngi che te strapa tüta la pèle da la crapa fino ai pie.
No' impòrta, mejór finìr magnàd de un jaguàr, de un puma o de un crocodrìil pitòst che de fenìre aròsto.

The village was protected by a circular barricade of wooden stakes enclosing it all around. I tiptoe up to the big barricade. There are no guards. I climb up to the top of the poles . . . Dammit! I see shadows of armed men climbing up the outside of the fencing.

They are enemy savages, who have come secretly to creep in and attack while everyone's asleep.

A prutég ol vilàzz gh'éra tüta una zinta de palón de lègn intorna, che ol seràva. Arìvo quàcc de bass a la gran cinta. No' gh'è nisciün de guàrdia. Mé rampéghi in zima ai palón . . . Bòja! Te vedo de le ómbre de zénte armàta che i è drìo a saltà deréntro la palisàda.
I son selvàzz nemìsi, che i végne de nasconduo, de supiàt a catàrli in del sògn!

I don't know what possessed me . . . maybe it was instinct . . . I started shouting: "To arms! To arms! Wake up, people. Your enemies have come to slaughter you!"

What a dope! What should I care about saving the skin of these savage cannibals, who on top of everything else want to eat me?

Oh, well. It was the least I could do.

"To arms! To arms!"
That wasn't enough for me. I grab a big pole and beat those savages senseless.

No' sò cosa m'è ciapàt . . . così, per l'enstìnto, mé son bütà a criàre: "Alàrme! Alàrme! Svegéve zénte, che gh'è dei nemìsi che i ve végne a scanàre!"
Ma che cojòn! Cosa mé ne intregàva a mi de salvàrghe la pèl a 'sti selvàzz canìbali, che oltretütt mé vòl magnàre?
Ohi, no' podévi farne a mén.
"Alàrmi! Alàrmi!"
No' conténto, càti un gran palón e gió a menàr stangàt' mé orbi a 'sti selvàzzi.

My sleeping Indians wake up.

A tremendous battle begins: darts and spears fly in all directions!

The women fight too, throwing stones and beating men.

Of all the enemy savages who succeed in getting inside the barricade, only ten are left alive and they are taken prisoner.

On our side, one was killed and many were seriously wounded.

'St'Indios indorménti se desvégia.

'Coménza uno scontro treméndo: saète e lanze che vola da partüto! Combàte anche le dòne a tiràr sasi e a menàr bastonàde.

De quèi selvàzz nemìsi che son reusìt a saltàr deréntro de la stacionàda, sojaménte diése i son restà vivi e i han catàd presòn.

Dei nostri, vün l'è restàt masà e quàtro son restàdi ferìdi, pròprio cunsciàt.

One of them was the shaman: a knife stab had opened his belly and his intestines were coming out.

Vün de quèi o l'è ol stregón Sciamàno: una cültelàda gh'ha dervìt la panza e gh'è sortìt tüte le busèche.

Poor man. I felt sorry for him . . . Look, the least I could do was to try to save him.
I ran to my hut, took a metal blade, an awl, and a needle for sewing sails that I had kept hidden, and approached the dying chief of the wizards.

Póver crist, mé despiàs . . . Varda, vöri tentàgh aimànco de salvàl.
Vò coréndo ne la mia capàna, ciàpi una lama de fèro, una lésina e la gügia per cüsìr le véle che avévi tegnüt de nascondòn e ghe vago arénta al capo dei stregón morebónd.

I heated up the metal and passed it over the wound.
"Aiaooooh!" An awful scream from the shaman. Savages armed with spears made moves to impale me . . . but the shaman lifted his arm a bit, as if to say: "Let him do it."
I, with my needle and thread, and with one eye on the spears of the nervous savages, started to sew, like I was used to doing with the wounds of the horses: knit one . . . purl two . . . cross one sideways . . . it was a great piece of embroidery.

'Rovento el fero e ghe lo paso su la ferìda.
"Aiaooh!", un crio treméndo dei Sciamàn. I seivàzz armàdi de lanza fan ol movimént de zagaiàrme . . . ol Sciamàn ol valza apéna un brasc, come a dir: "Lassélo fare".
Mi, co' la gügia e ol refe, sémpre con un ògio a le lanze dei selvàzz nervüs, 'coménzi a cüsìre come févi co' le ferìte dei cavàli: punto drizzo . . . do' punti a cróse . . . vün de travèrso . . . pròprio un bèl ricamìn.

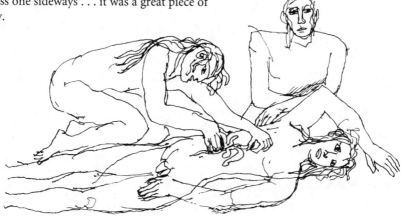

I had barely finished sewing when the shaman opened his
eyes and gave me a half-smile . . . He grabbed my hand and
kissed it. Everyone around us started
kissing my hands, caressing me . . .
then they lifted me up and carried
me to where there were others who
had been wounded in battle.

I found people sliced up all over! I had to cauterize and sew
without taking a breath until the sun set.

No' gh'ho gnanca fornìt la cusidüra, che ol Sciamàn
dèrve i ògi e el mé sorìde apéna . . . mé cata
una man e mé la basa. Tüti intórno
mé basa i man, mé fa i carèsi . . . po'
i mé vaiza su de péso e mé
pòrta dove gh'è i altri ferìdi in
de la batàja.
Trovo zénte tajàda in dapartüt! Mé tóca cauterisàr
e cüsìr sénza ciapà un respìro fina ché cala ol sole.

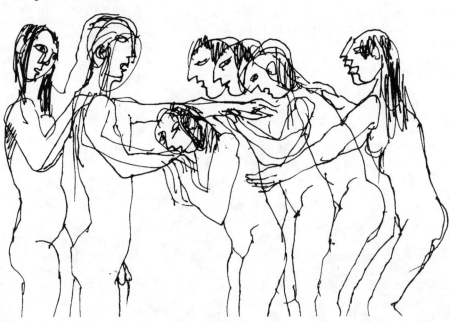

By the end I was dead tired. They took me to a hammock. I slept and sewed. Sewed and slept.

I was awakened by a soft tender warmth around my shoulders and back. I open my eyes. Oh, God. Thank the Lord! Two girls were embracing me all over! Hooray! Of course! This was the reward for having saved the whole village. I let myself go in their arms like a baby and I slept. I don't know how much later it is when I hear the shouting of the cacique: " Eh, Johan Padan, you marvel! You saved us! If you hadn't been there to sound the alarm, our enemies would have slaughtered us . . . Bravo!" And he kissed me! "All the wounded that you sewed up are alive. They're in great shape. The shaman is even walking . . . a little lopsided . . . but he's walking!"

He kissed me on the mouth, which for me was a little disgusting! "So I'm saved. You're not going to eat me," I said.
"Eat you?! How could we eat you, who sounded the alarm so wonderfully . . . No, no . . . don't worry, we're not going to eat you. We're going to make you our guard dog!"

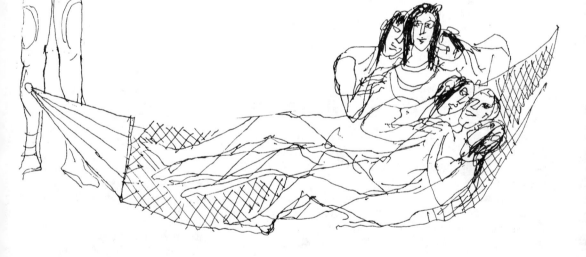

"Thank you! And my companions?" I ask. "Have you decided to free them too?"
"No. Them, we'll eat. They weren't the ones who saved us." And there was no way to talk him out of it. They were going to eat them and that was it.

A la fin, straco morto, m'han catà, m'han portà su l'amàca . . . mi dormivi e cüsìvi, cüsìvi e dormìvi!
A farme desvegiàr l'è stàit un savòr de tenerìn morbedóso intórno a le spale e a la stcèna. Dèrvo i ògi: segnór deogràsia! . . . S'éri embrasà tüto da dóe fiòle! Evìva! Quèlo o l'era de següro ol prémi per avérghe salvàt tüto ol vilàzz. Me so' lassàito andare in de le lor bràse come un bambìn e ho dormì. Ho sentì, no' sò quanto dòpo, el cacìco ch'ol criàva: "Ehi, Johan Padàn, maravégia! Ti te gh'hai salvàt! Se non l'era per ti che te dàvet l'alàrme ghé scanàva tüti, i nostri nemìsi . . . Bravo!" . . . E me basàva! "Tüti quèi feriti che ti gh'ha cüsìt i son vivi, i stan benone. A gh'è pò o! Sciamàn ch'ol camìna . . . ol va un pò de pandarlón . . . ma ol camìna!"
Me basàva su la bóca, che me faséva schìvio proprio!
"Alóra son salvo, no' me magni pu? . . . " gh'ho dit.
"Magnàrte?! Figürat se te magnémo a ti, così bravo a dar l'a!àrme . . . . . . No, no . . . stàit trànchio, no' te mangnémo: te fémo fare ei can de guàrdia!"

"Gràssie! E i mé compàgn?—ghe dimàndi—Gh'avìt desidü de liberàrli anca lori?"
"No, quèli i magnémo. Non gh'han miga salvàt lori."
E non gli é stait manera de convinserlo li se magna e basta!

Outraged and saddened, I go outside the barricade toward the sea. I was walking with an awful depression on my shoulders. "How could I save them?"

I come to the bay. I sit on the sand and look up at the moon, because, now, I always like to keep an eye on the moon. The moon is large and clear with all those little clouds round and round it . . . like that time in Venice when my girlfriend the witch showed me a similar moon just before a raging storm.

"I love you, pale witch."

The cacique came to me and said: "What are you doing, talking to the moon?"

"Yes . . . I do it all the time!"

"And she answers you?"

"Of course . . . she's my mother!"

"Ah! Ah! You are the son of the moon? And what does she say, your mother?"

"She says that she's steaming mad at all of you, and that if you don't immediately save my companions from being eaten, she's going to throw thunderbolts and send down a tempest to kill you all."

"Oh, oh!" the cacique laughs. "Oh what a wily rascal! We all know that you're good at sewing up wounds and sounding the alarm, but to expect us to believe that you're also a wizard child of the moon is a bit much, Johan. We may be savages, but we're not idiots!"

"Ah, so it's a little too much for you, is it? All right, if I were in your shoes, I'd give orders to pull in all the boats, pack up every piece of furniture I could carry, and escape as quickly as possible to the big cavern on top of the hills to save myself, because in a little while the sea will rise up as high as the sky!"

Incasà e intristìt vago föra de la zinta, invèrso el mare. Caminàvo co' adòso un gran magòn. "Come i pòdo salvàre?"

Arìvo a la marina, mé sètto sü l'aréna e vardo la lüna, che mi, oremài, ghe do sempre un ögio a la lüna. La luna l'era granda, ciàra, cun tüte le nuvolète intórno tonde tonde . . . come quèla vòlta a Venésia quando la mia 'morósa stròlega mé gh'avéva mostràt una lüna iguàle e che de lì a pòch gh'éra stàito ol finimünd.

"Stròlega smorta te vojo ben!"

L'è 'rivào ol Cacìco, me fà: "Còssa te fai, te pàrlet co' la luna?!"

"Sì! . . . NORMALE!"

"E lée, la te responde?!"

"Vorìa veder, l'è la mia matre!"

"Ah! Ah! Ti te sèt el fiòl de la luna ? E còssa la dise 'sta tòa madre?"

"La dise che l'è incasàda negra cun voi altri, che se non salvìt sübeto i me' cumpàgn de magnàrli, ve manda adòso fülmini e tempèsta de copàrve a tüti!"

"Oh, oh!"—ol Cacìco ol ride—Ohi, che furbàsso! D'acòrdo che ti sìo dimostràt bòn cüsidòr de ferìde e che ti gh'ha salvà co' l'alàrme, ma farte créder anco stregón e fiòl de la luna . . . a l'è un po' grosa Johan, sémo selvàzz ma miga cojòn!"

"Ah, l'è un po' tròp? Bòn, se fuèssi nei pagn' de vüi, mi, darla l'órden de tiràr sü tüte le barche, de far fagòtto de ógne maserìa che ve pudìt caricàrve e andèria a infricàrme all'imprèscia derénto a quèla gran cavèrna in zìma a la colìna a salvàrghe, che fra poco qui ol mare s'erampicherà nel ziélo!."

"Ohaaa! Ha!" The cacique was choking with laughter. "Don't be ridiculous. The sky's as clear as if it's just been washed. The sea is calm, serene, and placid as piss."

He had barely finished saying that the sky was clear when SWUAFF! At just that moment the sky flashed with lightning and thundered like the sound of two hundred cannons! Then there was a terrible gust of wind carrying clouds of sand . . . A horrible black stripe appeared on the horizon over the sea. All the savages, filled with fear, went running to pull in their boats.

"Ohaa! Ah!"—ol Cacìco ol se soféga del rid—"No' di' stronsade! Ol ziélo l'è cìàro che ol par slavà, ol mare l'è pìàto, calmo, tranquilo 'mé 'na pisàda."
No' gh'avéva dito "el zièl tranquìlo che . . . SWUAFF!, a l'istante un gran ciarón . . . un luminón de saète e un tron 'me dosénto canonàde! Po' 'na treménda sbafàda de vénto tira sü un nivolón de pòlver . . . 'na orébil riga négra l'è aparüda al'orisónte del mare. Tüti i selvàzz, catàt de spavénto, i va coréndo a tiràr sü le barche.

"A hurricane!"
they shouted. "A
hurricane's coming!
Save us!"

L'uragàn!—i crìa—Arìva
i'uragàn! Salvémose!"

They ran to the village, packed up everything they could,
let out all their animals and prisoners, including my
companions, and off they went. Goats, babies, turkeys, wild
pigs. They all went streaming into the big cavern!

Córe al vilàzz, caréga tüto quèl che i pòl, tira föra le
bèstie e anca i prisonér, comprési i mé compàgn, e
via tüti: cavre, fiolìt, tachìni, porsèi
selvatéch, tüti a intrupàrse derénto a la
gran cavèrna.

We didn't have time to get there before the deluge burst loose. A raging wind uprooted the trees like they were made of straw. The huts in the village were flying like dried leaves. The sea vomited boiling breakers . . . OIHCSCHIACH . . . that swept everything away . . . they even came up to the cavern!

Come sémo stàiti al repàro foera scòpia el finomùnd. Un vént fursenàt strapa i arberi cume fudès de paja. I ca' del vilagg volan via come fòje sèche. Onde a cavaloni vomitàite dal mar che boìre: OIHCSCHIACH spàssan via ogni cossa . . . 'rìvan anca a la caverna!

But we were lucky: a heap of uprooted trees, tossed by the wind, rolled up to the entrance of the cavern and formed a dike against the waves that were crashing into our refuge. It was an earthquake, an unhinging, a smashing, a thundering . . . women cried and screamed . . . men cursed. Dammit to hell! After two days and three nights this blockbuster of a hurricane underwent a sudden scene change, like the kind you see in the puppet theater when the backdrop of the tempest is lifted and one with good weather and a shining sun is rolled down in its place. It happened just like that . . . a burst of light, a sudden silence . . . and from inside we saw shooting rays of sun. There was a silence as awful as death . . . no song of a parrot . . . not even the yell of a monkey.

Ohi, che gran culo che gh'avèm: 'na caterva d'àrbori stciuncunàt la zónze a rotolón, frombolàt dal vento a stopàr l'entràda de la caverna e a fagh de bastión a le onde che se stciàntan de contra la nostra tana. Ma gh'era un tremamòto, un bracàr, uno stciànto, un rumòr . . . che le done le piagnéva, le criàva, i òmeni i biastemàva . . .
Orco can! Dòpo dói ziórni e tri notti de 'sto sburlotàr treméndo d'uragàn, come sucèd nel teatro de le marionète, a l'impruvìsa càmbia la scèna: va sü ol fondale de la tempesta e végn giò srotolàndose quèl del bèl témp serén col sol che splende!

With difficulty we unblocked the entrance to the cavern.
We went out.
Dammit! What a disaster! Outside it looked like two hundred wild and furious giants had plowed up the whole coast and all the forest.
The village had disappeared!
After a while it became clear that of all the villages, and there were thousands and thousands of them in the area, ours was the only one to be saved. And I, who was an anti-Christ, saw my hand rise up on its own and make the sign of the cross.

I turned around and saw behind me, with their faces bowed flat on the ground, all these savages on their knees, at my feet, like so many sheep: men, women, children, prisoners. I even had the impression that the goats and pigs were also kneeling, and maybe even some turkeys too.

"Forgive us," they begged, crying, "for not paying attention to you right away. We swear we won't eat you anymore, not you and not your Christian companions! We've understood in the end that you are not only the son of the moon, but also the son of the rising sun, and that you've come from the other side of the heavens to save us! A prophecy foretold that one day there would arrive from the sea a man with a beard like you, with white skin like you, a little ugly like you, who would speak with the moon like it was his mother. That one is you. Holy Man of marvels, Holy Man who is the son of the sun, help us. A Holy Man. A Holy Man." They all shouted, "A Holy Man. A Holy Man."

O l'è stai uguale . . . un ciarón grande, de colpo un silenzio . . . e deréntro s'è vedü li raj sparài dal sol. Un silénsio che faséva criàr de morte . . . no' gh'era un canto di un papagàl, nemanco il criàr d'una scìmia.
A fadìga destòpum l'entràda de a la cavèrna.
Se sòrte.
Bòja!, che desàstro! De föra ol pare che dosénto giganti furiosi, sca!manàt, l'àbbino aràto tüta la còsta e la furèsta intréga.
O! vilàzz l'è disparüt!
Vegnémo a savér apèss che, de tüti i vilàzz che gh'éra intórno per mìlia e mìlia, nojàltri s'éremo gli üneghi a èserghe salvàt. E mi che sun un anticristo me so' vedüo la man montàrse, da sè sola, a farme el segno de la crose.
Mé revòlto de drìo, e mé vedo lì, co' la fàcia basàda, schisciàda nel terén, tüti 'sti selvàzz in genugiün, ai me' pìe come tanti pecurón: òmeni, dòne, bambìn, prisonéri . . . Gh'ho avüt fina l'impressiòn che se fuèsser inginugià ancha le cavre, i pursèi e perfino i tachìn.
"Perdònaghe—i soplegàva piàgnendo—se no' te ghe avémo sübeto dàito atensiòn . . . tel ziurémo che no' te magnerémo più, né tì, né i to' compàgn cristiàn! Émo comprendìdo, al fin, che ti no' sét sojaménte el fiòl de la luna, ma anca ol fiòl dei sol che nasse, 'gniüdo apòsta de l'altra parte dei ziélo per salvàrghe! La profezìa ol gh'aveva avertìdo che de là del mare, un ziórno, ol sana 'rivàt un òmo co' la barba come ti, bianco de pèle come ti, un po' brutìn come ti, che ghe parla con la lüna come fuèsse sòa matre. Quèlo te set ti! Santo meravegióso, santo fiòl dei sol aiüdaghe ti! Santo, santo." Tüti che i criàva: "Santo, santo . . ."

I almost shouted out, "Hallelujah. Hallelujah!"

What a braggart! Me, a lowly blasphemer, son of a whore, saved by the scruff of my neck from the shit of cows and pigs, running from the fires of the Inquisition . . . in one stroke I had become a Holy Man, wizard, doctor, son of the moon and also son of the sun!

Look at what fate can do!

But I couldn't believe what an exhausting occupation it was to be a shaman-wizard-Holy Man!
First, there were all those baskets and basins full of things to eat: at least a hundred vases, baskets, and chests, all merchandise saved from the disaster. They got down on their knees and said: "Behold, Holy Man, it's all for you: Eat it!"
"Oh, are you crazy? Do you want to make me explode? And what will you others eat?"
"All right, if you want to hand over some to us . . . thank you . . . but first you have to bless it."

"Bless what?"
"The food!"
So I had to get down on my knees for this parade of baskets: I blew softly on the rice, then again on the cassava bread, another breath on the fruit, on the fish, the crabs, and the turkeys: "Ahaa!" I also had to blow on their heads to free them from evil spirits: "Ah, ah . . ."
I almost had a spontaneous pulmonary convulsion.

Mi per poch no' me scapa: "Alelùia! Alelùia!".
Oh sacragnòn! Mi, un canàja blasfémio, fiòl de puta, saivà scrofàndo in de la mèrda de le vache e dei porsèi, scapàndo dei föghi de l'Inquiosisiùn . . . in un sòl bòto son divegnüt: santo, stregón, médigo e fiòl del sol!
Varda tì ol destìn!

Ma mi, credéva miga che ol fuèsse un mesté tanto fatigóso tremémd fà ol stregón-santo-Sciamàno!
Tanto per 'comenzàr, i arìva con una mügia de baslòti rempegnìdi de ròba de magnàre: zento tra vasi, canéstri e cavàgne tüta marcanteria salvada dal desàstro. S'inginògia e i mé dise: "Ecco, santón, l'è tüto par ti: magna !"
"Ohi, sit matti? Mé vorsì far stciopàre? E vialtér cosa mangìt?"
"Bòn, se ti vòl 'vansàrghe quaicòs anca par nojàltri . . . grazie . . . ma prima ti ghe dévi fare ol plagér de lo benedìre."

"Benedìre cosa?"
"Ol magnàre!"
Mé tóca mèterme ginugióni devànti a 'sta desfilàda de baslòti: e giò una bofàda sül màis, po' un'altra sül pane de magnòca, un'altra bofàda sü i früti, sü i pèssi, le granséole e i tachìni: "Ahaa!"
Mé tóca bofàrghe anca süi lór teste per liberàrgheli dei spìriti malvàz: "Ah ah . . ."
Per poch no' m'è 'gnüt ol pnéumo toràcico spontànego.

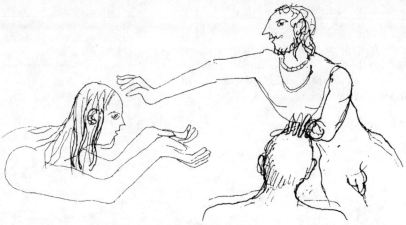

And then I had to touch every one of them on the forehead and the mouth. By the end, even my companions were hugging me with tears in their eyes: "Thank you for saving us! You saved us twice: first from being eaten and then from the hurricane . . . These savages are right . . . there's some kind of witchcraft in those eyes and hands of yours! Touch us too, come on!"

"Embrace us . . ."

"Touch us . . ."

"Me too, touch me too!"

"Me first!"

They were all over me, and the savages threw themselves at me too.

"Eh! Slow down! Eh! Ah no, that's enough!"

I grabbed a stick and started spinning it around! "Give me space! The first one that touches me gets bashed on the head with this stick!"

E sont obligàt a tocàrli sü la fronte e sü la bóca vün per un. A la fin anca i mé cumpàgn i mé ambràssa co' le làgrime a i ògi: "Gràsie che ti gh'ha salvà! Salvà do' volte: prima, de vèss magnà e po' salvà de l'uragàn . . . Gh'han resòn 'sti selvàzz . . . quaicòss de stregonìa t'el gh l'ha de següro in quèi ògi e in quèi man! Tòcheghe anca a nojàltri, fèite bòn!"

"Ambràsaghe . . ."

"Tòcaghe . . ."

"A mì, toccame a mì!"

"Prima a mì!"

E tüti che i mi végne adòsso e i se büta anche i selvaggi.

"Eh! pian! Ehi! Ah no, basta!"

Ho catà un bastón e l'ho fàit pirietà d'entórno.

"Slargheve! El primo che me tóca ghe sctèpo 'sto bastón in su la crapa!"

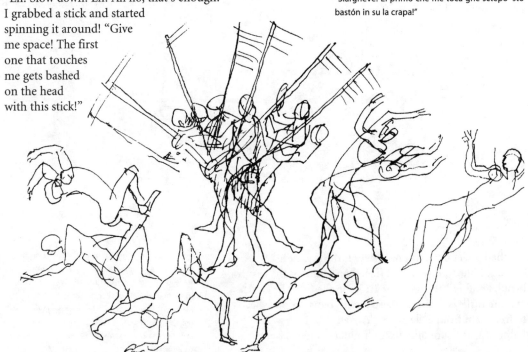

That resolved the situation, but there was another more serious one: the cacique got down on his knees in front of me again.

"You, who can speak to your mother the moon and your father the sun . . . ask them where we should go . . . you have seen that we can walk in any direction for days without finding a tree that still stands or an animal to eat . . . even the lizards and crabs have disappeared . . . we have to escape this place! But where should we go? We have to go someplace that was beyond the reach of the storm. But where? To the north or the south? Should we go to the west? Should we go to the east? Where should we gooooooooo?"

"Stop shouting!" I said. "Go west!"

"How can you say it so clearly and sure?"

"I'm a Holy Man! I should know a thing or two, shouldn't I?" I knew for certain that in those years many Spanish armadas, with fifteen or twenty ships in each expedition, went west of these shores to establish a large colony. So, after a few months' march we would surely encounter those Christians . . . and finally we would have the chance to make a sweet return to our homes. Home . . . because to tell the truth . . . these damned Indians were beginning to get on my nerves!

Because after the voyage in the ship's hold covered with the shit of horses and cows, and our salvation embracing the pigs . . . and being enslaved . . . and plucked like a turkey, painted with circles, and then beaten . . . winds, storms, lightning bolts, followed by: Holy Man! Holy Man! Blow on us, pat our heads, our butts, our balls . . . I've had enough! Home! I want to go hooooome!

Risòlta la situasiòn, la ghe n'éra un'altra un po' più seriòsa: ol Cacìco ol s'éra metü 'n'altra vòlta in ginugiöni devànti a mi.

"Ti, che ti pòl parlàrghe a to' matre la lüna e a to' patre el sol . . . ti, ti gh'ha bén vedüo che tüto intòrno per jornàde e jornàde de camino no' ghe se ritròva un àrbaro sano, né ninghiüna bèstia de magnàre, che perfino le lusèrtole e i càncari son desparude . . . dovémo scapàre da 'sto lògo! Ma dove andémo? Dovémo andàr in d'un liògo dove non è 'rivàt la tempesta. Ma dove andémo? De nord o de sud? Andémo de ponente? Andémo de oriente? . . . Dóe andémooo?"

"E no' criàr!—fagho mi—Se va, per ponénte! ""Come te fai a dirlo così ciàro e segùro?"

"Sunt un santo! Savrò qualche cosorìna!"

Mi savévo de següro che una mügia de armàde Ispagnòle, in quèl témpo, con quìndese, vénti nàvi per ògni spedisiün, i era deséndue a ponente de quèla còsta per fondàrghe una colònia granda. Dònca, con quàlche mese de camìno, gh'avrìamo de següro encontràdi 'sti cristiàn . . . e, finalménte, avrèsmo üt la sciànsa de far bòn retòrno a casa. A casa che, davéro . . . de 'ste Ìndie malerbète comensàva ad avérghene de vomegàre! Che fra ol viàzo ne la stiva ne la merda dei cavàli e de le vache e ol salvaménto ambrasà ai porzèi . . . e l'éss fàito stciàvo . . . e spenàto 'mé un tachìn, coloràt a zérci, e po' bastonà . . . vento, tempesta, fuimeni-saète e dòpo: santo, santo!, bofàrghe adòso, tocàrü sü la crapa, sü le ciàpe e süi cojòn . . . Basta! A casa! Voi tornàrme a casaa!

Part Two

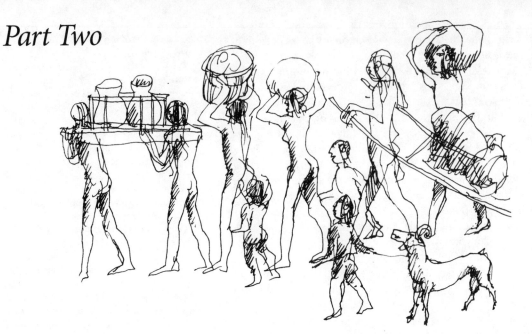

"So let's go! Forward march!"
The cacique gave a sign of agreement, but he warned me that these parts were inhabited by a race called the Junicacio, who were not at all friendly . . . and another called the Inca, who were even worse.
"We'll go there anyway. That's the end of the discussion!"
After all, was I or was I not the holiest son of the sun, and the moon too! "So keep quiet and start walking!"
And so we made a caravan, me in front with a big leaf on my head to keep off the sun, and all the others behind me, including the prisoners captured in the battle at the village: all with ropes tied around their necks.

"Alóra, se va! In camìno!"
Ol Cacico ol fa segno che sì, d'ecòrdo, ma ol ghe da avisàda che de quèle bande, se retròva una rassa de zénte che la se ciàma Junicàcio, che no' so' miga bòni . . . e altri che se ciàma Incas, che anca loro no' scherza.
"Beh, se va' iguàbe per quèle tère. E no' gh'è discussión!" Bòja, l'ero o no' l'ero, ol santissimo fiòb dei sole e anca de la lüna! Dònca cìto lì: in marcia!
E così se forma 'na gran carovana, mi d'innanzi tegnéndome in testa una fòja granda per reparàrme dol sol, e tütti i altri, adrè a mì, comprés i presonér caturà in quèl scontro deréntro al vilàzz: tüti ligà con le corde al col.

We walked for days and days across territory that had been ravaged by the hurricane, devastated. You couldn't even find a grasshopper, or a worm to eat, not even sweet roots. Day after day the supplies of corn, goat meat, and pork were running out, until in the end we were left with nothing to eat. We were dying of hunger. People were groaning, babies were fainting, and finally the cacique said: "That's enough. Tonight we eat!"
"What do we eat?!"
"We eat the prisoners that we brought with us."
"Are we going back to that barbaric vice of cooking human flesh?"
"Why," replied the cacique. "Are you Christians more civilized? You, who kill your enemies in battle, butcher each other, massacre each other . . . and then leave ripped-up bodies to rot on the battlefields? Fresh food, meat killed that very day! What a waste! And we're the barbarians?"
"Who told you these things?"
"A Christian that we ate last year."
"Enough! That's the end of the discussion. From now on, no more eating the flesh of Indians or Christians! Otherwise I'll tell the moon and she'll get furious and send another earth-shaker."
"Dammit," they shouted. "This moon is a real ballbuster!"

Émo caminà per ziórni e ziórni in un terén che l'üragàn l'avéa revoltà, scardena. No' se trovàva una cavalètta, un vèrmeno de magnàre . . . nemanco le radìsi dólze. Così, ziórno per ziórno, le masserìzie de màis e le scorte de cavre e porsèi i andàva deslenguéndose, fino a che sèm restàdi sénza pì nagòt. Se moriva de fam, gh'era la zente che la crìàva, los chicos, i fiulit che desvegnìva e alóra el Cacìco gh'ha dit: "Basta, 'staséra se magna!"
"Cossa se magna?!" "Se magna i prisonér che ghe sémo portàit aprèso!" "Ah, ghe se retròvemo un'altra volta co' 'sto vìsio de bàrberi de cüsinàrse carna de òmeni?" "Perchè—mé respünd ol Cacìco—sit più sivìl vojàltri cristian? Pròpri vüi che masét i nemìsi in batàja, se scanì, ve smassacrì . . . e po', tüti i morti squarciàdi e lasét marsìre sü i campi de lo scontro? Roba frèsca, carne 'massàda de giornàda! Strasoni! E nüi sarèsmo i bàrberi!"
"Chi te l'ha 'cuntàda 'sta storia?" "Un cristiàno che émo magnà l'anno pasà." "Basta, no' gh'è discussión. De 'sto moménto, carna de indio o de cristiàn no' se ne màgna più! Se no, ghe lo digo a la luna che s'incàsa 'e ve manda 'n'altra volta el tremamóndo!"
"Bòja—i crìa—'sta lüna che rompicojón!

Two days later, when no one had eaten as much as a dried leaf, and we were staggering like drunks from hunger, we suddenly saw coming from a far-off hill a long thin stream of smoke rising to the sky.

"We made it," shouted the cacique joyfully. "There in the distance are the Conciuba."

"Who are the Conciuba?"

"The're savages like us, from the same race as ours . . . They're called Conciuba because they have shaved heads. They're a friendly tribe . . . And they too must surely have been saved, because the hurricane didn't get that far."

Our savages quickly stoked up a fire and threw some wet herbs on it so it would give off a lot of smoke. And they moved around it with some big leaves like the ones I used for protecting me from the sun . . . they were fanning, covering, uncovering, and putting cut leaves all around the fire: making smoke clouds, long, short, big, puffed-up, and long again . . . and then a string of little clouds in clusters. It was unbelievable stuff! With this smoke-play the cannibals could talk to the savages on the hill in the distance. They made words from clouds of smoke. So effectively that when the Conciuba arrived they were carrying all kinds of food! They brought it because . . . the ones over here had notified them with the smoke: "Listen . . . we haven't eaten for days and days, not a bite . . . bring us something to eat because we're hungry as cows!"

As soon as they came close, they threw themselves onto their knees in front of me and gave me all the food, saying: "Touch us, blow on us too . . ."

What was going on?

Witchcraft! Our Indians had warned them with the smoke: "Listen, we've got an important Holy Man with us. He comes from the rising sun and he's the son of the moon . . . he talks to the moon . . . to the mooooooon!! Be careful because she gets mad as a rattlesnake if you don't do what he says!"

Doi ziórni apprèss, che nisciüno l'avéva magnà nemànco una fòja sèca, e se caminàva ciondolón me' embrìaghi per la fàme, a l'improvìsa, de una colìna in fóndo, émo visto spontàr ün lòngo fum sutli . . . che montàva in ziél.

"Ghe sèm,—l'ha crià ol Cacìco tüto festüs—là infónda gh'é i Conciùba . . ."

"Chi enn i Conciùba?"

"I enn dei selvàzzi come noialtri, de la mèsma rassa nostra . . . i ciàman Conciùba perchè i gh'han la crapa pelàda. I è una tribù amìsa . . . E anca lori de segùro se son saivàt, che l'uragàno fin là-lòga no' l'è 'rivàt."

All'imprèscia, 'sti selvàzz nostri, attìsa un fògo e po' ghe sbàtten de soravìa de le erbe bagnàde per fà 'gnir fóra un gran fumo. E movéndose intórno con de le fòje larghe come quèla che dovràvi mi per riparàm del sole, i le sventolàva, i le covriva, i le destacava, i le tajava intórna ai fògo: i fàseva 'gnir fóra di nìvolete lònghe, corte, siarghe, sgionfie, longhe de novo . . . e ancóra, de colpo, una fila di nivolètt a gràspolo. Ròba de no' créderghe! Con 'sto ziògo dei fumo, 'sti canìbali, i era drìo a parlàrghe a quèi selvàzz, che stéveno in fónda sü la colìna! Coi nìvoli de fumo faséa paròle! Tanto è vera che quèi Conciùba quand so' 'rivàiti, éreno carigài de roba de magnàre! Han portàito tante robe . . . chè loro, quèsti qua, co' il fumo l'avéan avertìdi: "Aténti . . . che l'è ziorni e ziorni che noialtri no' "sgraniamo", no' magnémo miga . . . portéghe de magnàre che gh'émo una fame bestia!!"

Come i son 'rivà a diése passi, i se son bütà tüti in genögio devànte a mi, e me dava tüta la roba de magnàre e i mé diséa: "Tócaghe, bófaghe adòso anca a nüngh . . .".

Se l'era capitàt?

'Na strologorìa! I nòster indiàn, col fumo, li gh'avéva advisàt: "Aténti che co' noialtni gh'è un santón che vien dal sol che nasse, e l'è ol fiòl de la luna . . . ghe parla a la luna, a-ll-a-luunaaa!! . . . Aténti che quèla s'encàssa 'me üna bissa se non ghe de' trà!"

They had a dozen savages with them who had big heads with bleached hair gathered in braids. . . . they were dark-skinned, almost red . . . and they had rings in their noses . . . they had thick jaws, with lots of teeth . . . and evil faces . . . Their chief came over to me, looked at my feet a little, and then SPIU SPIU, he spit on my feet!

"Hey, you miserable savage, what's got into you?"

"We will not revere you, even if they say you're a Holy Man. You look too much like those Spanish Christians we met at a four-and-half-month walk from here. They disembarked from a dozen big ships about a year ago, a hundred men completely covered in metal, helmets, armor, and they had sticks that spit fire. And then they attacked us with hideous monsters that they call horses: a huge beast that has a man growing out of its trunk . . . alive, all covered in metal, as one with the animal . . . and with the other soldiers they butchered everyone. They threw themselves on our women. They screwed them right there in front of our eyes and then carried them off as slaves.

In tramèzo a quèi, gh'éra una donzèna de selvàzz che gh'avéa de' testón co' dei cavèi ingiaidìdi racòlti a tresìne, scüri de pèle . . . squàsi ross, e i gh'aveva dei anèli sul nas . . . i gh'aveva perfino de le ganàsse co' tanti dénci . . . una fàcia de catìvi . . . Gh'è stàito e! loro capo che l'è vegnüd devànti a mi, m'ha vardà un pochetìn i pie e po' SPIU SPIU, m'ha spudà su i pie!

"Oh vilan d'un selvàz, cossa te cata?!"

"Me cata che no' gh'avémo nissciùna reverénza per ti, anche se i dise che te s'è santo. Te somèie tròpo a quèi cristiàn spagnoli che noialtri gh'avémo incontràt a quatro mesi e mèso de camìno de chi loga. I sünt sbarcàdi, oremài fa pì de un ano, de una donzéna de navi grandi, una centéna de òmeni recovèrti al complét de fèro, elmi, coràse, e i gh'ha dei bastón che spüda fògo. E po' ghe sont vegnüdi adòso con dei mostri tremendi, che ion i ciàma cavàl: una gran bestia, che del gropón ghe spunta un òmo . . . vivo, tüto covèrto de fèro, una roba sola con st'animàl . . . e coi i altri soldàt i fa' matànze de tütt. Ghe so' saltàiti adòso a le nostre done, le han fotü lì, davanti ai nostri ògi e po' le gh'han portàito via stciàve.

It's lucky for you that you're surrounded by all these people defending you, because if we ever find you alone, we'll eat you alive." And they went off cursing.

Later I discovered that these savages were from a special race that called themselves Incas . . . which was the extreme short form for: inconsolably pissed off!

I knew what role to play. I feigned indignation: "Is that so? Well! I'm going to go right there, to that plain, and denounce them to the grand admiral governor . . . who is a great man of honesty and justice. He surely knows nothing about this looting and murder. And when he finds out, you'll see . . . he will deliver a horrible punishment to these butcherous assassins! So it's settled, tomorrow we leave and all of you together will accompany me to the mountains in that valley."

Not a chance! No one made a sound. They sat on their asses, put their heads between their knees, and without looking me in the face said: "No, no, no, no, we're not going! Those Spaniards are too evil. They kill, they butcher . . . we're not going!"

"I don't care. You can stay here. I have my own savages. Cannibals, let's go!"
No one moved.
"Cannibals, are you coming with me?"
The cannibals stayed seated with terrified faces.
"So even you won't come with me? After all I've done for you? . . . I blew on your food till my lungs burst . . . I chased away evil by patting your heads, your butts, and even your balls . . . I sewed up your wounds when your intestines were falling out . . . and now, the one time I ask you a favor, you answer no, we won't come with you? No? To a Holy Man? Then you know what I say to you? Up your asses, you savage pricks!"

Bon per ti che te s'è contornàdo de tüta 'sta zénte che te defénde, chè, se te trovémo de solo un'altra volta, te magnémo vivo!" E via che so' andàit blastemàndo. Po' ho scovèrto che 'sti selvàzi son d'una raza spesiàl che la se ciàma Incas . . . che l'è üna estremasiùn curta de incassà!

Mi cognosévo bén 'sto progràma-spetàcol. Mé sont fingiüt endignàt: "Ah sì? Bon! Ariverò mi là, in quèla piana e ghe farò denünzia al gran Almirante Governadór . . . che quèl l'è un gnand'òmo de onestà e justìsia. De següro lü no' cognóse nagòtt de 'ste roberìe e de 'sti 'masaménti. E quando ol savarà, vedarét . . . ghe darà una tremenda punisión a quèi macelàri asasin! Alóra d'acòrdi, domàn se riparte e viàiter, tüti insèma, me' acompagnìt de là dei monti in quèla vale!"

Gnanca per idea! Tüti i stà cito sentà sül cül, la testa infricàda in fra i ginògi . . . no' mé varda in fàcia e i me dise: "No, no, no, no, noiàlter no' vegnémo miga! Quèsti spagnòi i son tropo catìvi. I massa, i scana . . .
no' vegnémo miga!

"No' me interesa, resté chi tranchìli, tanto mi gh'ho i mé selvàzzi. Canibali, andémo!" Nisciùn che se mòve.

Canibali me compagné?" I canibali i stéva sentàdi co' una fàcia de spaventàdi.

"Alóra no' vorsìt acompagnàrme nemanco voiàitri? Con tüto quèlo che ho fàito mi?! . . . V'ho bofàt sü le vivande de stciupàm i polmón, v'ho descasà ol maligno sparpignàndove la crapa e i ciàpp e anca i cojóni, recusìt le ferìde con le busèche föra . . . e adèso, per una volta che ve dimàndi un plasér, voàltri mé respondì de no, no' vegnìmo cun ti? De no? Al santo?! Alóra savét cosa ve disi? Andì a da' via ol cüi, selvàzz dol cazz!"

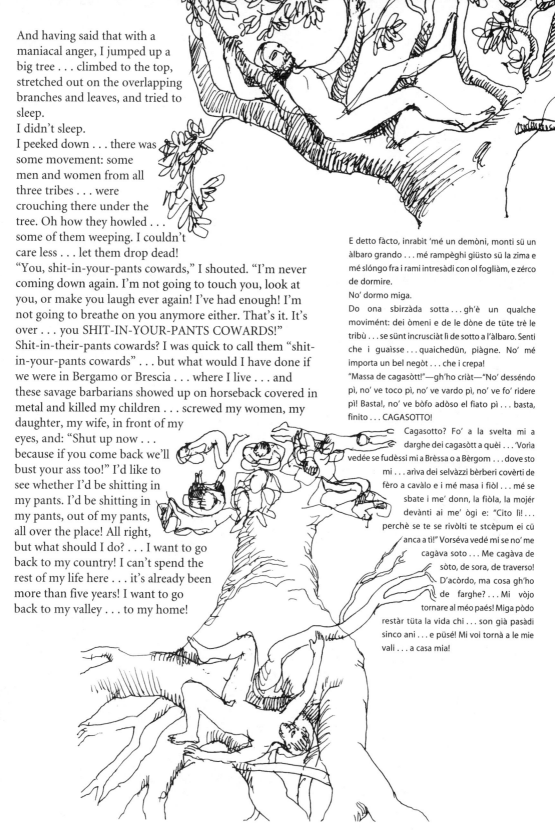

And having said that with a maniacal anger, I jumped up a big tree . . . climbed to the top, stretched out on the overlapping branches and leaves, and tried to sleep.

I didn't sleep.

I peeked down . . . there was some movement: some men and women from all three tribes . . . were crouching there under the tree. Oh how they howled . . . some of them weeping. I couldn't care less . . . let them drop dead!

"You, shit-in-your-pants cowards," I shouted. "I'm never coming down again. I'm not going to touch you, look at you, or make you laugh ever again! I've had enough! I'm not going to breathe on you anymore either. That's it. It's over . . . you SHIT-IN-YOUR-PANTS COWARDS!"

Shit-in-their-pants cowards? I was quick to call them "shit-in-your-pants cowards" . . . but what would I have done if we were in Bergamo or Brescia . . . where I live . . . and these savage barbarians showed up on horseback covered in metal and killed my children . . . screwed my women, my daughter, my wife, in front of my eyes, and: "Shut up now . . . because if you come back we'll bust your ass too!" I'd like to see whether I'd be shitting in my pants. I'd be shitting in my pants, out of my pants, all over the place! All right, but what should I do? . . . I want to go back to my country! I can't spend the rest of my life here . . . it's already been more than five years! I want to go back to my valley . . . to my home!

E detto fàcto, inrabìt 'mé un demòni, monti sü un àlbaro grando . . . mé rampèghi giüsto sü la zima e mé slóngo fra i rami intresàdi con ol fogliàm, e zérco de dormire.

No' dormo miga.

Do ona sbirzàda sotta . . . gh'è un qualche movimént: dei òmeni e de le dòne de tüte trè le tribù . . . se sünt incrusciàt lì de sotto a l'àlbaro. Senti che i guàisse . . . quaichedün, piàgne. No' mé importa un bel negòt . . . che i crepa!

"Massa de cagasòtt!"—gh'ho criàt—"No' dessèndo pì, no' ve toco pì, no' ve vardo pì, no' ve fo' ridere pì! Basta!, no' ve bòfo adòso el fiato pì . . . basta, finito . . . CAGASOTTO!

Cagasotto? Fo' a la svelta mi a darghe dei cagasòtt a quèi . . . 'Vorìa vedée se fudèssi mi a Brèssa o a Bèrgom . . . dove sto mi . . . arìva dei selvàzzi bèrberi covèrti de fèro a cavàlo e i mé masa i fiòl . . . mé se sbate i me' donn, la fiòla, la mojér devànti ai me' ògi e: "Cito lì! . . . perchè se te se rivòlti te stcèpum ei cü anca a tì!" Vorséva vedé mi se no' me cagàva soto . . . Me cagàva de sòto, de sora, de traverso! D'acòrdo, ma cosa gh'ho de farghe? . . . Mi vòjo tornare al méo paés! Miga pòdo restàr tüta la vida chi . . . son già pasàdi sinco ani . . . e püsé! Mi voi tornà a le mie vali . . . a casa mia!

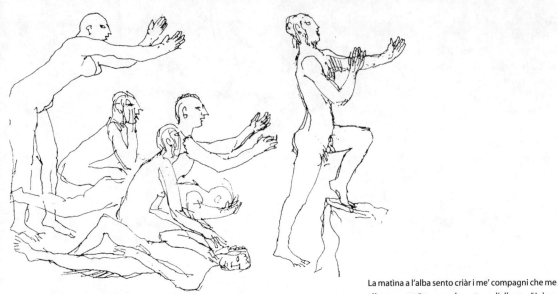

The next morning at dawn I heard my companions
shouting at the tops of their voices: "Johan, come down.
Disaster has struck. Last night, these savages, the moment
you stopped looking at them, fell into a tremendous state
of desperation, and forty of them were stricken sick with
grief. Come down please, do something, because you're like
the light for them, their breath, their life!"
"Stop it, you wretches. Who am I now, Jesus Christ? Put
me under a glass bell and I'll come out with my arms wide
open and bless you! All right . . . I'm coming down."
When I got down to the ground, I found a bunch of people
flat on their backs, pale and trembling.
One by one I breathed on them, patted their faces, their
stomachs . . . but most of all, I tried to show them I was
happy, smiling big smiles . . . giving them friendly slaps . . .
to make them see I wasn't angry anymore.

La matìna a l'alba sento criàr i me' compagni che me
ciàmano a tüta vos de sota a l'albero: "Johan
desséndi che chi l'è stciopà un desàstro. Sta note 'sti
selvàzz, dei momento che ti no' te li vardi più, son
burlàt deréntro a una desperasiün tremenda e in
quaranta se son immorbài de tristìzia. Desséndi te
pregi, fai quaicòssa, perchè ti te s'è devegnüt la lüse
per loro, ol fiàt per loro.., la vita!" "Desgrassià, adèss
so' Jesus Cristo? Metéme sòta una campana de
vedro . . . vegni föra con le mani slargàt a benedìrve!
Va bén . . . deséndo . . .
Ziónto de baso, retrùovo una mügia de gente slargà
par tèra sbianchìda coi' tremori, e mi, vün per vün,
ghe bòfi adòss, ghe palpo sü la fàcia, ol stòmego . . .
ma sóvra tüto, mé tóca mostràrme contento, con
gran sorìsi . . . molàrghe de sgiafòt de sempatìa . . .
insóma farghe inténder che no' son più inrabìt.

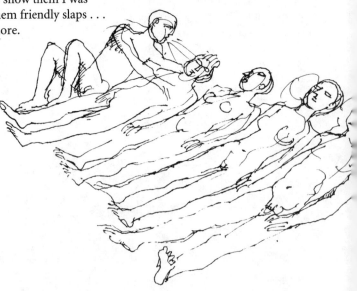

But that wasn't enough: for the most grief-stricken ones I had to let loose with a pantomime of clownish joy . . . I threw myself into a dance, leaping, bouncing . . . And I shouted: "Dance, come on, jump, let's go . . . PAPARAAPPAPUM . . . dance, dance!"
The grief-stricken ones all danced! In less than a half hour, they were all healthy again . . . except eight who died! From dancing!
"Forgive us, we're all coming with you!"
Olé! Let's go! We're leaving!
Finally, we're leaving!

E no' l'è basta: devànti a quèi che son morebóndi mé tóca scatenàm in una pantomima d'alegrèsa spajasénta . . . mé büti a balàr, saltar zompando . . . e vusi: "Balé, avanti, salta, via andémo . . . PAPPARAPAPPAPUM . . . balàre, balare!"
Tüti i moribondi che i balàva! Dòpo neanca meza ora i eran tüti sani . . . salvo oto che eran morti!
Balàndo!
"Perdónaghe, vegnémo tüti con ti!"
Alé! Adelànte! Se parte! A la fin se parte!

We crossed a forest for days and days . . . looking up through the leaves of the overlapping branches, we could only occasionally catch sight of patches of sky. We progressed with great difficulty . . . branches and undergrowth blocked our path. All of a sudden someone shouted, "A monster!"
My companions and I took some long spears and went to see what it was.

Se 'travèrsa una foresta per ziórni e ziórni . . . vardàndo in sü fra i rami entresàdi de fojàme, se reussìva sojaménte a endovinàr qualche sfèrzola de ziélo. Se va en avànti con gran fatìga . . . rami e arbùsti che ghe blòca ol camìno. A l'impruvìsa, s'è sentì criàre: "Un mostro!!"
Mi e i mé compàgn, prontàndo de le lanze lònghe, vémo a védar.

Oh, mother of God! It was a horse! A wild one. A young skinny stallion . . . kicking up its hooves, biting big chunks out of anyone who happened to be nearby. We had to capture it.

"Hey, Indians, let's go capture this monster! Where are you?" I looked up . . . they had all climbed up to the top of a tree.

"Oh, you've found yourselves some comfortable seats for the show!"

Oh, sangre de dìos! L'era un cavàlo! Enselvadeghìd. A l'era un stalónin magró . . . ol tirava scarcagòn coi' zòcol, o! sgagnàva co' gran cagnàde ognùn che ghe capitava a tir. Bòn, bisogna farghe la catüra.

"Ehi zénte de indios, fémo la catüra de 'sto mostro! Ma dove sit?!"

Valzo la fàcia i eran tüti rempegà in zima ai alberi.

"Ah, ve sit piasà comodi par ol spetàcolo!"

And so, assisted by my companions, we stretched cords of rope round and round the tree trunks in a circle so that the beast was surrounded. Then we took a long reed . . . he was in the middle of a clearing . . . and I began: "Come here, good boy . . ." he reared up, snorted, and pawed his hooves on the ground . . . trembling: "Look, the monster's scared! What is a horse, after all? It's just a donkey with an inflated sense of self-importance. Careful now, I'm going to try to mount him."

I climbed up to the top of a tree and straddled a branch. I waited until the horse came close enough, and I jumped on his back. I grabbed his mane . . . And he began to thrash around, from side to side, he bucked . . . all of a sudden he reared up, I flew through the air . . . AHH . . . PAA . . . and then: FLAT ON MY ASS!

And all the Indians laughed, shouting: "The Holy Man's lost his touch."

How quickly a reputation can be lost!

e alóra, aiudàt dei mé compàgn andémo a destènder de le còrde lónghe tüte tórno-tórno, de tronco a tronco d'àlbaro . . . in zìrcolo, de manéra de zircondà tüta 'sta bestia. Pò emo ciapà una cana lònga, lü l'era in mezo a una radura, ho comensà: "Vié, bravo . . ." se rampegàva, sbonconcìàva, o dava de sòcolo,el tremava "Vardé, ol gh'ha pagüra el mostro! Cossa l'è a la fin un càvàl? . . . A l'è un asino che se dà un poco d'emportansa! Atensión che adèso zérco de montàrghe en gròpa mi."

So' montà in sima a un albero, me so' metùo a cavalción d'un ramo, ho specià che il càvàlo drisàse, sunt andàit de gropa, l'ho catà de sgàrgola, gh'ho ciapà la criniera . . . e lü coméncia a sgargagnàr de qua, de là, ol spintornàva . . . de bota m'ha dàit una strinzonàda, sunt andàit per aria AHHH . . . PAA! . . . UNA CULADA!

E tüti i Indios che rideva criàndo: "Ah . . . , ol santo el s'è ingripào!"

Come se fa imprèscia a pèrder una reputasiòn!

Fortunately the Negro came to my rescue . . . he slapped the horse's rump, jumped onto its back, and straddled it. He gripped the mane with one hand and the tail with the other . . . and the horse began to jump, stand on its hind legs, twist sideways, and kick, but the Negro didn't move . . . he was glued on. After a half hour of this dance, up, and down, and around, the horse was out of breath. (*Shows how the horse breathes when it is out of breath.*) AH, AH . . . Then the Negro got him to do whatever he wanted. First a nice gallop . . . TRUN, TRUN, TRUN, TRUN, then a trot, TRUN and TRUN, then the side-cross: "Cross your legs. One in front, the other behind, there you go . . . Now take a bow . . . Now hop . . . Sit down!" and "Good night!"

Meno male che gh'è stàito el Negro che m'ha salvàito . . . gh'ha dàit una paca su le ciàpe al cavàlo, gh'è saltàit inforcà de gropa, gh'ha brancài con una man la criniera e co' l'altro la cua . . . e quèlo ha comensà a saltare, a 'nvrogognàre in pie, de traverso, el caracolàva, ma lü ol Negher no' se movéva . . . ol era inculà! Dopo mèsa ora de quèsta ronda de su, de qua, 'sto cavàlo ol gh'aveva la bonfarìa. (*Rifà il cavallo che respira col fiatone*) AH, AH . . . Aióra ol Negher gh'ha fàit far quèl che vorséva lü . . . prima un bel galòpo . . . TRUN TRUN TRUN TRUN, po' il tròto, TRUN e TRUN, po' la cróse: "Incrosàre le giàmbe!, v'una davanti e v'una de drio, via! . . . Fà la reverénza! Fa la zòpa . . . Sentàito!", e bonasìra!

There was a savage who shouted, "Bravo Negro!" He hugged the horse. He wasn't afraid anymore. "I want to ride it!" he shouted. "Me too, me too!" they all shouted. Even the women wanted to ride that horse. And so we set up a riding school for the whole tribe.

A few days later we heard the ear-splitting whinny of another horse from not far away. Ah, ah, ah . . . it was a female horse: the mother of the young stallion who had escaped from the Spaniards and given birth to him in the forest. She was used to saddles, and when we mounted her she didn't even move. But then a little later the young stallion's father arrived, a huge male: he was a bull with a mane! He jumped, kicked up his hooves, and had the teeth of a lion. No one could touch him.

When the Negro jumped on his back, the stallion bucked him off so hard that he smacked into a tree . . . it almost crushed him!

Then I had the idea of trying an incredible taming technique I'd seen in Bergamo.

Gh'era un selvàzo che criàva "Oh, bravo Negro!" L'embrassàva el cavalo, no' gh'avéa pu' pagùra. . "Voj montàrghe!" vusàva. "Anch' mi, anch' mi!" vusàvan tütti. Anche le done vorséven fa la monta a 'sto cavàlo . . . e alóra emo fàito la scòla de monta a tüta la tribü!

Qualche dì aprèss arìvom a sentì una nitrìda a squàsa-orègi d'on altro càvàl de miga tanto lontàn. Ah, ah, ah, l'era una cavaba femena: la madre del stalunìn che l'era scapàda dei spagnòi e l'aveva sfornàito ne la foresta. A l'era 'bituàda a la sèla e quand sémo andàit a montarla no' s'è neànca movùa. Solamente che de lì a pòch l'è 'rivàt el pader dei stalunìn, un màstcio tremendo: a l'era un toro co' la criniera! Dava dei sgiampàd, dei zocolàd, gh'aveva dei dénci da leon, nisciùn ol podéva tocàrlo.

Gh'è stai oi Negro che gh'è saltàito in gròpa, ol stalón gh'ha dàit 'na sgropàda de stcèna che l'ha sbatüdo contro un albero . . . che momenti l'impatàca!

Alóra a mi m'è vegnù in mente 'la dòma a la bergamasca' . . .

The hardest part is putting on the bridle, because the horse would bite anyone who came near him . . . so you put the bridle on the ground tied to the ends of two reeds that are laid down like a trap . . . he walks over and sees the bridle on the ground, and, being curious, puts his head down to look at it: "What is this thing," he wonders . . . and TRAK, the two people who've been hiding with the reeds in their hands lift them up all of a sudden and the bridle gets pulled on to the stallion's snout up to his ears. But at this point you have to attach ropes to the bridle to make the reins, one on the right, and one on the left. You can't approach him from the front because he'd bite you, so you pretend to talk to someone who's standing to your right . . . and you tie it over there . . . and he, the horse . . . gets curious . . . so he comes over to listen and . . . then you go to the other side, but make sure you change the man that you're talking to . . . otherwise the horse will get suspicious (*mimes the harnessing of the horse: the linking of the reins to the bridle*). You let the two ropes fall loosely in a line . . . (*mimes extending the ropes so that they reach the testicles of the stallion, and tying a knot around the testicles*) . . . next it's the pectorals, you slide the ropes along the pectorals, then you slide them along the belly . . . when you get to the balls you make a little ring, you loop it around one testicle, without pulling . . . then another loop, also very gently, around the second testicle . . . then you wait for him to put his head down, you straddle onto his back as fast as you can. (*Mimes jumping on the back of the horse, who reacts by lifting his head and neck so that he squeezes his testicles by his own action, and neighs desperately.*) TAN . . . right away he goes: TAK! "AHHIIII!" . . . he lifts his back: "AIIIHHHHIIIII!!!" . . . he raises his neck, TAK!: "AHHOIIII!" . . . by the third bucking . . . he's a new beast (*mimes the walk of a horse on parade*). "What elegance!"

che l'è tremenda! La prima roba difìzil è infilàrghe la cavèssa, chè lü, come te ghe va aprèso, te cagna . . . e alóra se büta per tera la cavessa, la se lega a la punta de do cane mese apòsta come trapola . . . lü el camìna e come el vede la cavèsa par tera, curiosso come a l'è, se abàsa a vardàrla: "Se l'è 'sta roba?" el se domanda . . . e TRAK, i dòi che stan nascondùi con i cane in man, i tira sü in alto de bòto e la cavèssa la ghe se enfila su la fàcia del stalón sora a le orège. Ma a 'sto punto te ghe deve atacàr le corde a la cavèssa per far le briglie, una a derécio, l'altra de manca, no' bisogna andàrghe de fronte perchè te cagna e alóra ghe se fà finta de parlàrghe con un altro e ghe se liga de qua . . . chè lü, el cavàlo . . . l'è curioso . . . el vègne a ascultàre, a sentire e alóra . . . Po' se pasa de l'altra parte, ma se cambia òmo che ghe se parla se no a lü, al cavàl ghe végne el sospècto. (*Mima l'imbragatura del cavallo: le briglie legate alla cavezza*) Le dóe corde se làssan tomberlàr così par lóngo . . . (*mima di stendere le corde fino a raggiungere i testicoli dello stallone e di annodarle ai testicoli stessi*) ghe ol petorón, te la fé slissigàre sul petorón, po' slissigàre su la panza . . . quando se arìva al cojón te fé un anelo, te gh'infórchet il cojón, sensa strìgnere . . . po' l'altro, dolzo anco lü sul segóndo cojón . . . po' te spèci che lü l'è gió basso co' la crapa, te ghe l'infórchet de bòta a gropón: (*mima di saltare in groppa al cavallo che reagisce rizzandosi con la testa e il collo così da strizzarsi da sè solo, i testicoli, con relativi nitriti disperati*) TAN . . . lü a l'estànte: TAK! "AHHII!", el dà de stciéna: "AIIIHHIIIII!!!" . . . se rissa de colo TAK! "AHHOIII!" . . . alba tèrsa ingropàda . . . te vedet 'sta bestia . . . (*mima la camminata del cavallo da parata*) Un 'elegànsa!

In two months all the Indians learned to ride.
And we resumed our journey with a cavalry.
We crossed rivers and gullies, climbing up through the
mountains.

Dòpo doi mesi, tüti 'st'indiàn gh'avéva imparàt a
cavalcàre.
E via che se reprénd ol camìno co' la nostra
cavalerìa.

Once in a while we met some of the tribes that were
scattered throughout the valleys and dales.
My reputation as a Holy Man was growing. Everyone
bowed down in front of me. There were some people who
brought me gold and silver, and I told them: "Are you
crazy?! Do you expect me to go around loaded down with
gold and silver and all these precious stones like a porter?
Keep them yourselves! I don't want to be burdened!"
And they all bowed down before me with great reverence.

Andévimo travèrso fiümi, canalòn e rampegà sü per
montàgne. Ogni tanto ghe se incontràvemo con de
le tribù sparpajàde sü per i brìchi e le valàde.
La mea reputasión de santo la creséva, gh'era de la
zente che me portava ori e arzénti e mi ghe diséva:
"Ma si' mat?! Adèso vò' in giro caregàt de oro e
argento e tüte 'ste pietre presióse?! Così, come un
fachìn? Tegnévela voialtri! No' voj portàr de pesi,
mi!"

66

And then there's the story of the two miracles I performed . . . (*He turns to the public, as if offended by the incredulity he senses he has provoked.*) I PERFORMED TWO MIRACLES!! (*Then he downplays it.*) A COUPLE OF LUCKY BREAKS!

The first one happened when we came to a plateau where there was a big lake. On the lake was a village with houses on stilts . . . with canals, bridges, and narrow passageways . . . a little Venice, made of wood.

These Venetian-Indians came to meet us and complained: "We would like to offer you all the gold in the world and precious stones too, but we don't have anything! All we have are the tears in our eyes . . ."

"What happened?"

It had been two years since their last "fish-geyser." A fish-geyser is a phenomenon that occurs in these regions . . . something like a "cascade of fish" that rises up out of the water. Every two months, on the full moon . . . the moon pulls, pulls, and pulls on the lake, in a way that makes the fish come bursting out of the water and fly. These Venetian-Indians come out with their baskets and bowls and collect the fish as they rain down from the sky. Then the fish are smoked, salted, and dried so that there's enough to eat for the whole year . . . and everyone's happy! But now they were desperate: "You, son of the rising sun and the moon . . . speak to your mother . . . tell her to end this punishment!"

E tüti i se pròstava in gran reverénze devanti a mi. Po' gh'è stàito anche il facto dei dóe miracoli che ho fàito . . . (*Rivolto al pubblico, quasi risentito dell'incredulità che immagina di aver suscitato*) HO FÀITO DÓE MIRACOLI!! . . . (*Poi minimizza*) DÓE COLPI DE CULO!!! Ol prim l'è stàit quand sémo 'rivàit sü, in cima a on altipiàn doe gh'é on gra lagh. Sül lagh gh'é una ciutàd pìcola co' le case sòra a palafìicte . . . co' le cale, i canàl e i ponti . . . una Venésia pìcola, fada de lègn.

'Sti ìndios-venesiàn ghe végne incontra e i se laménta: "Noialtri ve vorèssimo portare tüto l'oro de 'sto mondo e anche le pietre presióse ma no' gh'avémo negòta! Gh'avémo soltanto ol planto dei nostri ògi . . ."

"Cosa gh'è succedüd?"

I era dóe ani che no' gh'era pu' la risciàda. La risciàda l'è un fenomeno che végn da quèste bande . . . ol sarìa come un fropotón che végne föra de l'acque e i vola. Ogni dòe mesi, co' la luna piena . . . la luna la tira, la tira, la tira dentro il lago, la fa vegnì föra dei stciopón de pessi che i vola. Loro, 'sti Indios venessiàn, végnen föra coi cesti, le canèstre e i cata tüti quèi che i piòve de l'alto e po' i sistema a fùmegare, i mèten sòto sale, i schìscia e i magna pèssi pe' tüto un ano . . . che i so' contenti! Ma ora i era desperàd.:" Ti, fiòl del sol che nase e de la lüna . . . pàrlaghe a toa madre . . . dighe de no' darghe 'sta punisiòn."

"I don't know . . . my mother the moon is a little eccentric . . . the moon can be moody, you know!"

Dammit, what could I do? I wait for the moon to appear, plop myself down in front of her, and start talking: "Mama! Hey, mama, can you hear me? . . . Yes, it's me, your son . . . the son of my father too . . . the rising sun . . . listen, mama, could you do a little something for me! Could we get the fish to jump out of the water like they do every year . . . What? They're taking a break this year? Come on, mama, have a heart . . . We can't let these people starve to death just because those lazybones don't want to be eaten . . . Threaten them . . . tell them you'll fire up the volcano that's under the water if they don't start moving!"

Then I turned back to the Venetian savages and calmly said: "Maybe tomorrow morning. I think I persuaded my mother."

And the next day, early in the morning, those Indian fishermen were ready: baskets poised, nets open . . . Some of them had three or four baskets tied around their waists . . . and they stood in the lake with the water up to their stomachs. God, what a fool I'd look if the fish didn't move.

"No' so . . . la mia matre la Luna, l'è stramba . . . La Luna a l'è lunàtega!"

Bòja, cosa ghe pòdo far mi? 'Spècio che ghe spunta la lüna e me piàsso lì de fronte e fo' mostra de parlarghe: "Mama! Ehi mama, ti mé sénti? . . . Sì, son mi, ol to fiòl . . . fiòl anca de me pare, el sol che nasce . . . ascólta mama, ti no' te pòl farme 'na ròba così! I péssi i déve saltàr föra de l'acqua come tüti i ann! . . . Cosa? Quèst'ano sünt de repòso? E no mama, zérca de mèterte una man sül còre . . . 'sta pòra génte no' te poi lasàrla morì de fame per via che quèi pelandròn no' gh'han vòja de farse magnàre . . . Minàzzaghe che se no' se mòve ti fe stciopàr ol vulcàn che gh'è sòta l'acqua!"

Po' mé revèrsi ai venesiàn selvàsi e ghe fo tranquil: "Forse sarà per domàn matìna. Crédo che la gh'ho convénza mia matre."

E l'endomàn, de matìna presto, tüti 'sti Indios pescadòr son pronti: canèstri, rèttendüde . . . ghe n'éra de quèi che intorno a tüta la vita s'éren ligà tri quatro, cavàgne-cèste . . . e stéva in mèzo a l'acqua del lagh immergìüi fino a lo stòmego. Dio che figüra che fo' se 'sti pèssi no' se mòve!

And that's when I got that lucky break I was talking about. The sun came out . . . and: RAM! The water in the lake starts to boil. Hordes of catfish, perch, whitefish, and cod burst into the air. Bluefish and snappers splashed out of the water and fell into the baskets by the thousands! Pike and trout leaped out of the water onto the roofs of the houses . . . Sturgeon were falling into the boats . . . and if a fish, by accident, fell back into the water: "Oh, I'm sorry!" it would come right back up and hop into a basket! Fish would jump into your mouth, and, if you weren't careful, between your buttocks as well!

You can't imagine what a party they threw for me afterward. They took me in their arms, threw me up in the air like a mackerel, and almost broke my back.

E chi, la m'è 'rivàda 'sta gran bòta de cüi che ve disévi!

Spònta ol sole . . . e: VRAM!, coménza a büìr davéro tüta l'acqua del lagh. Stciòpa risciàde de arborèl, coregón, piòte, pèrseghi per l'aria! Cavéden e lavarèll sprìssa fòra de l'acqua e te bòrla in tüti i canèstri, a mila a mila! Luzzi e tròte che fa gran zómpi fòra da l'aqua fin süi tècc dei ca', barbi-storión burlàn derénto le barche . . . e se quarche pesse, per erór, rebòrla deréntro a l'acqua: "Oh, pardon!" ol torna sùbit indrìo e i resàlta in de le cèste! Te salta in bóca . . . e se no' stàit aténto te se infrìca anca in fra i ciàpi!

No' se pòl imaginàrse la fèsta che m'han fàito aprèss. Mé catàva in brazo e i me bütàva per l'aria compàgn d'un merlüz, da stcepàrme la stcèna.

The second embarrassing stroke of fortune happened when we went down to the plains. What a disaster! There hadn't been a drop of rain for four months. Everything was parched: carobs on the ground, corn on the ground, corncobs, animals dead of thirst, covered with hungry ants . . . and men were dying of thirst too. And there were these poor savages on their knees in front of me, begging me: "Oh, son of the rising sun and the moon . . . make us a miracle!"

"Enough of that! The sun and the moon have nothing to do with water!"

"We know that, but you are just the laughing buffoon who can save us. If you can make the rain god's son laugh, his father will be moved and water us with his tears . . ."

"Stop! Stop! Stop! I don't understand! What is this story about the rain god?"

"The rain god is the one who makes it rain. He has an only son who never laughs . . . But if you can make him burst into laughter, the rain god will see it and be flooded with so much emotion that he'll cry with joy, and his weeping will wash over us all!"

"And where is this son of the rain?"

"There!" and they pointed to a rag doll, a bundle of sticks, a patchwork puppet filled with straw and rags, dangling there on a chair, with an expressionless face: it had no eyes, no ears. "How can he laugh if he has no mouth?"

"It's pretty hard . . . that's why he never does. But you're a clown-buffoon who knows how to get a laugh . . . go on, dance, jump . . ."

Ohi! Ohi! I had no choice, I had to dance . . . play the clown . . . hurl myself into pirouettes . . . make faces. All the savages are clapping their hands, beating their drums . . . they're shouting . . . they're singing . . . and I'm performing all the buffoonish contortions I know!

La seconda fortüna pròpi de svergognàs la m'é capitàda quando sèm desendüi in bas ne la piàna: che desàstro! L'era quatro mesi e passa che no' pioveva manco üna lacrima. S'era secàdo tüto: le carube par tèra, mais par tèra, formentón, le bèstie assetade, morte, con tüte le formìghe che le magnàvano . . . e anca i omeno i moriva par la sete. E a gh'era 'sti poveri selvazzi in ginögio devanti a mi che i me suplicàva: "Oh fiòl del sol che nasse e de la luna . . . faghe ün miracolo!" "Oh, basta! Adèso la luna e il sol no' ghe c'entra co' l'acqua!" "Lo savémo ben, ma ti è tanto un bufón, ün ridanciàn, che te poi salvàrghe. Se ti è capàz de far rìdar ol fiòl dei dio de la piòva, ol dio padre se comòve con tante lacrime che ghe inonda . . ."—"Fermi! Fermi! Fermi! No' capìsso nagóta! Cos'è 'sta storia del deo de la piova?"—"Ol deo de la piova l'è quèlo che fa piovere. Ol gh'ha ün fiòi ünego che no' ride mai . . . Ma se ti è capàzze de farlo stciopàr in üna ridàda, ol deo de la piòva a véder ol so' fiòl che ride ghe cata ün magón de tanta felizidàt che se comòve, piàgne, piàgne de ziòia, piàgne che ghe bagna a tüti!" "E dov'è 'sto fiòl de la piòva?" "Là!" e i me mostra ün pigotón, ün fagòtt, ün pupàsso de pèssa con la pàja deréntro, ciondorlón, sentàdo su üna caréga, Co' la fàcia piàta: no' gh'ha i ògi, no' gh'ha le orègie.

"Ma come fa a rid ün che no' gh'ha neanca la boca?!" "L'è pròpri lì ol difìzil . . . che inscì ghe riésse mai! Ma ti è tanto paiàsso che te lo poi far rìder . . . Dai bala, salta! . . ." Ohi! Ohi! No' gh'è verso, mé tóca balàre . . . fa el pàiasso . . . mé slànzo a far piroètt . . . bocàsse. Tüti i selvàzz i bate i man, bate tambür . . . i crìa . . . i canta . . . e mi mi me stòrsego intorno a fa el bufón!

70

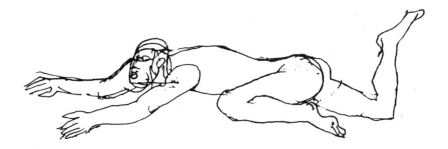

I stand upside down with my feet in the air . . . I sprawl out on the ground and start rolling all over the place. Everyone bursts into laughter. Then all of a sudden a woman shouts, "He's laughing. He's laughing too!" A miracle! Unbelievable: On the face of the scarecrow was a sideways slit with the trace of a twitch that looked just like a laughing mouth . . . and two little holes that seemed like shining eyes!

Mé stragiàmbo co' i pie per aria . . . me stravàco spatascià per tèra a rutulùni.
Tüti i sbòta in una gran ridàda. Po', de i'istànte, una dòna la vusa: "Ol rid! Ol rid anca lu'!"
Miràcui! Ròba de no' crèderghe: deréntro la so' fàcia vòda del fantòzz, s'éra sgarbelà 'na svèrzuia a tàj de travèrs compàgn d'òna bóca ridént . . . e dò' bogìt che paréva ògi slusighénti!

"He's laughing! Rain god, your son is laughing . . . Feel
something! Cry!"
TON! TON!
"He's feeling something!"
TON! TON! TON!
"He's crying!"
PTON! PTON TON . . . TON . . . PTIN!
(*He makes gestures that indicate the drops coming down ever
more slowly until they stop. He looks at the sky angrily.*) Is
that it? Are those all the tears you have? You must be a little
constipated! Rain! Rain! Cry!
PTON PTON PTON TONTONTONTONTO!!!!!! The water
started coming down in torrents! By dawn we were flooded
with water up to our knees! And all the savages were dancing
and singing. (*Mimes a dance to the rhythm of the rain.*)
PTENPTERNPTENPTEN!
When night came the water was up to our waists!
"Hey god, that's enough!"
PTENTPENPTEN!
"Enough!"
PTENPETNTPEN!
"Enough!! Do you want to drown us? (*Threatening*) Careful
or I'll strangle your kid! . . . Enough!! Watch out or I'll
come up there and wallop you! Enough!!!"
(*The rhythm of the rain diminishes, but then starts again
timidly.*) PTON PTON.
"Enough!"
PTIN!
"Enough!"
PTIN!

"Ride! Deo de la piova, ol to fiòl ol ride! Comòvete!
Piàgne!"
TON TON
"Se comòve!"
TON TON TON
"Piàgne!"
PTON PTON TON . . . TON . . . PTIN!
(*Si arresta col gesto di indicare le gocce che scendono
sempre più lentamente sino a bloccarsi. Si rivolge al
cielo, ristentito*) "Basta cosi?! Son tüte chi le tòe
làgrime?! Te set ün po' stitico! . . . Piovi! Piovi!
Piàgni!"
PTON PTON PTON TONTONTONTO!!!!! Comincia a
vegnìr giò un acqua treménda . . . A l'alba éremo
immergùo ne l'acqua fino ai ginögi! Gh'era tüti i
selvàzz che i balàva e cantava (*mima una danza a
ritmo di pioggia*) PTEN PTENPTENPTEN!
Arìva la nòce che l'acqua l'era fino a la vita.
"Beh, deo . . . adèso basta cossì!"
PTENPTENPTEN
"Basta!"
PTENPETNPTEN
"Basta! Te ghe voi' 'negàre?! (*Minaccioso*) Guarda
che te stròso ol fiòl! . . . Basta!! Aténto che végno sü
e te pico! Basta!!"
PTON PTON PTON "Basta!"
(*Il ritmo della pioggia diminuisce, ma poi riprende
timido*)
PTON PTON
"Basta!"
PTIN!
"Basta!"
PTIN!

The water was up to our necks and all the savages swam to me with only their heads sticking up out of the water and shouted: "Son of the rising sun . . . stay with us!" (*Mimes swimming.*)

"No thanks, it's a little too humid for my taste. Maybe some other time!" (*He mimes swimming rapidly away from them.*)

"I have to get to Cacioche!"

We resumed our journey and the rain savages followed us.

We crossed a river, another river . . . then suddenly we found ourselves caught up in a horrible storm . . . there were horses everywhere . . . in the river sixty horses were swept up in the tempest. I don't know where they came from, but they were drowning! We took all the rope we had with us and made lassos . . . we hurled them into the water and roped all the horses, pulling them onto land one by one. We saved all sixty horses. Now we had sixty-three beautiful steeds . . . the Indians went riding every day . . . they couldn't get enough!

L'acqua era 'rivàda fino a la gola e a tüti i selvàzz vegnìva fora solo la crapa e i nodàva verso mi e i me vusàva: "Fiòl del sol che nasse . . . resta con noialtri!"—"(*Mimando di nuotare*) No, gràsie, l'è tropo umido per el me caràtter, se vedémo un'altra volta! (*Si allontana sempre mimando di nuotare con foga*) Debbio arivàre a Cacioche!"

Sémo ripartìdi e 'sti selvàzz de la pioggia i son vegnù appresso a nunch.

Emo 'traversàt un fiüm, un altro fiüm . . . ghe trovémo a l'improvìsa in üna büféra tremenda . . . a gh'era cavàli dapartüto . . . int un rivo slargo a gh'era sesanta cavàli che i se rotolava ne la tempesta. No' so da dove i vegnìsse ma i stava 'negàndo! Avèm catà tüte le corde che gh'évemo aprèso, em fàito un lanzo . . . le em lanzàde imbragàndo i cavàj e, uno a uno li emo tràit a tèra. Così sémo riusìti a salvar tüti i sesanta cavali. Adèso gh'avévimo sesantatre bei cavali. I Indios i andava cavalcando tüto el ziorno . . . una festa!

Just a year earlier they didn't even know what horses were. They thought they were monsters.

And now it was as if they'd been born together! They rode the horses standing up: "Eehaaheeh!" . . . bareback: "Ahaaa!" . . . standing on their hands: "Eheeplom!" . . . They could ride backwards and upside down too. I saw one of them riding while balancing calmly on the horse's rump. Then a horse came with three Indians on its back . . . standing up. Another horse came trotting alongside them with three other enthusiasts, also on their feet, shouting: "Do you want to switch horses?" One over here . . . one over there. . . . another one here . . . another one there! Then I saw something even more incredible: an Indian on a horse rode up behind another horse, and when he got close to the other horse he, the Indian on the first horse, gave it a walloping kick with his heels, and his horse jumped up onto the back of the other horse: a horse riding another horse, with an Indian on top!

In those days I have to admit I was a little absentminded . . . we were supposed to head east and I don't know how, but we ended up walking in the wrong direction . . . So all of a sudden we found ourselves facing the other ocean. We were looking for the Atlantic, but we had found the Pacific! Holy smoke! We had to turn around. Four months of walking for nothing! . . . But after all, we didn't have anything else to do!

Solamente un ano àntes no' cognosséva i cavali, i credeva che fosse mostri e adèso era come se i fosse nasciüdi ensémbia! I montava a cavàlo de drisso: "Eehaaheeh!", sénsa la sela: "Ahaa!", e po' se revoltàva: "Eheeplom!", e andava de rovèrso. Gh'ho vedüo un che andava tranquilo in echilìbrio sü la culatta del cavàlo. Po' è 'rivàit un cavàlo con tn Indios sul gropón . . . in pie . . . al gran tròto se gh'é: "Fémo stciàmbio de cavàl?" Pasa de qua, pasa de là, pasa de qua, pasa de là! Po' gh'ho vedùo una roba gimài capitàda al mondo: un Indios su un cavàlo che andava de drio a un altro cavàlo, quando son 'rivàit in para al cavàl, lü, l'Indios a cavàl gh'ha dàit una sfropàda coi talón, ol so cavàl l'è saltàit in gropa a l'altro cavàl: un cavàla a cavàl d'un cavàl, con l'Indios a cavàl!

In quèi ziórni mi de segùro ero un po' svèrgulo . . . dovévemo puntàr a oriente e no' so com'é, se sémo stortài de diresiòn così de trovarghe de fàcia all'altro mare de contro. Noiàltri se cercava il mare Atlantico, émo incontràt el Pacifico! Cramento! Ghe tóca tornar indiro. Quatro mesi de camino per negòta! . . . Ma tanto no' gh'avévimo niénte de fare!

After four more months we came to a hill . . . and on this marvelous hill I smelled an odor that I knew well: sulfur! I went scrounging and found a nice big slab of it, long and in one piece. I dug it up and then I hid it. Later I prepared some charcoal, then I looked for some magnesium and found it in a cave . . . there was some saltpeter there too: "I'm going to make some fireworks! I'll go load up some reeds!"

While the Indians were sleeping in carefree tranquillity, I cut the reeds, then I hollowed them out, I put in the black powder, saltpeter, and sulfur, then the magnesium, then I braided the fuses . . . and I lit them (*mimes a sequence of noisy explosions*): PTIN PTAN PHIIIIII! PAM! PAM! PAM! PAM! (*pictures the Indians trying to escape*) "It's the end of the world! The world is exploding!"

They ran in all directions.

PIM! PIAM! PIAM!

"The stars are exploding."

PIAM! PIAM! PIAM!

"Forgive us, moon!"

Dopo altri quatro mesi sémo 'rivàit a üna coìina . . . e in 'sta colìna meravegiósa gh'ho sentìt un odór che mi cognossévi ben: sólfero. Sont andàit a sfrugugnà, gh'era un filón de sólfero belo, intrégo, lóngo . . . L'ho tirào föra, po' l'ho nascondüdo. Aprèso ho preparào de la carbonèla, po' gh'ho zercàt del **manganésio,** deréntro una grota l'ho trovào . . . gh'era anca del salnitro: "Fago i fòghi d'artifizio, fago le cane!"

Mentre gli Indios i dormiva tranquili e beati, gh'ho tajàt le cane, le gh'ho sbusàite, gh'ho metùo dentro la polvere negra, sainitro e sólforo, po' ol magnanesio, po' gh'ho intrezzà tüte le mizze . . . e a gh'ho daìto fógo (*mima esplosioni fragorose*): PTIN PTAN PHIIIIIIIII! PAM! PAM! PAM! PAM! PAM! PAM! (*Fa immaginare gli Indios che fuggono*) "La fine del mondo! Stciòpa e! mondo!" I scapàva de qua e de là! PIM! PAM! PAM! PAM!

"Stciòpa le stèle!"

PIAM! PIAM! PIAM!

"Perdónaghe lüna!"

They were all on their knees . . . and I was laughing and laughing! They looked at me: "Oh, Johan Padan, were you the one making all that bombastic thunder?"

"Yes, but I didn't do it just to scare you, but because we're about to meet the Spaniards in Cacioche, and we're going to make a big party out of it! They like fireworks and we're going to give them a show that will knock their eyes out, but first you all have to learn how to make fireworks."

So they learned . . . and they got a little carried away! They made fireworks and set them off for any reason at all: We'd take a walk: PAM! I'd go for a pee (*mimes the explosion and a leaping somersault*): PAM! I'd eat a meal: PAM! I'd be making love: PAM! PAM! "Enough already!"

Tüti in ginögio . . . e mi ridevo, ridevo! I me varda: "Oh, Johan Padan, te s'è stàit ti a far tüta 'sta stcioperìa?" "Sì, ma no' l'ho miga fàito per spaventàrve, ma per ol fato che adèso noiàltri se incontrémo coi spagnòl a Cacidòche e tüti in coro ghe faremo una gran festa. A loro ghe piàse i fóghi d'artifizio e ghe farèm dono de bòtti da inchiuchìrli, ma besógna che viàltri tüti aprendìt a far i fòghi d'artifizio."

E i imparàvan . . . Esageràt! I faséva fòghi d'artifizio e i faséva stciopàr anche quando no' era el caso. Se stava a caminàr: PAM! Stavo a pissàre (*mima botti e zompi a soprassaito*): PAM! Stavo a magnàre: PAM! Fasévo l'amore: PAM! "Bastaaa!"

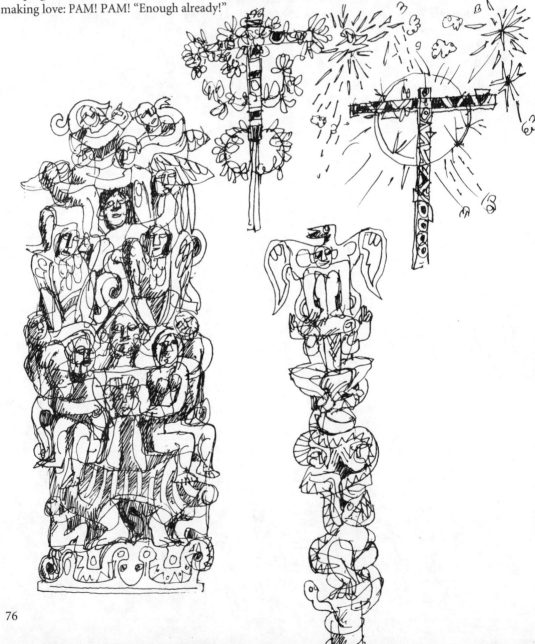

We came to the edge of a peak at the top of a mountain chain. From there we had a clear view down into a large valley . . . it was a city (*stretches out his arms in a triumphant gesture*). Cacioche! It was Cacioche! The city of Cacioche! There was the sea, the Atlantic, a harbor . . . ships . . . Cacioche! (*almost shouting insanely*) "Finally I found you, Cacioche! What a city . . . vibrant, towering walls of wood . . . and look at the houses, the mansions . . . those big buildings there are the storage houses . . . the other one is the cathedral, see how the bell tower is made from tree trunks . . . That big one there is the palace of the governor . . . and those are the soldiers' barracks . . .

Sémo 'rivàt infine in zima a üna cadéena de montagne. De là se vedeva tüto ol valón, largo, ciàro . . . e üna *citàd:(allarga le braccia con gesto trionfante)* Caciòche! A gh'era Caciòche! La citàd de Caciòche! A gh'era ol mare!, l'Atlantico, col porto . . . le navi . . . Caciòche! (*Quasi gridando impazzito*) "Finalmente Caciòche t'ho ritrovàita! Vardé che citàd, viva, le grandi müra tüte de legn, i palón, e vardé le case, i casoni . . . quèi casón là grandi sono le conserve de fóndago . . . quell'altra l'è la catedràl, vedìt che gh'ha il campanìl tüto fàito de tronchi . . . Quell'altro là grande ol l'è ol palàge dèl governadór . . . e po' altre case dèi soldàit, le guarnigión . . .

and just outside the walls are the plantations of cotton . . .
corn . . . wheat . . . Look how huge they are! On the other
side are the hollowed-out mountains . . . the gold mines . . .
you can see the slaves in chains! Indians, Indians chained
like slaves . . . carrying bales of cotton . . . all Indians . . .
loading up the ships . . . all Indian slaves! And over there
are ten of them, ten Indians, hanged by their necks!"
I can see from the corner of my eye that all the Indians
around me have gone pale, all white in the face. Women
were trembling. Some of them fainted. "Don't be fright-
ened, don't be afraid. I'm not going to take you to
Cacioche . . . I'm not going to take you to the Spaniards.
Don't make any noise. Let's go back two days' walk. I have
to talk to you!"

e apéna föra dai müri i piantagión de cotón . . . de
mais . . . de formentòn . . . Vardé che grande! Sbüsà
de la, ghe son le montagne . . . le miniére de oro . . .
tant'è vero che gh'è i stciàvi con le cadéne. Indios . . .
Indios incatenàd . . . 'me stciavi . . . anche quèli che
i porta bale de cotón . . . tüti Indios . . . anche quèli
che i caréga le navi . . . tüti Indios stciavi! E ghe n'è
diése, diése Indios impicàd . . ."
Mi i sbìrzio con la coda de l'ògio: visìno a mi i Indios
éran tüti bianchi, smorti in fàcia, a gh'era le dòne che
tremava, a gh'era quèi che desvegnìva. "No' féve
terór, no' gh'èite pagüra, che tanto no' ve porto a
Cacròche . . . No' ve porto dai Spagnòl. No' fe' de
rumor . . . Tornémo indrìo de dòe ziórni de camìno,
che ve dévo parlare!"

When we had retreated from Cacioche to a hidden valley, we sat ourselves down very calmly, and I gave some orders: "Men on one side, women on the other! Count yourselves!"

"A thousand, two thousand . . . eight thousand men!"

"And the women?"

"Almost seven thousand!"

"And the elderly? How many elderly?"

"More than three thousand."

"Children?"

"Another three thousand."

"The older ones?"

"Four thousand."

Twenty-five thousand . . .

"Too many . . . too many! We can't all go to Cacioche . . . we'll create too much confusion . . . we're double the population of the city, including the Indian slaves! I want to tell you the truth. If I turn you over to the Spaniards they'll enslave you, in chains . . . and they're right . . . no offense intended . . . but you are not normal men . . . for them you are kin to the animals. Let's level with each other . . . You have no religion, you have no doctrines, you have no souls, and you don't even have a God. To save you from becoming slaves I have to make you fellow Christians. Then the Spaniards won't be able to touch you . . . it's the law! But we need a priest, a priest who can teach you the doctrines, a preacher . . . (*He is spurred on by the looks of the Indians.*) I can't teach you the doctrines. I'm an anti-Christ, a foul-mouthed blasphemer . . . I can't! I can't teach you the doctrines! I don't even know the doctrines! . . . (*Brief pause. Then with determination*) I'll teach you the doctrines. But you better pay attention, because I'll quiz you afterward."

Quando se sémo ritrovàit lontàn de Caciòcle in un valón nascondùo, se sémo **sentadi bei** calmi e tranquili e gh'ho ordenàt: "I mastci de una banda, le fèmene de l'altra! Contéve!"—"Mila, domìla . . . otomìla mastci!"—"Le fèmene?"—"Quasi setemìla!"—"E i vègi? Quanti sono i vègi?"—"Più de tremila"—"I bambìn?"—"Anca lori tremila"—"E quèli plu grandi?"—"Quatromila" . . . Venticinquemila . . . "Massa tropi, no' podémo andare a Caciòche . . . fémo tròpa confusión . . . sémo il dòble de tüta la popolasión che gh'è in 'sta città, compreso i Indios stciàvi. Ma ve vòi dir la vertàd, se mi ve porto in boca ai spagnòl, i spagnòl ve fan tüti stciàvi, ve incadéna . . . e gh'han anca resón . . . sénsa ofénderve . . . ma viàltri no' sit miga òmeni normàl . . . per lori vui sit dei parenti de animal . . . Guardémose in fazza . . . vuit no' tegnìt religión, no' gh'avìt dotrina, no' tegnit anima e no' gh'avìt nemanco un deo! Per farve salvaménto de stciàvi dovrìa farve devegnìr fradèli cristiani . . . Si voiàltri sit fradèli cristiani, i spagnòl no' ve pol tocare . . . per lézze! Ma a ghe vòl un prévete, un prévete che ve fa dotrina, un fràite . . . (*In progressione come incalzato dallo sguardo implorante degli Indios*) No' pòdo miga farve dotnina mi che son ün antecristo, un blasfemadór . . . mi no' pòdo!, mi no' pòdo far dotrina! Ma no' cognosso manco la dotnina! . . . (*Breve pausa. Poi determinato*) Ve fago dotrina. Ma guai chi no' sta aténto che dòpo ve intèrogo.

"First rule: The soul is eternal . . . the body decays . . . after it dies it gets put underground and the worms eat it . . . but the soul is eternal and there aren't any worms that can eat it . . . it goes to the sky, and is blessed in Heaven . . . if the body has been good on earth . . . if, on the other hand, it's been cruel, the soul falls deep down under the earth's bowels . . . it goes to hell and burns for eternity. Amen!
"Indians, how do you like that? . . . You don't like it. All right, we'll go on."
The hard part was explaining to the Indians about the original sin, of Adam and Eve . . . I said: "Adam and Eve were two Indians, naked as the day they were born, just like you . . . breasts, buttocks, bushes, birds' nests . . . little birdies, little turkey necks . . . all out in the open . . . and they loved each other and embraced each other and made love without shame or embarrassment . . . and in the midst of all this beauty the sneaky serpent arrived. The serpent was the devil, and with an apple in his mouth he said: 'Adam, eat the apple! Sweet, delicious, red apple! Adam, eat this apple!'
"'No. I don't like it . . . ask Eve.'
"'Eve, will you eat the apple?'
"'Let's split it. Half for me. Half for Adam . . .'
"While they were sharing the apple . . . the archangel Gabriel appeared out of nowhere . . . or maybe it was Michael. . . . it could have been Raphael . . . I don't remember any-more. . . . but he jumped down with a sword in his hand: "'Get out! You wretches! You ate God's forbidden apple! Get out of Paradise! . . .'"
And all the Indians shouted: "That one must be a Spaniard!"

But with the savages it wasn't easy getting this idea into their heads about punishment linked to divine fruit. Because they don't know what apples are . . . they don't have apple trees, not even pear trees. So I had to change the story a little and put a mango in the serpent's mouth . . . big as a watermelon . . . (*demonstrates*) . . .
"And the poor beast of a serpent had his face all distorted saying: (*speaks with difficulty, almost slobbering*) 'Adam, eeeeaatzhisssssmaaaanggmaaang-maaaango!'"
It was also hard to explain the idea of

Prima régula: l'anima l'è eterna . . . ol corpo marzìse . . . dòpo ch'el mòre va soto tèra e i vèrmini se lo magna . . . ma l'anima l'è eterna e no' gh'è vèrmini che la magna . . . la va in ziélo, beata in Paradiso . . . se l'è stàito bón ol corpo in tèra . . . se l'è stàito cruèl l'anima la sfónda de soto, la svàrga dentro . . . va int ol inferno e la brüsa in eterno. Amen!
Indios, ve piasùo? . . . No' v'è piasùo. D'acòrdo. Andémo avanti!"
La roba difìzil l'era spiegàrghe ai Indios quèsta question del pecato original, de Adamo ed Eva. Mi gh'ho dit: Adamo ed Eva erano dòe Indios, a l'éren desnüdi quando son nassùdi proprio come voiàltri, le zinne, le ciàpe, la pàsera, le paserìne e ol paserìn col pìndorlón tüto a descovèrto . . . i se voléva bén, i se embrasàva, i faséva l'amore, no' ghe importava de pudór e vergognànza . . . sul plü bèlo l'è 'rivàto ol serpentón canàja, el serpénte ch'ol era ol diaòl, co' üna póma in bóca e ghe diséva: "Adamo magna la póma! Dolze, bona, rosse le pome! Adamo magna 'sta póma!" "No' a mi no' me piase, dìghebo a Eva!" "Eva, te màgnet la poma?" "Fémo metà per ün, mi e l'Adamo . . ." Magna ti che magno mi, salta föra l'arcanzélo Gabrièl . . . Michèl . . . adèso no' me regòrdo pù se l'è Rafaèl . . . salta föra co' la spada in man: "Föra! Desgrasià! Avé magna la póma proibìda de Dio! Via dal Paradiso!". E tüti i Indios che han criàt: "Quèlo de següro l'è ün spagnòll". Ma ai selvàz no' era fàzile fàrghelo entrare in crape 'sto fato del castigo per via del frùcto divìn. Che loro le pome no' le cognósse miga . . . no' gh'han piante de póm, e nemanco de pere . . . e alóra gh'ho doüt mèterghe in bóca al serpentón ün mango . . . ün angüria così (*indica*) con 'sta povera bèstia del serpentone con tüta la fàcia sgaracàda che ghe diséva: "(*parla con difficoltà quasi biascicando*) Adamo . . . amghailangoangoango!". Difìzile l'era spiegàrghe

shame . . . because first they were living calmly, walking around with the bird's nest and the turkey neck right there out in the open with the buttocks and the breast, and it didn't matter at all . . . then all of a sudden shame came! When? When the archangel Gabriel came out with the sword in his hand and said:

"Did you eat that forbidden mango?! Get out of Paradise!"

"Oh, we're so ashamed!" (*Quickly covers his genitals with his hands.*)

"Like I said, Get out of Paradise!"

"Oh, we're so ashamed! Oh, the shame of it! Oh, my bird's nest . . . please give me a fig leaf to cover myself!" The Indians didn't understand this idea of a fig leaf for covering yourself . . . because they don't have figs . . . they have prickly pears . . . imagine one of those leaves with all the spikes . . . a cactus between your legs . . . "AHAAAAA!"

On the other hand when I told them about Jesus, sweet, gentle son of God, with all that long hair . . . they liked him, this son of God . . .

"How beautiful. Jesus is so loving and compassionate that he holds little babies in his arms . . . and forgives them all: 'Have you committed a big sin? Oh, what a sin . . . I forgive you! . . . You, how many sins have you committed? Three sins, four sins? Five sins? All forgiven!' When he met a man who walked all twisted: 'Oh, straighten up!' 'Thanks for the miracle, Jesus!'"

They liked the fact that Jesus brought the dead back to life . . . he knew how to have a good time. But they didn't like the apostles. The Indians didn't like those apostles at all! They were all so serious, always with their hands clasped together, walking around one after the other with gold circles over their heads . . . and they were all men . . . always men . . . only men . . . it made the Indians a little suspicious . . . so much so that I had to put a woman in with the apostles: Mary Magdalene.

Oh how they liked Mary Magdalene! . . . with her round firm breasts, her buttocks, all naked, covered only with a long cascade of hair that went: "IHIAAAAAAA!" (*He shakes his head and mimes the undulating movement of the hair that reveals her nude body.*)

anche quèsto fatto dèl pudór, che loro prima vivévan tranquìli col passero, la passerina, andavano in giro co' le ciàpe, le zinne . . . tüto descovèrte, che no' ghe importava negóta . . . de colpo ghe végn la vergogna! Quando? Quando salta föra l'arcanzélo Gabrièl co' la spada in man che ghe dise: "It magnà el mango proibìdo?! Föra del Paradiso!"

"Oh che *vergogna!*".(*Rapidamente si porta le ani a coprire il pube*)

Come gh'aveva dito "Föra del Paradis!"

"Oh che vergogna! Oh che pudór! Oh la pàsera . . . dame per piasér una fòja de figo de covrìrme . . ." I Indios no' capiva miga 'sto fato de la fòja de figo . . . da covrìrse!Anca parché loro del figo i conósse solo quèlo d'India . . . el figo d'india . . . Pensa a 'sta föja co' tüte le spinerìe . . . te la pichi in fra le giambe: "AHAAAA!"

Invece quando ghe gh'ho racontà de Jesus, fiòl de Deo, dolze, zentìl, con tanti cavèii lònghi, a tüti gh'é piasù 'sto fiòl de deo . . . "Che belo Jesus!" Così amoroso, pasionàt che valzàva i bambin in brasso . . . e po' faséva perdonànsa a tüti: "Te gh'è *ün pecàt* tremèndo? Oh che pecàt . . . Te lo perdono. Ti quanti pecàt? Tri pecàt, quatro pecàt, cinque pecàt? Tüti perdonati!" Quando ghe n'era un che caminava un po' sbìrgolo: "Oh, va drisso!" "Grazie, miracolo Jesus!" Ghe piasèva Jesus che faséva resuscitàr tüti, faséva le feste . . . Invece chi no' ghe piasèva miga éran i apostoli, ai Indios i apostoli no' che piasèva per nagòta! Tüti seriósi, tüti co' le mani giònte che caminavan ün de drio a l'altro coi cerción d'oro in crapa . . . tüti mastci, sémpre mastci, solamente mastci . . . che ai Indios ghe faséva ün po' sospècto . . . tanto che gh'ho dovut mèterghe intramèso a 'sti apostoli üna fèmena: la Madalena . . . Come ghe piasèva la Madalena!, co' le zinne tonde e puntàde, le ciàpe . . . tüta desnùda, covèrta sojaménte de una gran cascàda de cavèli che la faséva: "IHIAAAA" (*scuote la testa e mima il sollevarsi ondeggiante dei capelli, che lascia nuda tutta la sua. figura*).

81

It was awful when I told them about Jesus, son of God, being nailed to the cross, with all his blood trickling down, as he was dying, dying, gasping . . . the Madonna under the cross crying . . . Mary Magdalene pulling out her hair. As they listened to this story all the Indians were weeping in desperation: "He's dying! He's dying! The son of God, the son of Heaven is dying!" And they pulled out their hair, as if it were one of their sons dying . . . and they scratched at their own skin . . .

And they slapped themselves and punched themselves in the face, they beat their stomachs, weeping, they threw themselves on the ground . . . One day, one night, two days, three days, three nights . . .

"That's enough!! Why all this desperate lamentation over nothing? You're getting carried away. It's an old story, ancient history . . . no one remembers it anymore . . . And anyway you can calm down, because three days after he dies Jesus is resuscitated and comes back to life!"

El tremendo i'é stàito quando gh'ho racontàdo de Jesus fiòl de Deo che l'era inciudàt su la cròse con tüto ol sàngo che ghe colava da baso, col moriva, ol morìva, ol rantolàva e la Madona de sotavìa la cróse che la piagnéva, gh'era la Madalena che se strassàva i cavèli. Devànti a 'sta conta a gh'era tüti i Indios che i piagnéva deseperàdi: "Mòre! Mòre! Ol fiòl de Deo, ol fiòl del ziélo mòre!". E se strassàvan anche loro i cavèli, come se fuèsse un loro fiòi che stava morendo, e se dava de le sgarbelàde, se tiravàn dei sgiafutùn in fàcia, i se picàva in sul stòmego, i piagnéva, i se butàva per tèra . . . ün ziòrno, una nòte, dóe ziórni, tre ziórni e tre nòti . . .

"Basta! Ma cos'è 'sta caragnàda de piaghe, andémo! Esageràt! A l'è üna storia antìga, vègia, no' se recòrda pù nissùn . . . E po' stet tranquìli che dòpo tre ziórni che l'è morto Jesus el resciùscita, torna in vita!"

82

(*In the voice of an inconsolable cry*) "It's not true. You're just telling lies to console us, but we know that the son of Heaven is dead. He's dead!"

"I don't tell lies . . . I'm a Holy Man! But watch out, because there was another Holy Man named Thomas who didn't believe in the resurrection of Jesus either. He went in person to the tomb from which the son of God had just risen. He was alive! He still had all the sores on his ribs . . . And he, this doubting Thomas, had the audacity to stick his finger into a bloody hole in Christ's ribs . . . and a thunderbolt came down: NIAAAAA! (*puts both hands under his armpits so they look like stubs*) Big halo, little stubs! Watch out!"

And all the Indians were singing: "He's alive! The son of Heaven is alive!" And they were hugging each other and throwing themselves onto the ground and making love. They were drinking. They were getting drunk . . . Some of them had brought white powder that they called "boracero," which means inebriated . . . They put this white powder into their nostrils . . . and instead of sniffing it up like this (*demonstrates*) . . . they stick reeds up each other's noses and (*mimes blowing through the reed*) PIUM! PIUM! "You too!" "Me too!" PIUM! PIUM! . . . . "I see God!"

"You miserable wretches! How dare you drug yourselves, get drunk, and jump around like that in front of the Lord!"

(*Con voce di pianto sconsolato*) "No' è vera, te ghe conti üna busìa sojaménte per consolàrghe, ma noiàltri savémo che ol fiòl del ziélo l'è morto, l'è morto!"

"Mi no' digo miga busìe . . . mi sont ün santón! Ma aténto che gh'è stàito un altro santón, Tomaso, che no' credeva miga a la resuresiòn de Jesus. L'è andàito lü de persona do' gh'era la tomba de Jesus che l'era apéna spontàito föra: vivo l'era! Gh'aveva tüte le piaghe ancora in tèl costato . . . e lü, 'sto Tomaso malcredente, gh'ha üt el bèc de infilàrghe i didi in ti bögi sanguagnénti . . . gh'è arivàito un fùlmin: NIAAAA! (*Si porta entrambe le mani sotto l'ascella apparendo come monco*) Cerción, 'uréola e moncherìn! Aténti!"

E tüti i Indios che cantàvan "L'è vivo! Ol fiòl del zièl l'è vivo!" i se embrassàva, i se butàva per tèra, i fasévan l'amore, i bevéva, i se imbriagàva . . . A gh'era quèli che gh'han portàit de la polvere bianca che loro i ciàman boracéro, boracio vol dir imbriàgo . . . 'sta polvere bianca se la incarcàvan in te le narìzz . . . invece de tirar su così, se infricàvano de le cane in ti böc del naso l'un l'oltro e (*mima di soffiare dentro la canna*) "PIUM! PIUM! Anca ti, anca mi!" PIUM! PIUM! "Vedo Dio!!"

"Desgrassiá! Ve droghè, bevé, salté davanti al Segnór!"

"It's not allowed?"

"No it's not!"

"You can't dance in front of God?"

"NO!"

"You can't make love in front
of God?"

"NO!"

"You can't drink?"

"Only the priest drinks. Everybody else watches!"

"And we can't blow through the reeds?"

"NO!!"

"Not even a little snort?"

"NOOO!!!"

"Oh, what kind of dead religion is this?"

"It's not a dead religion. It's a religion of life, of life!
Because when we celebrate the resurrection of Jesus on the
day of Holy Easter in my village, in my valley, everyone
sings and dances and is filled with great happiness . . . and
they sing sweet songs that give you goose bumps when you
listen . . . I'll sing one of them for you, a song of great
tenderness:

"Oh what joy and oh what wonder
The son of heav'n is still alive
The son of Mary is still living!
The Virgin Mary is full of cheer now
And there's nothing for us to fear now
Not the Turks or the stormy winds now
Not the winds or the Christian soldiers
Not the Turks or the Christian soldiers."

"Beautiful! Beautiful!" All the Indians were dancing.
"Again! Again!"
I sang it for them again and they learned it by heart, word
for word . . . and they sang it . . . a little too quickly
(*demonstrates the same tune in a rhythm somewhere between
a samba and a saltarello*).

Oh what joy and oh what wonder
The son of heav'n is still alive . . .

At this point I said: "Let's all go to Cacioche! . . . Let's get
our crosses ready . . . No, not everyone . . . just a thousand.
The first time we go, a thousand: eight hundred men, two
hundred women. You other twenty-four thousand, stay out
of sight. If we need you I'll send a signal and you can come
forward . . . forward with the horses!"

"No' se fa?!"

"No' se fa no!"

"No' se baia davanti a Dio . . ."

"NO!"

"No' se fa l'amor devanti a Dio?!"

"NO!"

"No' se beve?!"

"Beve solo il prévete, i altri sta a vardare!"

"E no' ghe se spara le cane?"

"NO!!"

"Ma nemanco üna canèta?"

"NOO!!!"

"Oh, ma che religión de morte l'è, quèsta!"

"No' è religión de morte, l'è religiòn de vita, de vita!
Che quando al mèo paese, in de le mie valàde o gh'è
Jesus che resórze o gh'è la santa Pasqua de
resuresiùn, tüti i canta e i bala e inn contènti
d'alegrèssa e i tira föra de le canzón dolze che a
'scoltàrle te végne i sgrìsoi . . . Mo' ve ne canto una
de gran tendrèssa:

"Oh che bèlo o che 'legrìa
l'é ancamò vivo o! fiòl del ziél
l'é ancamò vivo ol fiòl de la Maria
Maria verzén lé in gran conténto
nesciün de nojàltri ol gh'ha più spavénto
né dei turchi né del gran vénto
né del gran vénto né dei cristiàn
né dei turchi né dei cristiàn."

Bello! Tüti i Indios che i balàva "Ancora! Ancora!"
Ghe l'ho cantada ün'altra volta e l'han imparàda
ugual preciso . . . la cantàvan . . . ün po' tropo
alegròta (*esegue lo stesso motivo a ritmo fra la samba
e il saltarello*):

"Oh che bèlo o che 'legrìa
l'é ancamò vivo ol fiòl del ziéi . . ."

A 'sto momént ho dito: "Andémo tüti a Cacìòche! . . .
Aprontèm le cròse . . . No', propri tüti no . . . mila . . .
Per la préma volta andémo in mila: otosénto mastci,
dosénto fèmene . . . Voiàltri invece ventiquatromila,
sti tüti nascondù . . . Se gh'è bisogn de voiàltri ve
fémo dei segni e vegnì avanti . . . avanti coi cavali!".

We had more than a hundred horses . . . everyone was riding horses now . . . "Let's get moving! Hold your crosses up high! . . . But I have to ask you please not to blow up your crosses!"

It was an obsession they had . . . you couldn't put a cross in their hands without them right away painting it all sorts of colors, covering it with colored feathers, filling some reeds with saltpeter, sulfur, and magnesium, and then lighting it: PAM! IHAAAAAAAAAAIII! PAM!

"No exploding crosses, please!"

We arrived at Cacioche singing.

Plu de zénto cavali, tüti andava a cavàlo . . . "Movémose! Con le crose alte nel ziélo! . . . Me racomando: no' fè stciopàr le cròse!" Che l'era üna mania . . . no' podévi darghe üna crose in man che subito loro la pintàvan de tanti colori, ghe metévano le plüme coloràde, ghe metévano le cane de salnìtro con lo sólforo, ol magnanése, po' i ghe dava fógo: PAM! IHAAAAAAIII! PAM

"No' se fa stciopàare le crose!"

Sémo 'rivàit cantando davanti a Cacìoche.

When we stopped in front of the towering walls of Cacioche, the Spaniards stuck their heads out of the high towers: "Hey, look! Amazing! There are Indians out there, Indians with crosses, singing church songs! Christian Indians!"

The governor immediately came out onto the big rampart and shouted: "Who's responsible for this? Who gave these Indians permission to practice our religion!"

I took a step forward and answered him: "Me. It was me, Lord Governor. My name is Johan Padan and they call me 'son of the moon and the rising sun.' I don't know if it was right or wrong to teach them our religion . . ."

Quando sémo ziùnti in faza le mura granda a Cacìoche, i spagnòl son spontàt de soravìa "Ehi, vardé! Meravègia! O gh'è de Indios, Indios co' le crose!, che i canta canti de giésa! Indios cristiani!"

Dal bastion grando l'è sortìdo sübito ol Governadór e gh'ha criàt: "Chi gh'ha dàit ol permèsso a 'sti Indios de far dotrìna!".

Ho fàito un paso en avante e gh'ho respondì: "Mi, son stàito mi. Siór Governadòr, mi me ciàmo Johan Padàn e loro i me ciàma "fiòi del sol che nasse e de la luna", mi no' so se ho fàito ben o mal a farghe dotrìna . . .".

He, the governor, looks around and notices that all these Christian Indians on their knees in front of the ramparts have basins and baskets full to the brim with pieces of silver and gold, and lots of necklaces. Curious, he asks: "And who is all this gold for, and all this silver?"

"For you. It's a present that the Indians are giving to you, Lord Governor."

"For me?!! You did well to teach them our religion."

Then he turns to his soldiers and says: "I'm talking to the Spaniards now: from now on it will be forbidden to enslave any of these Indians who are our brothers in Christ. They are subjects of the King and Queen of Spain! They will be allowed to work freely. They are free! They will work every morning in the plantations . . . as free men . . . they'll work in the mines too . . . compulsory, but free!"

None of the Indians understood the difference between compulsory and free but they were happy all the same . . . They launched themselves into drinking, singing . . . dancing.

Lü, il Govemadòre ol varda e si incòrge che tüti 'sti Indios cristiani che éran in ginògio devànti i bastiòn, gh'avévan dei baslòtti, dèi cesti-canestri impiegnìdi de tòchi d'oro, d'arzénto, e mügi de colàne, curioso el dimanda: "Ma per chi l'è tüto 'sto oro e tüto 'sto arzénto?"

"Per ti. A l'è ün présénte che i Indios te fa a ti, siòr Governadór." "A mi?! A t'hai fàito ben a farghe dotrina."

Po' se volta ai so' soldàt e ei dise: "Parlo ai spagnòl: de 'sto momento guai a chi se permètt de far stciàvi qualcun de 'sti Indios che sono fradèli nostri in Cristo, I son sudditi nostri, de la reìna e d'ol re de Spagna! I verà a lavorare liberi. Sono liberi! A lavorare tüte le matine in de le piantagión . . . liberi . . . anca in de le miniére i verà . . . obligati-liberi!"

E tüti i Indios no' i capiva ben la connessión tra obligati e liberà ma éran conténti uguale . . . Se son butà a bevar, a cantare . . . a balà.

Then at nightfall they all stretched themselves out on the ground, and at dawn when the morning bells began ringing to call them to work in the mines and plantations . . . all the Indians had vanished. You couldn't even find a shadow of an Indian!

Po' la nòte se son stravacàiti tüti par tèra e a l'alba, quando la campana curta l'ha comenzà a sonàr per ciamàrii tüti al trabàco, enfilàrse in miniéra, deréntro le piantagión, i Indios éran desparesìdi, no' gh'era più nemànco l'ombra de un Indios!

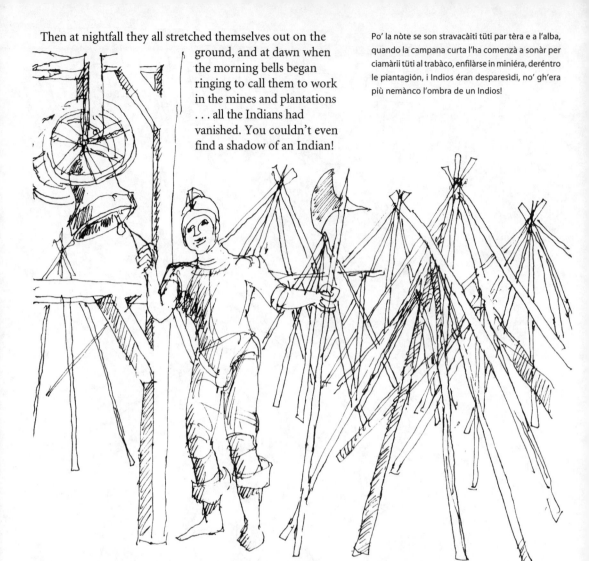

So they came looking for me instead. I was still sleeping. They grabbed me by the throat and dragged me in front of the governor.

E i son vegnüdi a ciamàrme a mi.
Mi dormivi ancmò, m'han catàit par la gola e m'han trascenà devànti al Governadór.

"On your knees," they said. And the governor: "So, Johan Padan, you're pretty clever, eh . . . you taught these Indians our religion . . . you prepared them . . . you came here to feel us out. And as soon as they heard, 'trabajo, work, mining' . . . they all disappeared, vanished. Now if these Indians don't get down here right away, if they are not back on their knees before me by the time the sun sets, I'm going to hang you from the highest pole! When the sun goes down, you'll rise with the moon!"

"In ginògio—m'han dito
E il Governatore: "Ehi Johan Padàn, furbo ti eh, ti hae fàito un po' de dotrina a 'sti Indios, ti i gh'ha preparà . . . ti végne qua a tastàrghe el polso a noialtri. Come i gh'han sentìo "trabàco, lavoro, miniére", tüti via, scapàti! Adesso se 'sti Indios no' dessénde sübeto qua, no' i retórna in ginögio avante a mi prima che cala ol sol, te impìco sul penón pù alto! Come descénde el soi ti te monti su la luna!"

89

Before the sun went down Jellybelly, Red, and Negro ran to get all the Indians, and they came down right away. They showed up all at once on their knees in front of the governor to implore him: "Lord Governor, we are ready to become your slaves immediately, but you must free Johan Padan, the son of the moon and the rising sun, our most precious shaman!"

Ante che dessendèsse ol sol o gh'è stàit el Negro, anca el Rosso e el Trentatrippe che son corúi a ciamàre tüti i Indios che son desendüi ràpedi. Tüti in un mumént son stàiti lì, in ginògio davanti al Governadór e ghe imploràveno diséndo: "Siòr Governadór, noiàltri sémo pronti a devegnìr stciàvi, ma ti te déve liberar Johan Padan, ol fiòl del sol che nasse e de la luna, oi nostro Sciammàn plu caro!".

The governor: "Look how dedicated these wretches are! All right! You all are free, because I have already given my word . . . but him I'm going to hang because he started a religion full of songs, dances . . . and laughter . . . blasphemer . . . Hang him!"

They put the noose around my neck and two hangmen tightened it. I could feel myself hanging, hanging there in the sky, my throat was choking . . . I saw red fire . . . the sky was burning: "Am I in hell?!" No! No! The sky was really burning! All the Indians, twenty-five thousand Indians, had come with torches and were standing on the bell towers, the plantations, and even the ships.

Twenty-five thousand Indians!

Fifty thousand torches!

The sky was burning! It was Red who shouted to the governor: "Be careful, Lord Governor. If you don't free Johan Padan immediately, they'll burn everything! They'll burn your plantations. They'll burn your storehouses and everything that's in them, they'll burn your churches, the cathedral, they'll make a bonfire of your palace, and your ships too! . . . How are you going to go home on ships of ashes!"

Infuriated, a captain shouted: "Fire the cannons!"

"No, stop! And you savages with the torches, you stop too . . . and think. You can set the whole city ablaze, Cacioche, fourteen years of work, thousands of gold coins went into its construction . . . all in flames . . . but in the end how many of you will be saved from the slaughter?

Ol Governador: "Ma varda che dedisiòn che gh'han 'sti disgrassió! D'acordo! Vialtri sit liberi parchè mi gh'ho üna parola sola . . . ma lü lo impìco perchè l'ha tràit in pìe üna religión tüta de canti, de balà e de rìder . . . Blasfémia! Impichélo!"

M'han tacà de le corde al colo e dòe boia m'han tiràito. Me son sentù pendùo, pendùo che montavi in ziélo, me se sgorgiàva la gorgia, ho vedùo rosso de fògo . . . el ziélo brusàva: "Sono a l'enferno?!" No! No! Ol brusàva e! ziélo davéro! Tüti i Indios, ventisincomila Indios che éran dessandùi co' le fiàcole in man, son montàit dapartüto, sui téci, sui bastión, anca su le gièse, in cima ai campanil, in de le piantagión, anca su le navi!

Venticincomila Indios!

Sinquantamila fiàcole!

Ei ziélo o! brusàva! Gh'è stàito ol Rosso che gh'ha vusà al Governadór: "Aténto siòr Governadór . . . se ti no' te liberi sübit Johan Padan quèsti te brüsa tüto. A fogo te 'nzendia a le piantagion, te brüsa i capanón con deréntro tüto o! racòlto, brüsan anca le gièse, catedràl, te fa un faló de tüto ol palàz e anca de le navi! . . . Dòpo mite vòjo véder tornàrte a casa co' de le navi de carbonèla!"

Infularmà ol capitàn gh'ha criàt: "Sparémo i canóni!"

"No, férma! E anca voiàltri selvàz co' le fiàcole sti' fermi, ragionè: viàltri podé brusàrme tüta in fógo la cità, Cacìoche, quatòrdese ani de trabàco, a gh'è ün milion de maravédi deréntro . . . tüta la brüsa . . . ma a la fin, quanti de voiàltri se salverà de vèss copàti?

How many of you will be blasted into the air by the cannon shots we fire? A thousand, two thousand . . . are so many of you ready to die just to save this wretched thief? Johan Padan, who passes himself off as the son of the moon and the rising sun, so he can come and rob you of all your silver and gold . . ."

It was the cacique who rose up on his feet: "Stop! Lord Governor, how long have you known Johan Padan? . . . You just met him! I have known him for five or six years, and he never robbed us of even a dried leaf. We gave him baskets and baskets of silver and gold . . . he didn't even touch it. 'I don't want to be a porter,' he said. You, Lord Governor, who arrived here without having been invited by anyone, you are the big thief! You came with all these armed men covered in metal, and you robbed us of our possessions, our land, the work of our hands, you robbed us of our men, our women, our gold! . . . and even of our language! You arrived full of self-importance, in plumed helmets . . . he arrived as naked as we were. You arrived triumphantly riding on stallions . . . he arrived riding too . . . on the back of a pig. He came here and brought to life men who were dead . . . you put to death men who were alive! He brought us a religion fashioned from songs, happiness, dances, and joy . . . you bring us a religion of sadness, melancholy, and death. You are always telling us: 'Remember that you have to die! You're alive now, but remember that one day you'll drop dead!' And we reach for our testicles in fear!"

Quanti salterìt per aria per le canonàde che ve sparèm? Mila, domìla . . . e vuisit pronti a crepare in tanti solo per salvar 'sto ladrón fotüt? Johan Padan che ol se fa passàr fiòl del sol che nasse e de la luna per vegnìrve a robàr tüti i ori e arzénti . . ."
A gh'è stàit ol Cacìco che s'è indrisàito in pìe: "Ferma! Siór Governadór, ti t'ol cognósset de quando Johan Padan? . . . Da adesso! Mi ol cognóssi da çinquo ani, sìe ani, e gh'ha giamài robàito nemanco üna foja sèca! Gh'émo donàt ceste e cavàgna de oro e arzénto . . . manco l'ha tocàito e l'ha dito: mi no' voi fare ol fachino! Ti sìor Governadór che te s'è 'rivàito e nisciün t'avéa invitàito, ti sì che te sèt ol gran ladron! Ti te sèit 'rivào con tüta 'sta zénte covèrta de fèro e armada, te gh'hai robàit ol nostro racólto, le nostre tère, ol trabàco de le nostre bràzia, te gh'hai robàit i òmeni, le dòne, l'oro! . . . e te gh'hai robàit anca la nostra léngua! Ti te sei 'rivàito tüto sburbanzóso co' le plume in crapa . . . Lü l'è 'rivàito desnùdo, sbiòto, come noiàitri. Ti te sei 'rivàit strónfio, a cavàld'un stalón . . . lü l'è 'rivàit a cavàlo anca lü . . . a cavàl de ün porsèlo. Lü l'è 'zonto chiloga e gh'ha metù in vita zénte che l'era già morta . . . ti te ghe mètet a la morte zénte che la sta ben in vita! Lü gh'ha tràito una relizión fata de canti, de 'legrèssa, de balo, de surìso e de felisità . . . Ti te ghe pòrtet üna relizión triste, de malconcìa, de morte. In ogni momént te ghe dìset: "Recòrdet che te dévet morire! Te sè in vita ma recòrdet che te dévet crepare! E noiàltri se tochémo i cojón!"

92

"Enough with the chattering!" shouts the captain. "Fire the cannons."
The artillerymen ran to light the fuses, but the fuses were wet and the gunpowder was drenched with dampness . . . The captain shouts: "Who peed in the cannon mouths last night? Bring out the horses! Mount the horses! Riders ready with your beasts! Get ready to charge the Indians!"
But the horses pulled back from their tethers. They didn't want to go out. They reared up and kicked their hooves. They rolled over on the ground . . . and they farted too . . . through their noses!

"Basta co' i ciànce!—vosà e! capitàn—Spengé 'ste fiacole o démo fogo a le mize dei canon!" A gh'è stàit o! capitan che l'ha criàt: "Sparémo coi canoni!". I artifiziér, coréndo, i va coréndo a dar fògo a le mize, ma le mize son bagnàde e anca le polveri maseràt de umido . . . El capitano el vusa: "Ma chi è che gh'ha pisàito deréntro le bóche dei canón 'stanòce?! Föra i cavali! Monté i cavali! I cavajér pronti su le so' bestie! Pronti che fémo la carica contro i Indios!".
Ma i cavàli, anco tirài co' le corde, no' i voleva vegnìr föra, i stragagnàva, i se rotulàva par tèra, i sgacagnàva co' le giàmbe per aria, i scorezzàva anca da le narìzz . . .

"What's gotten into these horses?" shouts the governor.
"Lord Governor," responded one of the soldiers. "Last night I saw some Indians who were filling up reeds with white powder . . . then they put them into the horses' noses, in the nostrils, and they blew in them: PIUM! They were pumping something into them . . . and the horses liked it!"
All of a sudden: PA! PA! PA! Fireworks were going off at the feet of the Spaniards, who were jumping all over the place and running around . . .

'Cosa gh'han fàit a 'sti cavali?' urla el Governatore. (Fa immaginare un soldato che gli risponde) "Siòr Governadór, gh'ho vedùo 'stanòce Indios che riempevàn de le càne lònghe de pùlvara bianca . . . po' ghe le infricàva deréntro ai narìz dei cavài, nei bögi del nas e i sbrofàva deréntro: PIUM!, e i pompàva . . . Ai cavàli ghe piàse!" risponde un soldato.
A l'impruvìso: PA! PA! PA! de bòto un gran fògo d'artifizio ghe 'riva in mèso a le giàmbe de i spagnòl, che i salta de qua e de là, i core . . .

93

"Stop! Stop, soldiers! Look, there's a cavalry charging at us! Whose cavalry is it? A hundred horses!!! INDIANS?! INDIANS ON HORSEBACK LIKE CHRISTIANS?! Nothing is sacred anymore!"

All the soldiers are on their knees shouting: "Don't kill us! Spare our lives! Don't kill us! Forgive us!"
"Come on, Spaniards, let's show a little dignity in front of these wild Indians! (*To the Indians*) Go ahead. Tie them all up. Tie the Spaniards to one another in a line and take them onto the ships! Unload their cannons, go on. (*To the Spaniards*) Spaniards, we're going to spare your lives. We're even going to send you back to your homes. We'll wait three days and three nights to see what the weather is like . . . If the weather is good, we'll send you back to your island. Happy? Good, get on your ships."
The first day went by . . . the moon was normal. The second day, still normal. On the third night the moon rose large and clear in the sky . . . with little clouds all round and round it.
"Hey, Spaniards, you can leave now! Bon voyage! Hoist the mainsail! Unfurl the jib! Haul up the yardarm!"

"Fermi! Fermi soldàt! Vardé a gh'è una cavalerìa che ghe végn incóntra in aiüd . . . De chi l'è 'sta cavalerìa? . . . Zénto cavali! ! . . . INDIOS?! INDIOS A CAVÀL COME CRISTIAN?! . . . No' gh'è pù religión!
Tüti i soldàt in ginoigio e i criàva: "No' maséghe! Déghe salva la vita! No' rnaséghe miga! Perdonéghe!".

"Ün po' de dignitàd, andémo spagnòl, davanti a 'sii forèsti de Indios! Avanti, (*agli Indios*) lighéli tüti, lighé i spagnòl ün a ün e portémoli su le navi! Scareghé tüti i canoni, via! (*Agli spagnoli*) A viàitri ve démo salva la vita a tüti, anzi ve fémo tornàr a le vostre case. 'Specièm tre ziórni e tre nòti a véder come sta el témpo . . . Se el témpo l'è bòn ve fémo tornar a le vostre isole, conténti? . . . Bon, monté tüti su le vostre navi!"
Il primo ziórno l'è pasàt . . . la luna normale. Al segéndo, normale almò. A la terza nòce monta una luna granda, ciàra in del ziélo . . . e tüto intorno de le nivoiète tonde tonde intorna.
"Ehi spagnòl, podé partire! Bon viàge! Vai con le vele! Tira el fiòco! Vai co' la randa!"

Then the governor came out on the quarterdeck and shouted: "Hey, Johan Padan, you imbecile! It was a big mistake to let us live! You should have killed us all, because now we're going to the big island of Santo Domingo and when we get there we're going to load up more cannons, and we're going to arm all the rest of the ships that arrive from Spain, and when we have enough ships and cannons we're going to come back here again to your shores and fire the cannons for weeks without end and slaughter you all: men, women, children, old people, dogs, and the fleas on your dogs too!"

A gh'è stàit o! governadóre che l'è spontà fòra del càssero e l'ha criàt: "Ehi, Johan Padan, imbezìi! Grave erór che t'hai fàito a lassàrghe in vita! Dovévet masàrghe tüti parchè adèso noàltri zonzerèm a l'isola grande de Santo Domingo e come arivémo là, careghémo altri canoni, armémo altre navi en arrivo da l'Espagna e quando sémo tante navi e tanti canóni tornerem chi de nòvo su le vostre coste, ve sparémo canonàde per setemàne intréghe, ve copémo tüti: òmeni, dòne, bambin, vègi, i can e anca le pùrese dei vostri can!"

"Lord Governor," I said. "There is an old proverb in my valley that says: Before you can go back to a place that you thought you could reach after having been to a second place to prepare to go to the first place that you wanted to get to . . . you have to arrive in the second place where you thought you were going to prepare to go back to the first place!"

"Siòr Governadór—fo' mi—a gh'è ün antìgo proverbio de le mie valàde che ol dise: ante de podér tornare int ün lògo dove se pensava de podér arivàrghe dòpo èserghe stato int ün primo lògo a preparàrse per arivàrghe in del segóndo, dove se voleva 'rivàrghe . . . bisogna 'rivàrghe al primo lògo dove se pensava de 'rivàrghe a preparàrse per poi arivàrghe al segóndo!"

The ships kept going, and going, getting farther away, about to disappear in the horizon, and I said to the moon: "Mother! Give them a nice big thrashing!" PUAM! A lightning bolt, a huge flash. For a second everything was clear,

Le navi andévano, andévano, se lontanàvan, stévano per desparìre a l'orisónte e mi gh'ho dito a la luna: "Matre, daghe ün stciopón!".
PUAM! Un fulmine grande, ün gran baleno . . . per un attimo s'è vidùoo ciàro

then the sea turned black . . . another flash of light . . . in the distance you could catch a glimpse of the Spaniards' tiny, tiny ships, and surrounding these tiny ships were funnels of twisting sea water. Another blinding flash! Next there was thunder exploding like cannons, then waves, waves that kept getting bigger and bigger until they arrived at the bay as tall as mountains! And inside these gigantic waves were pieces of broken wood from the shattered ships, drowned sailors, drowned soldiers, drowned captains, and the governor too, the vice-governor . . . the chaplain was there . . . All of them . . . they had all come back! Floating like waterlogged leather sacks.

po'ol mare l'è diventào negro . . . altro lampo di luce . . . in fondo, si scorgevano le navi dei spagnoli pìcole pìcole e intórna a 'ste navi pìcole de le trombetine de mare. Anmò dei luminón, stciopón! Apreso i tron che stciopàva come canóni e po' onde, onde sémpre pù grande che quando son zonte a la marina e l'era devegnüt alte come montagne!, e dentro 'ste onde grande a gh'era tòchi de navi. sgargarón fracassate e inframèso a gh'era marinéri anegàiti, soldàiti anegàti, capitani, a gh'era ol governadòr, ol vice-governador, ofiziàli . . . o gh'era anca ol capelàn . . . Tüti . . . éran tornàiti tüti . . . che galezàva come otre sgionfà.

We waited days and days to see if by chance we could catch sight of any returning ships, but since none of them had gotten to Santo Domingo there was no way for them to come back. We flattened the city. The city of Cacioche, we flattened it. We planted trees that, after five years or so, became a forest. We waited eleven years, but the Spaniards never showed up! One morning we saw the sea full of sails . . . The flag belonged to Leon of Castiglia. They were Spaniards. There was also the large flag of Panfilo Navares, a great leader, a captain famed for his glory. When they landed in the bay we Indians had disappeared, none of us were there.

They came down from their tall ships, followed by boats that carried their horses, studied some papers that they had in their hands, and said: "This must be a mistake. Cacioche should be here, but there's not even a log . . . no sign of a city in this place! . . . Let's go see if Cacioche is somewhere else!" And from where we were hidden we could see this huge army filing into the forest. And before they were halfway there . . . as the saying goes: "If misfortunes are supposed to happen, they happen!"

Emo 'speciàito ziòrni e ziórni par vidér se par caso se scorzéva spuntàr qualche nave de ritorno, ma dal momento che nesuno era zónto a Santo Domingo, no' podéva miga tornare indrìo. Noiàltri emo despianàd la cità, la cità de Caciòche l'emo spianàda, a gh'emo piantàd alberi che son dòpo zinque ani . . . i sont divegnut 'na foresta.

Emo 'speciàito ùndese ani ma i spagnòl no' i spontava miga. Una matina émo vedùo ol mare impiegnìdo de vele . . . le bandere éran quèle de Castija Leòn. i era spagnòl. A gh'era anca la bandéra granda de Panfilo Narvarèz, ün grande comandadór, gran capitan glorioso. Quando è dessandùo a la marina noiàltri Indios éremo desparùdi, no' gh'era nisciùno de noi. Loro i son dessandùi de le loro barche grande, e po' barconi che i portava anca i cavali e i gh'aveva le carte i man "De segùra qui gh'è un erór. Chi doveva èsserghe Caciòche, ma de 'sta zità, in 'sto logo, no' ghe sta manco un pilon! . . . Andémo a véder se Caciòche l'è en un'altra banda!" Noialtri éremo nascondùdi coi Indios dapartüto e avémo vedùo 'sta arrnada grande infricàrse intréga in la foresta.

Quando se dise: "Se le disgrazie devono capitare, capitano!": le robè, quando vol capitare, capita! . . .

99

The army hadn't even gotten to the middle of the forest when a little brush fire started burning over there (*points to his left*) . . . then another few sparks started burning there (*points somewhere else*) . . . then there was a big blaze, two fires, three fires, five fires . . . they were trying to escape every which way . . . "Oh, let's get the hell out of this forest! We'll all be burned! Out! We've got to get out of here! AHIAAAAIIIAA!"

They all burned! An entire army burned at the stake in a forest . . . How unfortunate!

Two years later the son of Panfilo Navares arrived, Michel Vasquez Navares, shrewder and more intelligent than his father. He looked around and said: "I don't like this! The Indians aren't coming out to meet us the way they usually do . . . Cacioche has disappeared . . . and look . . . there are burnt bones in the forest. I'm no half-cocked idiot. I won't fall for that trap in the woods. I'm going through the valley!"

He led his whole army toward the mountain where there was a large ridge above the valley. As they walked, the ridge got gradually smaller and smaller until it became very steep . . . a steep crevice . . . choked and narrow, so that they had to walk sideways, like this . . . (*he demonstrates*), which for horses is very hard to do! Suddenly they hear the gurgling of boiling water rushing downhill . . . a huge river with explosive waves that devastate everything in their path: (*As if the water is speaking*) "Stand clear of the flood . . . watch out . . . I'm coming down . . . move over there please . . . excuse me!"

They all drowned . . . in profile! Father and son . . . what an unfortunate family!

Tüta 'sta armàda no' arìva in mèso a la foresta, che gh'è ün fogherèl che brüsa lì, (*indica a sinistra*) po' gh'è ün foghìn che brüsa là, (*indica da un'altra parte*) po' ün fogàsso, dòe fóghi, tri fóghi, zinque fóghi . . . loro scapa de qua per andar de là.

"Oh, sgomberèm de la foresta! Ghe brüsa tüti! Föra! Scapémo de föra! AHIAAAIIIAA!"

Tüti brüsàt! Ün'armata tüta intréga brusàda in te la foresta . . . Ma varda che disgrassia!

Dòpo dòe ani l'è 'rivàito ol fiòl de Panfilo Narvalèz, Michel Vasques Narvalèz, plu furbo, plu inteiizénte del padre, infacti l'è 'rivàito e l'ha dito: "No' me piàse! No' gh'è Indios che ghe végne incontro come de normale . . . Cacìoche l'è desparùda . . . Vardé . . . in te la foresta gh'è le ose brusàde . . . no' son miga così cojón de' 'traversàrlo mi 'sto bosco tràpola, mi vago per el valón!"

Ol se indrìsa co' l'armàda intréga invèrso la montagna dove a gh'è la sfèrzula larga del valon. Mano a man che ghe entra el slargo ol se restrìgne, se restrìgne e ol devénta un tàjo profondo, 'na fèssa (*fessura*) fondo. strusàda, stretta e po' ghe tóca caminàr tüto de strasvèrso, così . . . (*mima una camminata tutta di fianco*) che per i cavàl caminar de 'sta manéra l'è difizil! De bòta se sénte el gargàio 'rebolénte de l'acqua che dessénde . . . un rivo tremendo stcìòpa frantolón d'onde che stravlòze ogni 'leménto (*come fosse l'acqua che parla*): "Atenti al srotolón, òcio che sbròcubo, tiréve in là, permesso!"

Son anegàdi tüti de profilo! . . .

Tra il padre e il fiòl, üna famija desgrassiada così!

Hernando de Soto sailed in there too, the greatest Conquistador in all of Spain. He arrived with nine hundred men and two hundred cavalry . . . more than they gave to Cortés. And with his nine hundred men and countless cannons Hernando de Soto met the Indians.

There was a chronicler who wrote: "These Indians arrived like demons! There were thousands of them shooting off fireworks . . . they came out of nowhere . . . two hundred more of them showed up . . . they vanished . . . then a hundred more appeared . . . they sprang from the ground like venomous snakes . . . they burned up the prairie . . . a river that came out of nowhere . . . a different trap every day!" After four months they all went back to the bay . . . Dammit what a disaster! Of the nine hundred men and two hundred horses, only thirty were left . . . and twenty-eight of them were horses!

Then there was Pedro Menderes de Vies. He was a captain who arrived with an army, went into the plains . . . and disappeared! And then another one named Erige Marco le Cronigador showed up with his army. Disappeared! Next came Luis Cansel Bavaraos: He went in . . . and vanished! Finally there arrived an army beyond counting commanded by someone named Tristan de Luna.

With a name like that you can guess what happened . . . He disappeared!

E l'è 'sbarcà anche Hernando de Soto, ol plu gran conchistadór de Spagna. Hernando de Soto . . . l'è 'rivàito con novesénto òmeni e dosénto cavali . . . plu importante de Cortèz l'era, con novesénto òmeni l'è 'rivàito, canoni che no' finiva . . . e lü l'ha incontràito i Indios. A gh'era ün cronigadór che ol scriveva "Ariva 'sti Indios, son dèi demoni! Sono in mila, i spara fóghi d'artifizio . . . compare a l'emproviso . . . ne ariva altri dosénto, i descompàre . . . po' ne ariva zénto . . . i sponta da la tèra come serpenti venenosi . . . brusa la prateria, un fium che sbota a l'improvisa . . . üna trapola ogni ziòrno!"

Dòpo quatro mesi i son tornàiti a la marina tüti . . . Boja che desastro! De novesénto òmeni e dosénto cavali erano restaiti in trenta . . . e ventotto erano cavali!

Alóra gh'è stàito Pedro Menderès da Viès, l'è 'rivàito lü un capitàn con üna armada, l'è entràido in dèl pianón: l'è desparùdo!

Po' l'è 'rivàito ün altro Herighe Marcos e! Cronigador . . . l'è entraito co' üna armada: desparùdo!

Po' l'è 'rivaido Luis Cansèl Bavaros: l'è entrado, l'è desparùdo!

A la fin ün'armada che no' finiva pù comandada de ün che se ciamàva Tristan de Luna . . . V'ün che se ciàma Tristan cossa ghe pol capitare? . . . L'è desparùdo!

At this point King Charles the Fifth proclaimed: "That's enough! That place called Florida is busting my balls! I declare the land of Florida to be impregnable territory! That means if any Christian Spaniard puts his foot there without my orders . . . even if he comes back alive . . . I'll hang him afterward, with my own hands!"

From that day on the Spaniards have never been seen here.

A Frenchman tried once . . . he was a little suspicious . . . he found the burnt bones . . . "Excuse me!" . . . he packed up and left.

Forty years went by, forty years since the day I showed up hugging a pig in the storm . . . I've become old, white hair, white skin, but I'm happy, I'm content, I'm healthy . . . I'm in love, I have wives and children that love me . . . I have so many children and grandchildren that I don't bother counting them anymore. There are children everywhere . . . sometimes I meet one that I don't recognize: "Who are you? My son? How about that! What a pleasure! Give me a kiss." I don't recognize all my grandchildren either. They come calling, "Father! Father!" . . . everyone calls me "Father!" Even "Holy Father!"

They love me, they are tender with me, compassionate. They're not scared of me anymore, never afraid. And when they have a problem, they always come asking me to resolve their arguments or give advice . . . I'm always there to take care of it . . . Respected, loved, happy . . . a king! . . .

A 'sto punto ol re Carios el Quinteros l'ha proclamàt: "Basta! 'Sta Florìda m'ha roto i cojóni! Declàro quèste tère Floride, tère inespugnable! Ch'el vol dir che se ün spagnòl cristian ghe mète pie sénsa l'ordine de mi . . . anche se torna indrìo vivo, dòpo lo impico mi co' le mie man!"

E de quel ziórno spagnòl no' se son pù vedui.

Gh'ha provàito qualche franzóso ün po' sospecto . . . gh'ha scoverto de le osa brusate . . . "Pardon!" l'ha faito fagoto. Son passaiti quaranta ani, quaranta ani dai ziórno che son 'rivàito imbrassàto al porsèlo in de la tempesta . . . son devegnu vègio, bianco de cavèli, bianco de pelo . . . ma son felize, son contént, son san . . . son amoroso . . . gh'ho muhèr, fiòl che me ama . . . Gh'ho tanti fiòli e fiòle e tanti nevódi che no' tégno nemànco più ol cunto. O gh'è nìnios dapartuto . . . ne incontro quaicun che nemanco recognosso: "Chi set ti? Me fiòl? Oh, varda, piazerz! Dame un basìn!"

No' cognòsso nemànco i me' nevódi che me ciàma "Padre! Padre!" . . . tüti me ciàman "Padre!" anzi "Santo Padre!"

Me voi ben, i gh'ha amor par mi, considerasion, gh'è mai terór, gh'è mai pagüra . . . Se gh'è üna questiòn i végne sémpre da mi, 'na dìsputa, ün consèjo . . . sémpre mi ghe pénso . . .

Respectàdo, amàdo, felìze: ün rèj!

The only thing that makes me nostalgic is the fresh smell of the wind from my valley. I don't know how it gets here, but I smell it . . . it wafts through my nostrils and gives me goose bumps. It's an aroma I smell whenever someone cooks venison . . . I smell the must of fermenting grapes from the tavern, I hear the wine bubbling in the barrels . . . the women singing, laughter, love songs . . . Oh, the love songs . . . Even the church songs make me nostalgic . . .

L'unica roba che me fa nostalghìa a l'è l'odor fresco del vento delle me' valàde, no' so de dove 'riva, ma lo sento . . . 'riva in del naso, me svìrzola, sénto ol parfùmo de quando cöse ol cavrïòl . . . mi me sénto ol stciopàr d'ol mosto dentro le osterie, me sento ol bujr d'oi vino in de le cròte . . . ol cantar de le dòne, ol rìder . . . i canti d'amor . . . Oh i canti d'amor . . . anche i canti de giésa me fan nostalgia.

There are moments when I'm struck by pangs of emotion that wring my heart. My gullet tightens, my heartbeat quickens . . . and I run desperately to the hammock . . . stretched out in the hammock I hug the netting . . . before long two young girls come by . . . and sing lullabies while they rock the hammock, they rock me slowly, slowly . . . I close my eyes and they sing me the song from my village that I taught them . . . with the very same words, the same idiom of my dialect from home.

"Oh what joy and oh what wonder
The son of heav'n is still alive
The son of Mary is still living!
The Virgin Mary is full of cheer now
And there's nothing for us to fear now
Not the Turks or the stormy winds now
Not the winds or the Christian soldiers
Not the Turks or the Christian soldiers."

A gh'è quèi momenti che me cata uno stciòpamagón che me stròssa ol còre, ol gargaròsso me stciòpa, ol cór me sbrüja . . . vado coréndo desesperàdo in de l'amaca . . . stravacà in de l'amaca me ambràsso la rete . . . dòe fìole végne aprèsso . . . i dónda . . . i nina l'amaca . . . mé dóndola piàn, piàn . . . mi sèri i ògi e lòro mé canta la cansòn del mé paése che mi gh'ho insegnàt . . . pròprio co' le stèsse paròle, col mèsmo idiòma del mé dialèct.

"Oh che bèlo o che 'legrìa
l'é ancamò vivo ol fiò! del ziél
l'é ancamò vivo ol fiòl de la Maria
Maria verzén lé in gran conténto
nesciün de nojàltri ol gh'ha più spavénto
né dei turchi né del gran vénto
né del gran vénto né dei cristiàn
né dei turchi né dei cristiàn."

104

Prima Parte

*(Fo's original text was written in dialect and translated into
Italian by Franca Rame.)*

Vai! Vai! Leva l'ormeggio! Arma la randa! Su il
trinchetto! Leva l'ancora! Su! Issa! Allarga tutto!
Issa! Va col paranello! Si va, si va! Via della
Giudecca! Via della Laguna! Via da Venezia . . .
Vai! Vai col fiocco!

Qualche giorno fa una signora che ha fatto:
"Oddio, non sarà tutto in questa lingua qua?!".
Ma d'altra parte, questo è il linguaggio dei
marinai del porto di Venezia nel '500. Volete
capirlo? . . . Non lo capisco io che lo recito da
due anni, e pretendete di capirlo voi, così,
d'acchito?!

Oh, che il vento tira e gonfia le vele . . . si va . . .
si vahaaa! Fuori! Siamo fuori! Fuori all'aperto.
Sono salvo! Salvo! Io, Johan Padan sono salvo!
"Salvo da chi?"
"Dall'Inquisizione! Dalla forca . . . da essere
bruciato! Quelli del Tribunale Santissimo, si
erano messi in mente che io fossi quello che
teneva mano a 'sta strega.
Sto parlando della strega che le guardie avevano
portato via in catene . . . Ma sì, quella che
dicono che fa le fatture, gli incantesimi! Che ha i
forconi, che ficca gli spilloni dentro i
pupazzi . . . che strozza i gatti e poi gli scruta gli
intestini per indovinare il futuro . . . che parla
col demonio, che parla anche con i morti . . .
con gli spiriti . . .
Esagerati! Ah, ah, ah! Parlare con i morti! . . .
Col diavolo . . . qualche volta . . . così per dire.
Non è vero che io le tenessi mano . . . io le stavo
appresso solamente perché sono innamorato.
Beh sì, facevo anche un po' d'assistente a 'sta
ragazza, ma solo come pretesto, per stare con lei.

Sapeste come mi faceva languire di gelosia, che
lei, 'sta bella strega, aveva intorno alle sottane,
tanti di quei serventi amorosi! E tutti che le
facevano un sacco di cortigianerie e regali.
Principi addirittura! Monsignori! Senatori
della Serenissima. C'erano i dieci della
Serenissima che le facevano la corte! . . . Non
tutti e dieci! . . . Due o tre dei dieci . . . ma non
era puttana!
Solo che, quando era attaccata a me, non
vedeva altro che me . . . mi parlava con quelle
parole da ubriacarti che ci si inventa facendo
l'amore.
Ma ohi, che amore!
M'ha insegnato tutti i trucchi per indovinare
quel che capita appresso leggendo le stelle . . . la
luna! Mi ricordo, stavamo stravaccati sulla rena
all'isola Paranello . . . era notte . . . era estate . . .
eravamo nudi a far l'amore . . . di colpo mi fa:
"Fermo! !"
"Cosa c'è?"
"Guarda la luna!"
"Perché? . . . Cosa c'è? . . . Hai vergogna della
luna?"
"No . . . Non vedi che la luna è chiara, grande,
con tutte le nuvolette tondo tondo d'intorno?"
"E allora?"
"E' un segno tremendo che tra poco ci sarà
tempesta! Ci sarà un vento che straccerà
tutto fino al campo di san Marco!"
"Non dire stronzate, ragazza, andiamo!, ma se
non c'è neanche un segno . . . una nuvola
intorno . . . il mare è tranquillo . . . la laguna è
piatta che pare una pisciata. Non c'è nemmeno
un uccello che vola . . ."

"Proprio perché non ci sono uccelli è un altro segno che sta venendo la tempesta! Via! Salta sulla barca!" e via a remare come matti.
"Ma dove andiamo?"
"Voga! Vogaaa! Andiamo a san Marco!"
Siamo arrivati giusto a San Marco, abbiamo buttato la barca correndo, abbiamo attraversato tutto il campo, siamo arrivati dietro all'angolo . . . quando siamo stati al coperto s'è sentito un uragano che stravolgeva: BRAAM! . . . Uno squarciamento! Le onde che arrivavano dentro la laguna, raspavano la laguna, strappavano su le barche dall'ormeggio, le sradicavano con tutti i pali . . . Sono arrivati due cavalloni, grandi, lenti che hanno preso una nave e l'hanno portata nel campo di San Marco davanti alla chiesa . . . È arrivato un altro cavallone che l'ha infilata dentro la chiesa . . . una nave nella navata!!
C'era il prete sul transetto "FERMAA! !" grida (*fa il gesto di benedire*).' BUAMM! . . . Se l'è portato via abbracciato a la prua!
Era un fenomeno 'sta strega . . . indovinava tutto!
Peccato che non abbia indovinato quello che è capitato a lei il giorno che sono piombate le guardie e l'hanno incatenata per ordine della Santissima Inquisizione. L'hanno portata sotto giudizio al Tribunale . . . Intanto che passava, io ero lì presente . . . E lì sono stato un vigliacco!
Ché l'ufficiale mi punta il dito contro e mi dice: "Tu non sei della congrega di questa?"
"Di questa? (*Pausa*) Mai veduta!"
Mi ero preso uno scagazzo da non dire! Io, all'idea d'essere portato al Tribunale dell'Inquisizione col giudice che mi punta il dito contro anche lui e mi dice: "Adesso, tu mi racconti tutti gli imbrogli che avete fatto voialtri con i diavoli, coi caproni dell'anticristo" mi sentivo male.
"Ma io non so niente!"
"Mettetelo subito alla ruota!" Io, all'idea di essere legato sulla ruota con tutti gli spunzoni . . . che mi dànno un fastidio!, e poi finiva di sicuro che mi bruciavano il culo!
Allora, col fuoco dietro alle chiappe sono andato correndo dove c'era il molo grande . . . c'era un brigantino che stava salpando . . . Ho detto: "C'è bisogno di un calafatore . . . uno che rattoppa le vele? . . . Pronto! Sono qua!" e via che sono montato.

Mi sono infilato sottocoperta ben accucciato come un ratto . . . poi quando siamo arrivati al largo sono venuto fuori con la testa, e mi sono detto: si andrà giusto dietro all'angolo . . . al massimo a Chioggia! "Dove si va?" domando.
"Siviglia!" Proprio dietro all'angolo!! Dico: "Per strada ci si fermerà a prendere fiato?"
"Sì"
"Dove'?"
"A Tunisi!!"
Io, sbattuto per mare, venticinque giorni di nave!!
Io, che sono nato come uomo di terra (e non di mare) . . . sono venuto al mondo fra Brescia e Bergamo, io, che l'acqua mi fa impressione solamente a guardarla . . . che mi ricordo la prima e unica volta che m'hanno buttato nell'acqua avevo due giorni . . . per il battesimo! . . .
Ho ancora gl'incubi!!
Siamo arrivati a Tunisi e da Tunisi siamo andati a Malaga e da Malaga siamo scesi a Siviglia. Ma Siviglia non è sul mare!!! Io credevo che fosse sul mare . . . No! Siviglia è in una piana tremenda con un canale, scavato ancora dagli arabi, che viene giù fino al mare. Tu arrivi con la tua nave, aspetti, arrivano i cavalli, arrivano i muli, ti attaccano come un carretto e ti trascinano come un barcone . . . così vai scivolando fino al porto della città dentro a 'sto fiume.
Siviglia . . . che città meravigliosa, bisogna vederla! Ci sono tutte 'ste cupole rosse e d'oro con 'sti spilungoni di campanili che si arrampicano in cielo . . . Ci sono tutte queste case con fontane dappertutto, vai per la strada con 'sti spruzzi che ti annaffiano.
Io ero incantato ad ammirare questa città . . . e come sbarco, mi ritrovo davanti di colpo una grande catasta di legna con quattro seduti in cima, comodi . . . che bruciano tranquilli
"Ma chi bruciano?"
"Eretici!"
"E chi li ha condannati?"
"Il Tribunale dell'Inquisizione!!" . . .
Sangue santo di Dio! Scappo da Venezia col fuoco dietro al culo . . . arrivo a Siviglia e me lo ritrovo davanti alle palle!!
'Sti fanatici davano fuoco alla gente in continuazione: agli eretici che non volevano abiurare, agli stregoni che non volevano

condannare la stregoneria, ai mori che non volevano la conversione . . . e ai giudei ebraici . . . per qualsiasi ragione!

Non lo facevano per cattiveria, gli bruciavano il corpo per liberargli l'anima . . .

Il corpo di carbonella e l'anima felice che andava in cielo! Pensa che cuore!

Una puzza di carne bruciata!

Ma questa gente di Siviglia non era triste, no anzi, appena finita 'sta funzione d'arrostita collettiva . . . buttavano via ogni paramento nero che avevano addosso, e si lanciavano tutti, donne e uomini, in una grande allegrezza e cantavano e ballavano . . . e mi ricordo che avevano delle nacchere, si chiamano così . . . robe da arabi . . . di legno, che loro battevano l'una contro l'altra e ci cavavano musiche . . . TRATATATATA TA. (*Canta mimando di danzare usando le nacchere*)

"Ahi! Ahi, dolce figliola . . .
per il grande calore
TRA TATATATA
dentro la fonte ci siamo bagnati
TRATATATA
e per asciugarti . . .
la mia camicia ti ho prestato
e nemmeno ti sei accorta che dentro
c'era nascosto il mio cuore!"
TRATATAT

E via! PIM-PAM . . . PAM!, i fuochi d'artificio . . . che venivano su nel cielo tutto illuminato!

Loro finivano tutto con i fuochi d'artifizio. E proprio lì, nei fuochi ho trovato subito da lavorare, che io sono un artificiere che non c'è al mondo . . . Facevo fuochi d'artificio luminosi da ubriacarli. Prendevo un tubo grande, lo riempivo di salnitro, gli mettevo dentro lo zolfo e poi la carbonella, poi facevo otto canne incatenandole una all'altra, poi dodici canne, poi tutte le micce: una lunga, una un po' più lunghina, una un po' più cortina . . . poi davo fuoco a tutto: PIAMM . . . BAAM . . . Artificiere d'oro, ero!

Tanto per la cronaca, devo ricordarvi che proprio in quel tempo era appena tornato dalle Indie il Colombo genovese, uomo di testa . . . che lui aveva fatto tutta la traversata in nemmeno un mese, però non andandoci per il dritto, ma arrivando alle Indie per il di dietro!

Pensa che testa! C'era arrivato per il rovescio! . . . Perché allora quando si andava alle Indie per il diritto, attraversando il Mediterraneo, si arrivava a Tunisi, a Tunisi c'era il deserto, si prendeva il cammello: (*accenna passi di danza mimando la camminata sbilenca del cammello*) cammello, cammello, cammello, cammello, cammello. Poi si arrivava alle montagne con un mulo o l'asino: asino, asino, asino, asino. Si discendeva, c'era il fiume, una barca, si attraversava, poi c'era il deserto: deserto, deserto, deserto, cammello, cammello, cammello, cammello, poi c'erano le montagne di nuovo, un mulo, un cavallo, un mulo di nuovo . . . poi si arrivava al mare . . . Finalmente al mare! Barca, nave . . . Ohhhh . . . cammello, cammello, cammello di nuovo . . . Era un po' lunga!!

C'erano quelli che partivano che erano bambini, tornavano dei vecchietti.

La cosa tremenda è che si riconoscevano subito quelli che venivano dalle Indie . . . per come camminavano . . . guardate come camminavano . . . (*Esegue una camminata tutti sussulti e sbirolamenti*) Avete in mente il cammello? . . .

Bene, guarda che testa 'sto Colombo Cristoforo! È andato per mare in trentacinque giorni prendendo "l'inverso" mondo per il di dietro! . . .

E bisogna dire, che per il di dietro l'ha preso anche lui, perché, con tutta 'sta grande scoperta, nessuno lo cagava.

Lui diceva: "Ci sono andato attraverso le Canarie in trentacinque giorni!" "Sì, sta buono, sta buono . . ."

Non interessava a nessuno perché non aveva portato niente! Ori, non ne aveva portati, pietre luccicanti non ne aveva portate, coralli non ne aveva portati . . . aveva portato quattro perle marce, dieci selvaggi, tutti immusoniti con le piume tutte spampanate . . . dei pappagalli spaventati, terrorizzati . . . con le piume tutte ritte . . . con gli occhi tondi che facevano: "Aiuto!" . . .

Invece le scimmie belle . . . col culo pelato . . . rosso infiammato . . . che si masturbavano dalla mattina alla sera.

"Ma Colombo Cristoforo che razza di schifezze hai portato?" "Io ho preso quello che ho trovato."

Io lo conoscevo e lui mi diceva: "Johan Padan dammi fiducia . . . io so di sicuro, che in questo mondo nuovo c'è oro a secchiate . . . Se tu vieni con me, ti copro d'oro, ti faccio ricco!"

Hai capito? Lui mi tampinava perché montassi sulla sua barca. Bella forza, io sono un fenomeno! L'Astrolabio io lo so leggere . . . sono scrivano, scrivo in bella grafia, sono un geroglifico meraviglioso. Sono calafatore. Cucio le vele . . . posso andare ai cannoni. Conosco i venti. Conosco le lingue, non c'è idioma al mondo che io non parli. Io converso in tutte le lingue, i dialetti, le lingue morte, quelle vive, quelle che stanno così e così . . .

E poi sono uno che quando ascolta uno straniero che parla tutto intricato, che non si capisce . . . l'ascolto per una settimana . . . tach, alla fine parlo come lui!

Non capisco quello che dice, ma parlo!

Ancora mi domanda se ho in mente di andar via con lui per il terzo viaggio . . . e io gli dico: "Caro scopritore, se trovate una strada per andare a piedi in 'ste Indie . . . vi vengo dietro anche in groppa a un maiale!"

Mai parlare a vanvera, che vanvera a vanvera, dopo ti succede veramente di ritrovarti a cavalcare un maiale. Vedrete più avanti nella storia.

Tanto per incominciare capita che scoppia una tremenda persecuzione contro i giudei. Una grande trappola inventata dalla Santissima Regina cattolica e dal suo caro marito per scacciarli e portargli via tutti i loro beni, denari e le case.

C'erano a Siviglia degli italiani di Firenze e Genova, dei gran furbacchioni, banchieri che, approfittando dell'occasione, facevano dei grandi affari. Loro ritiravano di nascosto le case ai giudei prima che fossero confiscate . . . e in cambio gli davano un'altra casa a Livorno o a Napoli dei medesimo valore . . . sulla parola . . . scritta su una lettera di credito.

Io conoscevo bene tutto l'intrappolamento, per la semplice ragione che da tempo mi ero messo al servizio di uno di 'sti banchieri. A fare cosa? A stendere le scritture. Sì, ve l'ho detto, io ero uno scrivano geroglifico provetto. Io scrivevo a mano 'ste "lettere di credito" . . . d'una scrittura . . . ah!, loro poi, 'sti ebrei, arrivavano in Toscana e Lombardia e si ritrovavano quello che avevano lasciato alla banca. Era un marchingegno ingegnoso!!

Soltanto che è successo che alla Regina è venuto il gran dubbio che ci fosse un trucco da intrallazzo . . . le sono girate le corone a vortice, ha preso dieci ebrei, gli ha dato una bruciacchiata, quelli hanno parlato, poi hanno preso i genovesi e i banchieri fiorentini, gli hanno dato un'altra bruciacchiata.

E poi al giudice dell'Inquisizione gli sono capitate in mano le lettere di credito . . . quelle che avevo scritto io . . . Guarda un po' la rogna! Le legge e dice: "Belle! . . . Mi piacerebbe conoscere quello che le ha scritte!" E io che faccio? Aspetto che mi branchino (prendano)? Via!

Sempre col mio solito fuoco dietro al culo, come un fulmine mi presento al porto e monto, saltando come uno stambecco su una delle navi della flotta del genovese Colombo, che sta salpando per il quarto viaggio. Era già staccata dal molo: "Fermaaa!" Ho camminato sulle acque!

Quando siamo stati al largo mi sono presentato: "Io sono capace di fare tutti i mestieri, io sono artificiere, posso cucire, sono capace di leggere l'Astrolabio, posso stare ai cannoni . . .". "No! Non abbiamo bisogno di questi lavori, sono tutti coperti! L'unico lavoro vacante è quello di guardiano dei maiali, vacche, asini e cavalli in fondo alla stiva!"

Di 'ste bestie c'era stipato il sottobordo per via che in 'st'altro mondo, di queste razze nostrane, non c'è ne sono: cavalli, muli, asini, vacche e porci non si sono giammai visti. E allora tutte le navi che discendevano avevano le stive piene di 'ste bestie per fare il ripopolamento! E così a me è toccato viaggiare sottocoperta in mezzo a 'sti animali, che cagavano da mattina a sera! Non erano abituati ai cavalloni delle onde . . . come c'era un cavallone (*allude al defecare delle bestie*): PARAPUM uno, PARAPUN due . . . PAA!

Ah, ho capito perché i francesi, per dirti buona fortuna, ti gridano: "Tanta merda!".

Io ero proprio dentro alla fortuna fino al collo! Che una notte c'è stata una tempesta tremenda, c'erano le onde che caracollavano addosso alla nave . . . la alzavano e la sbattevano di qua e di là . . . 'ste bestie di sotto che "sballanzavano" . . . C'erano i cavalli che tiravano zoccolate alle vacche, le vacche che incornavano gli asini, gli asini che azzannavano i porcelli . . . i porcelli in mezzo: "Bastaaa!!" gridavano. Alla fine erano tutti sfregiati e sanguinanti.

Mi hanno chiamato: "Cucitore! L'ago . . . cuci!" Ho cucito le vacche, i porcelli . . . tutte le ferite . . . Le ho salvate tutte 'ste bestie . . . che poi mi volevano un bene!

Alla fine siamo arrivati all'isola di Santo Domingo!

Che splendore!

Non avevo mai visto un'acqua così chiara! Si scorgeva il fondo, i coralli, i pesci colorati . . . c'erano 'ste piante che si arrampicavano in cielo, le scimmie che volavano, gli uccelli che cantavano.

Appena buttata l'ancora, ci sono venuti incontro i selvaggi indiani su 'ste loro barchette che chiamano canoe.

Venivano cantando, ridendo . . . erano tutti colorati, nudi . . . con una piuma e basta! E il bindorlone che andava!

Remavano con remi corti, pagaie, che fanno andare rapide di qua e li là.

Bella gente . . . ben formata . . . puliti . . . che loro, in ogni occasione si buttano in acqua a lavarsi con gran piacere, e nuotano come i pesci, anche nel mare profondo! Prendevano le perle e i coralli e poi se le mettevano in bocca . . . così: "Vuoi una perla? Prendi! (*Mima l'atto di sputare*)" "Grazie!"

Proprio bella gente!

Soprattutto le ragazze . . . nude come sono nate . . . senza pudore . . . non hanno alcuna vergogna: zinne al vento . . . ventre al vento . . . chiappe al vento . . . tutto al vento! Dio che ventata!

Erano così gentili questi selvaggi! Una esagerazione!

Soprattutto le femmine.

Non c'era bisogno di fare tutte le manfrine di 'sto mondo . . . no! Bastava che tu facessi un po' di pantomima per farti capire che ti piaceva una, che subito quella ti abbracciava! 'Ste figliole avevano un rituale magnifico: venivano . . . sorridevano, abbassavano gli occhi, ti prendevano per una mano, ti portavano nella foresta! Ti saltavano al collo: tu sdraiato, lei stesa su di te e scoppiava un amore incantato di lamenti e risate! Ma non per terra! Sulle foglie . . . delle foglie grandi che si chiamavano foglied'amore . . . da

una piazza . . . una piazza e mezza . . . due piazze . . .

E quando si incominciava l'amore, c'era il canto e il controcanto degli uccelli, le farfalle che cantavano . . . c'erano le scimmie che volavano d'albero in albero . . . "UHUUUHHH . . . AHAAAA . . . Forzaaa!!—gridavano—Forzaaa! Per il mangiare poi, si cavavano di bocca loro i bocconi, per favorirti!

E noialtri, cristiani cattolici . . . brava gente . . . prima a far tutti i cerimoniosi . . . a offrirgli campanellini, vetri da ciarpame . . . e poi si è incominciato a far razzia di tutto quello che avevano: a strappargli via donne, figli e caricarli sulla nave, per traghettarli schiavi, nel nostro santo mondo dei cristiani.

Tanto che arriva il momento che a quelli gli girano i "fronzoli". Arrivano in mille e mille straripando da ogni parte, armati di archi e frecce incazzati neri e gridano: "Dateci indietro subito la nostra gente o vi saltiamo addosso!"

E i nostri capitani, tutti stupefatti: "Ma perché fate tanto gli arrabbiati?! Noi non si pensava di portarveli via come schiavi 'sti vostri parenti . . . si voleva solamente fargli fare un giretto . . . fargli conoscere un po' di bella gente . . . belle città . . . insegnargli la dottrina del Dio unico e trino che sta nel cielo! E poi presentarli al Re e alla Regina nostra cattolica, che è buona e dolce come il pane!"

E quelli gli rispondono: "No grazie, basta con i giretti . . . perché di quelli che avete portato via al primo e al secondo viaggio . . . nessuno è più ritornato. Avanti, dateci indietro questi qui . . . e subito!, se no cominciamo a lanciare frecce e lance!".

Non avevano detto "frecce e lance" che dal bordo delle navi sono spuntate un mucchio di cannoni e hanno incominciato a sparare bordate: TA-TA-A-BOOM!

e -si vedevano 'sti guerrieri che saltavano per aria maciullati . . . e uscivano i cavalli con i cavalieri seminando gran terrore . . . che loro i cavalli non li conoscevano, non li avevano mai veduti e credevano che cavallo e cavaliere fossero una bestia sola . . . una stramberia orrenda della natura:

"Il mostro!—gridavano—Il mostro!" e si facevano bianchi di terrore e scappavano.

E quelli, i cavalieri gridavano, ridevano, infizavano, bucavano, li tagliavano in due . . .

teste che volavano. Una mattanza proprio da imbecilli!

Sia chiaro che io non sono una femminuccia. Non sono infante di cuore, ché io a diciotto anni ero nelle fanterie dei Lanzichenecchi . . . e ne ho fatti di scannamenti in battaglia . . . e anche dopo . . . ma scannavo gente che voleva scannare me! Ma questa era un massacro senza cognizione. Accoppare, tanto per accoppare.

'Sti cristiani che abbrancavano i bambini e li sbattevano contro gli alberi: spiaccicati! Tagliavano in due le femmine, squartate. Da vomitare.

Il cappellano m'ha detto: "Johan Padan, basta con 'sto mugugno . . . Cosa fanno alla fine? Ammazzano dei cristiani? No, ammazzano gente che non ha spirito, non ha cuore, non ha religione . . . non hanno né anima né Dio . . . Quando accoppi uno di quelli è come scannare un cane! Non far tragedie!".

Non farò tragedie, ma non mi piace!

Avevo lo stomaco chiuso, tanto che volevo tornare a casa! Guardavo di continuo se scorgevo qualche nave che tornasse indietro . . . Ma non partivano . . . Discendevano solo! C'erano navi che arrivavano ogni settimana, quattro o cinque, scaricavano gli animali che stavano nella stiva, poi si rifornivano di acqua e di verdure e facevano rotta verso ponente: "Dove andate?" "Alla ricerca dell'Eldorado." rispondevano e bestemmiando, issavano tutte le vele e via che andavano.

A me non piaceva per niente stare con questi miei compari buoni solo di ubriacarsi, giocare a carte e a' dadi, scannarsi l'un l'altro in baruffa e poi, per contorno vederli arrazzati, sbattersi addosso alle donne. Ma era vita? L'unica cosa che mi piaceva davvero era cercare di intendermi con la gente . . . che l'avrete capito: io ho una fissa per l'idioma, il linguaggio . . . sapere come parla la gente . . . quello che pensa, che dice . . . infilare parole strambe e scoprire tutto un discorso. Ma era difficile andargli vicino . . . si spaventavano, avevano sempre il terrore che dopo, di colpo, saltasse fuori un mostro-cavallo.

Io, per convincerli a mettersi tranquilli, facevo il pagliaccio. Quando li incontravo fingevo di spaventarmi io, prima di loro: "Oh! Un selvaggio! . . . un mostro!" E loro ridevano . . .

Qualche volta.

Così io gli domandavo: "Indios, come si dice sole?". E loro: "Aleghé". "E il nome del mare?" "Criaba" "E come si dice uomo?" "Opplaca" "E come se dice dona?" "Feila" "E come si dice bambino?" "Icme!" "E come si dice donna che fa all'amore?" "Ci sono tante maniere per dirlo, perché ci sono tante maniere per farlo . . . e allora ci sono tanti modi di dire l'amore."

Io gli domandavo tutto, gli rubavo le parole . . . e me le segnavo . . . e sono arrivato un giorno . . . c'erano cinque o sei selvaggi che facevano baruffa . . . mi sono avvicinato, ho fatto: "Able esset ateré priall ti io mastico . . . (*improvvisa uno sproloquio in gramelotte : con gesti fa immaginare di interrompere la discussione tra due gruppi diversi, ascolta, polemizza, ride e accenna una danza a sfotto*) . . . mi guardano stupiti: "Un Indios bianco!" Parlavo Indios!

Mi è quasi dispiaciuto quando hanno dato l'ordine: "Si torna a casa!".

Ma era tanta la felicità che avevo di ritornare da fuori, che ho caricato il doppio di tutti gli altri: caricavo l'acqua, caricavo le verdure . . . ho caricato anche cinque porcelli grassi, grossi che dovevamo scaricare a Santo Domingo. Intanto altri spingevano sulla nave un mucchio di Indios, prigionieri schiavi . . . centoventicinque incarcerati nella stiva, sul fondo, al posto della zavorra . . . e per non farli gridare ci avevano infilato della stoppia in bocca sino al gargarozzo.

Si parte. Gran caldo, mangiare poco . . . poco da bere. Questi poveracci di Indios incominciano a crepare. I cadaveri li prendevano e li buttavano a mare.

Qualche giorno appresso, dietro alla poppa, lungo la scia, scorgiamo un branco di pesci grandi che ci seguono: aspettano il pasto degli indiani.

Gli piacevano gli indios!

Allora i marinai hanno detto: "Perché non peschiamo con 'sti selvaggi?". Hanno preso degli Indios morti, freschi di giornata, ci hanno infilato degli ami, li buttavano in mare e pescavano.

Solamente c'è stato Dio padreternò che ogni tanto gli gira il triangolo, che ci ha mandato una tempesta con tal vento, che si vedeva il mare a rotoloni che scodellava le onde. Ci siamo ritrovati con tutte le vele stracciate e andavamo ballando come tanti ubriachi.

Si sente un "crasch" tremendo, abbiamo sbattuto contro uno scoglio! "Picco! Andiamo a picco! Giù le barche!" Ce n'erano tre.

Chiedo al capitano: "Dove mi sistemo io?"

C'erano tre barche: "No, per voialtri ~ cinque, guardiani di animali, non c'è posto . . . andate a picco con gli Indios e con i maiali!"

Non so da dove mi sia venuto, forse per rabbia . . . forse per pietà: ho spalancato il boccaporto, saltano fuori tutti gli indiani, che mi vengono addosso . . . mi schiacciano sotto i piedi e si buttano a mare!

Per fortuna che ci sono gli alti~i quattro miei compagni guardiani, che mi tirano in piedi.

"Svelti! Veloce, che la nave va sotto!"

Giù nella stiva ci sono ancora i maiali che "sgriffiano" disperati.

"Salviamo i maiali!" "Perché?" "Non si va in mare senza i maiali!" Che 'sti animali hanno un senso unico, che non c'è uguale, di orizzontarsi in mare anche con la tempesta. Tu li butti in acqua, e loro: TAK!, puntano subito il muso sicuro verso la costa più prossima . . . quando fanno quattro volte: "UHO,UHO,UHO!" la, c'è la costa e non si sbagliano mai!

È anche per questo che i genovesi dicono: "Bisogna portare sempre, su ogni nave, un porcello verace . . . oltre al capitano . . . che è un porco normale!"

Io e i miei compagni andiamo di sotto e prendiamo cinque maiali, uno per uno ci imbraghiamo ai maiali con le corde legate intorno alla vita . . . e poi, tutti insieme ognuno abbracciato al suo proprio porco: "Andiamo a mare . . . OHOHHE—IH . . . BOOM!"

Non è che mi fosse scoppiata una improvvisa passione cristiana per i maiali.

E' che io sapevo da un racconto che fa Omero, il poeta . . . quando parla dei naufraghi greci che si sono salvati abbracciati ai porcelli, perché il porcello, così grasso, tondo, non va a picco! Va sotto un po' . . . poi: BLO, BLO, BLO . . . PLUF!, (mima il maiale che torna a galla) torna a galleggiare! E una boa di grasso! Ha quel codino tutto ricciolo, fatto apposta, ché tu lo branchi (lo afferri) e non ti scivola mai . . . ti

attacchi a 'sto codino, lui va . . . (mima la nuotata veloce del maiale) sscitss . . . tritri tn . . . è una boa con le zampette!

Eravamo così abbracciati a questi porcelli che quando arrivavano le onde: "E no, sotto non andiamo!" (Mima, appena risalito, di baciare il maiale) SMACK . . . un baciozzo! Un'altra onda e . . . "OHOOOO . . ." SMACK!, un altro baciozzo . . . E', che è cominciato a piacere anche al porcello . . . andava a picco anche senza onde!

Dunque, noialtri cinque, abbracciati ognuno al proprio animale da salvataggio, sbacciucchiandolo . . . siamo arrivati, attraverso onde scaracollanti che ci sbrandellavano brache e camicia, alla costa, nudi! Che se ci scopriva il Tribunale dell'Inquisizione, ci bruciava vivi!

Siamo arrivati alla costa! I porcelli ci avevano portato a salvamento . . . e adesso eravamo lì, sulla rena della marina, nudi, abbracciati ai nostri maiali . . . nudi anche loro.

Boia!, che freddo c'è venuto addosso! . . .

Guardo la mia pelle . . . era bluette, i miei compagni tutti bluette . . . i porcelli, ciclamino.

L'unico che stava bene era il catalano, che era così grasso che lo chiamavamo Trentatrippe.

'Sto panzone mica aveva bisogno del maiale . . . infatti era stato lui, che aveva salvato il suo maiale! Poi ce n'era un altro che era rosso di capelli e lo chiamavamo Rosso, poi c'era un negro, che era mussulmano di Tripoli, lo chiamavamo Negro, c'era uno magro che lo chiamavamo Magro . . . perché noialtri gente di mare abbiamo una fantasia per i soprannomi!

Io ho detto: "E' inutile che ci siamo salvati, che tanto, tra poco, co' 'sto freddo moriamo congelati!".

Guarda quando si dice il miracolo.

Guardo la costa, la collina . . . c'è della gente! Ci sono dei selvaggi che discendono correndo.

Ma cento, duecento, tutti armati di archi e frecce. "Boia—dico—se quelli hanno conosciuto i cristiani, siamo fottuti, ci fanno a pezzi!"

Mi faccio coraggio . . . e mi butto a gridare parole nella loro lingua che ho imparato: "Aghiudu, en lì salà . . . chiomé saridde aabasjia Jaspania . . .—Capivano tutto!—Mujacia cocecajo mobaputio cristian!" "Eheee?" L'unica parola che non avevano capito era "Cristiani", eravamo salvi! (Inizia un dialogo in grammelotte, *quindi traduce per i compagni quello che ha appena detto*) "Dateci qualcosa da coprirci che qui c'è un freddo che ci trasformiamo tutti in ghiaccio, morti stecchiti!""Ma cosa vi diamo da coprirvi che siamo più nudi di voialtri?"

Ma guarda l'intelligenza di questi selvaggi: hanno preso delle stoppie e le hanno bruciate, hanno fatto un falò e poi si sono messi tutti in cerchio intorno a noi e ci coprivano per proteggerci dal vento.

poi, siccome il villaggio era lontano, hanno fatto tanti falò . . . ogni cento passi c'era un falò . . . poi ci prendevano in braccio, che loro erano duecento e ci portavano dove c'era un altro falò . . . Una bruciatina e via di corsa, bruciatina e via . . . bruciatina . . . e anche con i porci . . . bruciatina, bruciatina . . . ahi ahi!

Ché loro non conoscevano i maiali e credevano che fossero cristiani di un'altra razza . . . un po' più ingrassati.

Arriviamo al villaggio con le capanne ben costruite e ci sistemano dentro una grande capanna col braciere nel mezzo. C'era roba da mangiare e da bere.

"A me—dice il Rosso—'sto trattamento troppo affettuoso, tanto per noi che per i maiali, mi puzza niente di buono. Non vorrei scoprire che questi sono selvaggi cannibali e che ci trattano bene soltanto per poi mangiarci."

"Non dire stronzate!—sbotta il Trentatrippe—È il terzo viaggio che faccio in 'ste Indie e non ho mai incontrato indiani che avessero dentro le loro capanne pezzi di gambe o di braccia appesi a seccare o sotto sale, come ti vanno a raccontare quei cacciaballe dell'Amerigo Vespucci e di Alfonso Gamberan . . . ché, 'ste storie, loro le raccontano per avere poi il buon pretesto di trattarli come animali: sono cannibali, possiamo farli schiavi"

Oltre ogni discorso, devo dire che questi selvatici erano certamente gli indiani più dolci e gentili che avessi mai incontrato.

Per farci dormire . . . non ci facevano sdraiare su un pagliericcio, magari con le pulci, no! Sospesi per aria, nelle amache . . . che voi non conoscete le amache! E' una rete sospesa tra due travi di legno, con delle corde che la tengono allungata da qui a là. Poi c'è uno scaldino sotto per darti il calore quando ti stendi. Però, difficile montarci sopra! Chi non

ha esperienza si siede di culo, e: (*mima che l'amaca si rovesci e di cadere a terra*) PATAPUM! Una culata! No! Bisogna andarci di ginocchio! (*Mima di montare sull'amaca, con una gamba ripiegata*) . . . Poi si allarga questa (*mima di allargare l'amaca*), poi si allarga quest'altra (*mima di stendere l'altra gamba*), poi . . . PATAPUNFETE! . . . (*Mima di cadere a terra*) Perché non è neanche questione di ginocchio, è questione di bilancia, di equilibrio, è questione della dinamica, che tu quando monti, devi sistemare il ginocchio così, ma poi dare una spinta più che bene! (*Mima di far oscillare l'amaca come fosse un'altalena*) Poi giri questo e quell'altro, poi fai JOM, ti allarghi, aspetti, uno, due, tre . . . Uno che ti tira, uno che va giù, ginocchio di secondo, volta di qui, gira di là!! (*Mima un'oscillazione lunga e regolare*) E' la forza della dinamica!

Io ero così bravo che in quattro tempi ero bello che disteso . . . il mio scaldino di sotto che mandava calore e dormivo come un bambino. Una notte mi sento una dolcezza tenera qui attaccata àlla faccia, poi due tondi meravigliosi . . . vado giù con le mani, sento altri due tondi . . . Era una ragazza . . . una, ragazza nuda che era venuta dentro l'amaca per abbracciarmi, per farmi tenerezze! E tutti gli altri miei compagni, anche loro in ogni amaca con una ragazza che li abbracciava. Pensa la tenerezza che avevano! Ma era già difficile starci in uno solo nell'amaca, figurarsi in due!! Ho fatto per andarle a cingere la vita e con le gambe cerco di abbracciarla a cavalcioni . . . OHHI'IFI AH . . . FAA! . . . Mi si ribalta tutto!

Sono andato col culo nel braciere. AHHH! (*Mima uno scatto a risalire come una molla*) PAAA! Ero già ridisteso sull'amaca! . . . La forza della dinamica!

Ma io volevo fare l'amore con questa ragazza. Meno male che lei m'ha insegnato:

"Stai attento . . . prima cosa: il trucco è che devi fare la forcella col ditone del piede e l'altro dito . . . poi allarghi le gambe in modo che l'amaca stia bella distesa . . . allargata . . . poi mi passi il braccio sotto alla vita TACCHETA . . . mi scivoli sopra scambiando la posizione delle gambe *e* delle forcelle e . . . PAA!!

Sono andato giù con la testa verticale contro il terreno . . . Non sono arrivato a terra! . . . I coglioni mi sono restati imbragati nella rete: "Ahhh!". E lei, la ragazza, distesa sull'amaca, che dondolava e rideva contenta! Ma io sono un caparbio tremendo! . . . Intanto che i miei compagni stavano stravaccati sotto le piante all'ora della siesta, io di nascosto, quatto quatto, entravo nella capannona con l'amaca, e facevo degli esercizi di equilibrio . . . andavo con un piede, andavo con una mano, andavo capovolto con la testa a rovescio . . . Sono diventato un ballerino da amaca che non ce ne sono al mondo ! . . . Facevo l'amore, mi attaccavo con tutto, con le unghie, con le dita dei piedi, con le orecchie, i denti . . . le chiappe . . . E quando mi prendeva lo sghiribizzo di follia, uno, due (*mima una giravolta completa dell'amaca*) IHHEHHOHHAHH, il giro della morte!

Era una meraviglia stare in quel luogo; soltanto c'era una cosa che mi dava veramente un dispiacere tremendo . . . Era come trattavano le bestie. Loro hanno degli animali, che voi non conoscete . . . il tacchino, che lo chiamano dindon, che è un gallinaccio schifoso . . . e invece crede d'essere un pavone! Ha un collo che sembra uno struzzo con le lebbra, due occhi da cataratta! . . . L'unica cosa che ha veramente bella sono le piume, delle belle piume bluette, nere . . . che lui, quando si dà un po' d'importanza BRUUUM . . . allarga 'sto ventaglio (*spalanca le braccia e mima i 'incedere regale del tacchino*), cammina tutto baldanzoso che pare dica: "Guarda che belle piume che mi sono uscite dal culo!"

Bene, in quel momento ci sono questi selvaggi che gli saltano addosso, gli strappano tutte le penne . . . da vivo! (*Mima l'indios che strappa le piume all'animale*) GNIAK-GNIAK!

"Ahiaahaahaa!" . . . degli strepiti! GNIAK-GNIAK . . . e questo tacchino che salta di qua e di là e loro: GNIAK-GNIAK- GNIAK! . . . Ma che crudeli!

"Non siamo crudeli—mi rispondevano—è perché noialtri prepariamo il pasto . . . che se tu prendi il tacchino, lo ammazzi e poi gli strappi le piume, le piume vengono via con la pelle e con la pelle anche pezzi di carne! E tutta la polpa che c'è sotto è legnosa, stoppposa, non sa di niente! Invece, se abbranchi il tacchino da vivo: SGNIAK-SGNIAK-SGNIAK, gli strappi le piume, si fa tutto un movimento, il sangue

circola, ci sono tutti i nervi che saltano, è come fargli un massaggio . . . la carne diventa morbida che quando la mangi è una dolcezza, è un burro!

E facevano lo stesso lavoro anche con i maiali selvatici che hanno loro, che sono pieni di setole. Gli strappavano i peli a ciuffi: PIO PIO PIO' TRALLA . . . ! Ma non lo facevano per cattiveria crudele, loro hanno questa religione che dice: "Il mangiare è la vita!" Far da mangiare per quei selvaggi era come una religione.

Noi siamo grossolani, siamo rustici, noialtri un pezzo di carne . . . una sbruciacchiata *al* fuoco e via! La granseola . . . una bollita e via! Loro nel cucinare mettono tutto il sentimento di un rituale. Per esempio quando cucinano l'iguana . . .

Cos'è l'iguana? È un animale, un lucertolone tremendo, che voialtri non conoscete. È schifoso . . . è un drago nano ! . . . Ha tutte le creste proprio come un drago nano, ha una bocca che se ti prende! . . . gli spuntano dei denti che ti squartano . . . degli occhi in fuori e in fondo alla coda ha un pungiglione che se ti becca: GNIAC . . . sei ingessato! Si muove su delle gambe con ai piedi delle unghie tremende! Non lo puoi afferrare in nessun luogo . . . l'unica è prenderlo sulla cresta della schiena, un gran crestone, l'ultimo dei crestoni, un grande osso . . . TAC, lo prendi (*mima di sollevare la gran cresta, l'iguana che si divincola sbattendo gambe, coda e testa*), lui: GNA' GNA'! Fermo! (*Stende il braccio per evitare le graffiate dell'animale*) Stai fermo là! Poi prendi un pentolone, una gran pentola di acqua che bolle, ci sbatti dentro il sale . . . e lui, il lucertolone lo sbatti dentro tutto bello vispo com'è, il coperchio sopra . . . che a lui piace! BIDUBUDON! Dentro fa un casino: PATAPAPAA! Gli parte la bocca: TAPATAPAA! Gli partono gli occhi: TROPETITOTOO, tutta la cresta: TOM PIM TOM, le ossa: TOM TOM, le gambe: PEM PEM . . . la coda: PAA (*fa il gesto di cavarlo dalla pentola e di mostrarlo al pubblico, esprimendo meraviglia*) Un pollo!

Mangi 'sto iguana . . . Io le prime volte che lo mangiavo, giuro, VLAAM, vomitavo subito! Perché non ero abituato a quel gusto, che li ha importanza farci il gusto . . . infatti, quando ci ho fatto il gusto . . . ma anche dopo una settimana . . . VOMITAVO lo stesso!

Questa gente era gente allegra, felice, ogni occasione era buona per far festa. Una volta sono arrivati dei selvaggi che venivano da un'altra costa . . . Erano dei i giganti meravigliosi! Stretti di vita . . . chiappe stagne da san Sebastiano, gambe lunghe da saltimbanco, mani lunghe, occhi luccicanti . . . Le donne che avevano con loro: femmine mai viste! Avevano un collo alto, 'sta faccina tonda, con degli occhi! I capelli che arrivavano fino alle ginocchia, le zinne che si arrampicavano . . . Mostravano delle chiappe a balcone . . . che se prendevi un vasetto di acqua pieno sino all'orlo e lo appoggiavi sulle chiappe . . . loro camminavan . . . ma neanche una lacrima si spandeva.

Delle regine!

E tutti insieme facevano un bordello! Ballavano, cantavano, ridevano, mangiavano, si ubriacavano di birra, che loro ne hanno di tanti gusti . . . una felicità!

Soltanto che alla fine della festa, senza né uno né due, ci saltano addosso a noi cinque cristiani, ci legano su tutti e cinque come porcelli e ci sbattono dentro le loro barche: schiavi!

I nostri gentili salvatori ci avevano venduti per una miseria!

Io ero stato dato come soprapprezzo. Una regalia!

Tutti ridevano da sganasciarsi.

Le uniche che non ridevano erano le ragazze che stavano abbracciate con noi nell'amaca, quelle avevano lacrimoni lunghi che scendevano dagli occhi . . . piangevano senza singulti né lamenti.

I nostri padroni hanno incominciato a remare cantando, ballando: facevano festa 'sti selvaggi! E noialtri sbattuti sul fondo delle barche.

Dopo due giorni e una notte siamo arrivati alla loro costa. C'è apparsa una meraviglia . . . una costa giammai vista! C'era l'acqua chiara, limpida, profonda, si vedevano tutti i pesci come nuotassero nell'aria, era così pulita che il pelo dell'acqua non si vedeva, non si capiva dove cominciasse il cielo e dove il mare . . . C'erano dei pesci con delle alette che saltavano fuori dal mare, volavano in cielo . . . e nel cielo c'erano degli uccelli che si fondavano in fondo al mare e nuotavano sott'acqua.

Una confusione!

E c'erano questi alberi meravigliosi pieni di fiori . . . ma quanti fiori! Tutto fiorita era 'sta terra . . . Era appunto la Florida!

Era il paradiso per 'sti selvaggi . . . per noialtri, l'inferno. Ci toccava lavorare da mattina a sera dentro l'acqua a raccogliere granseole, spaccarle, grattare manioche, il mango, bruciare, tagliare . . . e alla sera eravamo stravolti, stanchi da morire, ci si buttava nell'amaca: soli! Non c'era nessuno che ci abbracciasse . . . non una ragazza.

I miei compagni avevano una malinconia che non si può dire e io gli dicevo: "Non fatevi vedere intristiti. Non fate i musoni, che a questi non gli piace. A questi nostri padroni danno fastidio gli schiavi tristi. Schiavi . . . ma allegri! Tanto che io, quando incontravo 'sti padroni, facevo il buffone: "Eh . . . a me piace far lo schiavo! Bella vita! Guai a chi mi libera . . . lo ammazzo! !" gridavo.

Poi il giorno del cambio della luna . . . che diventa intera, che io faccio sempre attenzione alla luna da quando me lo aveva insegnato la mia strega . . . la guardo e scopro che è tonda e tutta chiara . . . senza alone! Di colpo mi sono detto: "Questo è un segnale! Qui, cambia tutta la mia vita!". La stessa notte io ero sdraiato nell'amaca, sono venute due ragazze, mi hanno preso, mi hanno portato in un'altra capanna da principe . . . c'erano delle stuoie, delle pelli. Mi hanno buttato su una amaca grande adorna di filapperi di cotone, netta e profumata, e poi, tutte e due 'ste ragazze, si sono distese abbracciate a me e hanno cominciato a sbaciucchiarmi, a farmi carezze . . . delle cose che non posso raccontare . . .

La mattina mi hanno messo sotto un getto d'acqua di una cascata a schizzo, m'hanno lavato, m'hanno tutto cosparso d'un olio profumato, un olio meraviglioso! Io avevo dei capelli lunghissimi, hanno cominciato a farmi delle treccine con dentro dei coralli; avevo lunga anche la barba . . . hanno cominciato a farmi treccina anche a quella! In aggiunta m'hanno messo dei fiori attorno al collo e anche sulle spalle e due fioroni sulle orecchie! . . . (Pausa) Una bagascia!

Per finire mi hanno fatto montare su un ciocco d'albero . . . e tutti intorno hanno cominciato a dipingermi. Mi facevano dei segni con un pennello a tondo sulla schiena, di colore giallo . . . poi arrivava un'altra donna e mi disegnava una rigona tutt'intorno alle chiappe, di un verdolino . . . poi un altro mi disegnava un cerchio color arancio sulla pancia . . .

E il pisello azzurro!

Aha, aha . . . il bell'uccellin del cielo!

I miei compagni mi guardavano allocchiti e frastornati: "Ma che gioco è questo? Cosa ti fanno?"

Anch'io non riuscivo a trarre una ragione da tutto 'sto strambo rituale. Sarà perché gli sono simpatico—mi dicevo.

Ma ohi, di colpo hanno messo in pedi un trattamento che mi ha fatto venire i brividi di terrore: donne, bambini e anche gli uomini hanno incominciato a strapparmi i peli un po' dappertutto . . . dallo stomaco . . . dalle gambe . . . peli della barba mi strappavano, dalle ascelle . . . anche più sotto . . . sotto all'ombelico . . . che è un dolore!

"Basta disgraziati! Mi avete preso per un tacchino?"

"Sì!"

"Mi volete mangiare?!" "Sì!"

Sono svenuto!

Appena mi sono svegliato, ho capito cos'era tutta 'sta manfrina di farmi cerchi colorati sulle chiappe, il petto e sulle gambe . . . era la prenotazione dei quarti di carne che preferivano!!

Mi sono sentito andar via l'anima e sono crollato a terra come uno straccio per il dolor-spavento. Ma anche loro si sono spaventati . . . gli è preso il terrore per la paura che gli crepassi lì. Che loro . . . la carne morta da sola, non la mangiano. Ti devono ammazzare loro . . . fresco di giornata! Se no, vomitano!

Con un fil di voce ho domandato allo Sciamano capo degli stregoni . . . era simpatico . . . aveva grandi corna: "Ditemi perché fra tutti noialtri cristiani schiavi, avete scelto di mangiare proprio me? Io, che sono tutto pelle e ossa. Potevate ben prendervi uno dei miei compagni che ce ne sono di più belli grassi e stagni. C'è quel Trentatrippe . . . mangiavate tutta una settimana!".

"Perché tu sei simpatico . . . Carne di uno che ride è carne buona, si digerisce bene, ti fa fare dei bei sogni! Invece la carne di musoni come

quelli, ti si strozza nel gargarozzo, ti fermenta nello stomaco, ti fa fare rutti tremendi, e poi, alla fine, ti puzza sempre il fiato!"

Intanto il sole scendeva e io ho capito che domani mi avrebbero sgozzato e appeso per i piedi infilzato ai ganci per farmi colare il sangue . . . come ad un maiale.

No, ma io non sto qui a farmi scannare! Durante la notte, con le unghie e con i denti ho spezzato la corda e mi sono liberato.

Mi era venuta l'idea disperata di scappare per la foresta, scavalcando la staccionata. Io sapevo bene che si trattava di un'idea scervellata, (fuori di cervello) che non c'era speranza di restare vivo nemmeno per due giorni nella foresta, con tutte 'ste bestie e serpenti che si incontravano. C'era soprattutto il giaguaro. Il giaguaro è una bestia tutta maculata . . . un leone senza capelli! Ti salta addosso . . . ha delle unghie che ti strappano la pelle dalla testa ai piedi.

Non importa, meglio finire mangiato da un giaguaro, da un puma o da un coccodrillo piuttosto che finire arrosto.

A proteggere il villaggio c'era tutta una cinta di paloni di legno intorno, che lo chiudeva.

Arrivo quatto quatto sotto la gran cinta. Non c'è nessuno di guardia. Mi arrampico in cima ai paloni . . . Boia! Ti vedo delle ombre di gente armata che stanno scavalcando la palizzata.

Sono selvaggi nemici, che arrivano di nascosto, di soppiatto per prenderli nel sonno!

Non so cosa mi sia preso . . . così, d'istinto, mi sono buttato a gridare: "Allarme, allarme! Svegliatevi gente, che ci sono dei nemici che vengono a scannarvi!"

Ma che coglione! Cosa me ne fregava a me di salvare la pelle a 'sti selvaggi cannibali, che oltretutto mi vogliono mangiare?

Ohi, non potevo farci niente!

"Allarme! Allarme!"

Non contento, afferro un gran palone e giù a menar stangate da orbi a 'sti selvaggi.

I miei Indios addormentati si svegliano.

Incomincia uno scontro tremendo: saette e lance che volano dappertutto! Combattono anche le donne a tirare sassi e a menar bastonate.

Di quei selvaggi nemici che sono riusciti a saltare dentro la staccionata, solamente dieci sono restati vivi e li hanno fatti prigionieri.

Dei nostri, uno è stato ucciso e molti sono rimasti feriti, proprio conciati.

Uno di questi é lo stregone Sciamano: una coltellata gli ha aperto la pancia e gli sono sortite tutte le budella.

Povero cristo, mi dispiace . . . Guarda, voglio tentare almeno di salvarlo.

Corro nella mia capanna, prendo una lama di ferro, una lesina e l'ago per cucire le vele che avevo tenuto nascosto e mi avvicino al capo degli stregoni moribondo.

Arrovento il ferro e lo passo sulla ferita.

"Aiaooh!", un grido tremendo dello Sciamano. I selvaggi armati di lancia fanno il gesto di "zagagliarmi" . . . lo Sciamano leva appena un braccio, come per dire: "Lasciatelo fare."

Io, con l'ago e il filo, sempre con un occhio alle lance dei selvaggi nervosi, incomincio a cucire com'ero abituato con le ferite dei cavalli: punto dritto . . . due punti a croce . . . uno di traverso . . . proprio un bel ricamo.

Non ho nemmeno finito la cucitura, che lo Sciamano apre gli occhi e mi sorride appena . . . mi afferra una mano e me la bacia. Tutti intorno mi baciano le mani, mi fanno le carezze . . . poi mi sollevano di peso e mi portano dove ci sono gli altri feriti della battaglia.

Trovo gente tagliata dappertutto! Mi tocca cauterizzare e cucire senza prendere respiro finché cala il sole.

Alla fine, stanco morto, m'hanno preso, m'hanno portato sull'amaca . . . io dormivo e cucivo, cucivo e dormivo!

A svegliarmi è stato un tepore tenerino-morbidoso intorno alle spalle e alla schiena.

Apro gli occhi: signore, deograzia! . . . Ero abbracciato tutto da due ragazze! Evviva! Quello era certamente il premio per aver salvato tutto il villaggio. Mi sono lasciato andare tra le loro braccia come un bambino e ho dormito. Ho sentito, non so quanto dopo, il cacicco che gridava: "Ehi, Johan Padan, meraviglia! Tu ci hai salvato! Se non fosse stato per te che hai dato l'allarme, i nostri nemici ci scannavano tutti . . . Bravo!" . . . E mi baciava! "Tutti quei feriti che hai cucito sono vivi, stanno benone. C'è addirittura lo Sciamano che cammina . . . va un po' sbilenco . . . ma cammina!"

Mi baciava sulla bocca, che mi faceva proprio schifo!

"Allora sono salvo, non mi mangiate più?" ho detto.

"Mangiarti?! Figurati se mangiamo te, così bravo a dare l'allarme . . . No, no . . . stai tranquillo, non ti mangiamo: ti facciamo fare il cane da guardia!"

Grazie! E i miei compagni?—domando—Avete deciso di liberare anche loro?"

"No, quelli li mangiamo. Non ci hanno salvati loro."

E non c'è stato modo di convincerlo: se li mangiano e basta!

Incazzato e intristito vado fuori dalla cinta verso il mare. Camminavo con addosso un gran magone. "Come posso salvarli?"

Arrivo alla marina, mi siedo sull'arena e guardo la luna, che io, ormai, do sempre un occhio (guardo) alla luna. La luna era grande, chiara, con tutte le nuvolette intorno tonde-tonde . . . come quella volta a Venezia quando la mia fidanzata strega mi aveva mostrato una luna uguale e che di lì a poco c'era stato il finimondo. 'Strega smorta ti voglio bene!"

È arrivato il Cacicco, mi fa: "Cosa fai, parli con la luna?!"

"Sì! . . . NORMALE!"

"E lei, ti risponde?!"

"Vorrei vedere . . . è mia madre!"

"Ah! Ah! Tu sei il figlio della luna? E cosa dice 'sta tua madre?"

"Dice che è incazzata nera con voialtri, che se non salvate subito i miei compagni dal mangiarli, vi manda addosso fulmini e tempesta da accopparvi tutti!"

"Oh, oh!—il Cacicco ride—Ohi, che furbacchione! D'accordo che ti sei dimostrato buon cucitore di ferite e che ci hai salvato con l'allarme, ma farti credere anche stregone figlio della luna . . . è un po' grossa Johan, siamo selvaggi ma non coglioni!"

"Ah, è un po' troppo? Bene, se fossi nei panni vostri, io, darei l'ordine di tirar su tutte le barche, di far fagotto di ogni masserizie che potete caricare e scapperei velocemente in quella grande caverna in cima alla collina per salvarmi, che tra poco qui il mare si arrampicherà fino al cielo!"

"Ohaa! Ah!"—Il Cacicco si soffoca dal ridere—"Non dire stronzate! Il cielo è chiaro che sembra slavato, il mare è piatto, calmo, tranquillo come una pisciata." Non aveva detto "il cielo tranquillo" che . . . SWUAFF!, all'istante un grande chiarore, una luce di saette e un tuono come duecento cannonate! Poi una tremenda sbuffata di vento solleva un nuvolone di polvere . . . una orribile riga nera appare all'orizzonte dei mare. Tutti i selvaggi, presi da spavento, vanno correndo a tirar su le barche.

"L'uragano!—gridano—Arriva l'uragano! Salviamoci!"

Corrono al villaggio, caricano tutto quello che possono, tirano fuori le bestie e anche i prigionieri, compresi i miei compagni e via tutti: capre, bambini, tacchini, maiali selvatici, tutti ad intrupparsi dentro alla gran caverna. Non facciamo in tempo a ripararci che fuori scoppia il finimondo. Un vento forsennato strappa gli alberi come fossero di paglia. Le capanne del villaggio volano via come foglie secche. Onde a cavalloni vomitate dal mare che bolle: OIHCSCHIACH spazzano ogni cosa . . . arrivano anche alla caverna!

Ohi, che gran culo che abbiamo: una caterva d'alberi sradicati viene rotolando, scaraventata dal vento, ad arginare l'ingresso della caverna e fa da bastione alle onde che si schiantano contro il nostro rifugio.

Ma c'era un squassaterra, uno scardinare, uno schianto, un rumore . . . che le donne piangevano, gridavano, gli uomini bestemmiavano . . .

Orco cane! Dopo due giorni e tre notti di 'sto 'sburlottare' tremendo di uragano, come succede nel teatro dei burattini, d'improvviso cambia la scena: va su il fondale della tempesta e scende srotolandosi quello del bel tempo sereno col sole che splende!

E' stato uguale . . . un grande chiarore, di colpo un silenzio . . . e dentro si sono visti i raggi sparati dal sole. Un silenzio che faceva gridare di morte . . . non c'era il canto di un pappagallo, neanche il gridare d'una scimmia.

A fatica "distoppiamo" liberiamo l'ingresso della caverna.

Si esce.

Boia!, che disastro! Fuori sembra che duecento giganti furiosi, scalmanati, abbiano arato tutta la costa e la foresta intera.

Il villaggio è scomparso!

Veniamo a sapere appresso che, di tutti i villaggi che c'erano intorno per miglia e miglia, noialtri eravamo gli unici ad esserci salvati. E io, che sono un anticristo, mi sono visto la mano salirmi da sè sola e farmi il segno della croce. Mi volto indietro, e mi vedo lì, con la faccia abbassata, schiacciata nel terreno tutti 'sti selvaggi inginocchiati, ai miei piedi, come tanti pecoroni: uomini, donne, bambini, prigionieri . . . Ho avuto perfino l'impressione che si fossero inginocchiate anche le capre, i maiali e perfino i tacchini.

"Perdonaci—supplicavano piangendo—se non ti abbiamo subito dato attenzione . . . ti giuriamo che non ti mangeremo più, né te, né i tuoi compagni cristiani! Abbiamo compreso, al fine, che tu non sei solamente il figlio della luna, ma anche il figlio del sol che nasce, venuto apposta dall'altra parte del cielo per salvarci! La profezia ci aveva avvertito che di là del mare, un giorno, sarebbe arrivato un uomo con la barba come te, bianco di pelle come te, un po' bruttino come te, che parla con la luna come fosse sua madre. Quello sei tu! Santo meraviglioso, santo figlio del sole aiutaci tu! Santo, santo." Tutti che gridavano "Santo, santo . . ."

Per poco non mi scappa: "Alleluhia! Alleluhia!" Sacripante! Io, una canaglia blasfema, figlio di puttana, salvato scrofando nella merda delle vacche e dei maiali, scappando dai fuochi dell'Inquisizione . . . in un sol colpo sono diventato: santo, stregone, medico, figlio della luna e anche figlio del sole!

Guarda tu il destino!

Ma io, non credevo fosse un mestiere tanto faticoso-tremendo *fare* lo stregone-santo-Sciamano!

Tanto per cominciare, arrivano con un mucchio di panieri, bacinelle colme di roba da mangiare: cento tra vasi, canestri e ceste, tutta mercanzia salvata dal disastro. S'inginocchiano e mi dicono: "Ecco, santone, è tutto per te: mangia!"

"Ohi, siete matti? Mi volete far scoppiare? E voialtri cosa mangiate?" "Bene, se vuoi avanzare qualcosa anche per noi . . . grazie . . . ma prima devi farci il piacere di benedirlo."

"Benedire cosa?"

"Il mangiare!"

Sono costretto ad inginocchiarmi davanti a questa sfilata di panieri: e giù una soffiata sul mais, poi un'altra sul pane di manioca, un'altra soffiata sulla frutta, sui pesci, le granseole e i tacchini: "Ahaa!"

Mi tocca soffiare anche sulle loro teste per liberarli dagli spiriti malvagi: "Ah, ah . . ."

Per poco, non mi viene il pneumotorace spontaneo.

E sono obbligato a toccarli sulla fronte e sulla bocca uno per uno. Alla fine anche i miei compagni mi abbracciano con le lacrime agli occhi: "Grazie che ci hai salvati! Salvati due volte: prima dall'essere mangiati e poi salvati dall'uragano . . . Hanno ragione 'sti selvaggi . . . qualcosa di stregoneria ce l'hai di sicuro in quegli occhi e in quelle mani! Toccaci anche noialtri, sii buono!"

"Abbracciaci . . ."

"Toccaci . . ."

"A me, toccami a me!"

"Prima a me!"

E tutti mi vengono addosso e si buttano anche i selvaggi.

"Eh! piano! Ehi! Ah no, basta!"

Ho afferrato un bastone e lo piroetto intorno!

"Allargatevi (spostatevi)! Il primo che mi tocca gli rompo 'sto bastone sulla testa!"

Risolta la situazione, ce n'era un'altra un po' più seria: il Cacicco si era messo un'altra volta in ginocchio davanti a me.

"Tu, che puoi parlare a tua madre la luna e a tuo padre il sole . . . chiedigli dove possiamo

andare . . . tu, hai ben visto che tutto intorno per giornate e giornate di cammino non si trova un albero sano, né nessuna bestia da mangiare, che perfino le lucertole e i granchi sono spariti . . . dobbiamo scappare da 'sto luogo! Ma dove andiamo? Dobbiamo andare in un luogo dove non è arrivata la tempesta. Ma dove andiamo? A nord o a sud? Andiamo a ponente? Andiamo a oriente? . . . Dove andiamooo?"

"E non gridare!—faccio io—Si va per ponente!"

"Come fai a dirlo così chiaro e sicuro?"

"Sono un santo! Saprò qualche cosarina, no?"

Sapevo di sicuro che molte armate spagnole, in quel tempo, con quindici, venti navi per ogni spedizione, erano scese a ponente di quella costa per fondarci una colonia grande. Dunque, con qualche mese di cammino avremmo di sicuro incontrati 'sti cristiani . . . e, finalmente, avremmo avuto la chance di fare un buon ritorno a casa. A casa, che davvero . . . di 'ste Indie maledette cominciavo ad averne da vomitare!

Che fra il viaggio nella stiva dentro la merda dei cavalli e delle vacche e il salvataggio abbracciato ai maiali . . . e l'essere fatto schiavo . . . e spennato come un tacchino, colorato a cerchi, e poi bastonato . . . vento, tempesta, fulmini-saette e dopo: santo, santo!, soffiargli addosso, palparli sulla testa, sulle chiappe e sui coglioni . . . Basta! A casa! Voglio tornarmene a casa!

Seconda Parte

"Allora, si va! In cammino!"

Il Cacicco fa segno di sì, d'accordo, ma avverte che da quelle parti si ritrova una razza di gente che si chiama Junicàcio, che non sono affatto buoni . . . e altri che si chiamano Incas, che anche loro non scherzano.

"Beh, si va egualmente per quelle terre. E non c'è discussione!" Boia!, ero o non ero ii santissimo figlio del sole e anche della luna! Dunque zitto lì: in marcia!

E cosi si forma una carovana, io davanti con in testa una foglia grande per ripararmi dal sole, e tutti gli altri dietro a me, compresi i prigionieri catturati nello scontro al villaggio: tutti legati con le corde al collo.

Abbiamo camminato per giorni e giorni in un terreno che l'uragano aveva rivoltato, scardinato. Non si trovava una cavalletta, un verme da mangiare . . . neanche le radici dolci. Cosi, giorno per giorno, le scorte di mais, di capre e maiali andavano dileguandosi, fino a che siamo restati senza più niente. Si moriva di fame, c'era la gente che gridava, i bambini che svenivano e allora il Cacicco ha detto: "Basta, stasera si mangia!" "Cosa si mangia?!" "Si mangiano i prigionieri che ci siamo portati appresso." "Ci ritroviamo un'altra volta con 'sto vizio da barbari di cucinare carne di uomini?"

"Perché,—mi risponde il Cacicco—siete più civili voialtri cristiani? Proprio voi che ammazzate i nemici in battaglia, vi scannate, vi massacrate . . . e poi tutti i morti squarciati li lasciate marcire sui campi dello scontro? Roba fresca, carne ammazzata di giornata! Spreconi! E noi saremmo i barbari?"

"Come te l'ha raccontata 'sta storia?"

"Un cristiano che abbiamo mangiato l'anno scorso."

"Basta, non c'è discussione. Da 'sto momento, carne di indio o di cristiano non se ne mangia più! Altrimenti lo dico alla luna che s'incazza e vi manda un'altra volta il tremamondo!"

"Boia—gridano—'sta luna che rompicoglioni!"

Due giorni dopo, che nessuno aveva mangiato nemmeno una foglia secca, e si camminava ciondoloni come ubriachi per la fame, all'improvviso, da una collina in fondo, abbiamo visto spuntar un lungo fumo sottile . . . che montava in cielo.

"Ci siamo,—ha gridato il Cacicco tutto festoso—là in fondo ci sono i Conciuba . . ."

"Chi sono i Conciuba?"

"Sono dei selvaggi come noialtri, della medesima razza nostra . . . li chiamano Conciuba perché hanno la testa pelata. Sono una tribù amica . . . E anche loro di sicuro si sono salvati, che l'uragano fin là non è arrivato."

Velocemente 'sti selvaggi nostri, attizzano un fuoco e poi ci sbattono sopra delle erbe bagnate per far sortire un gran fumo. E muovendosi intorno con delle foglie larghe come quella che adoperavo io per ripararmi dal sole, le sventolavano, coprivano, distaccavano, le tagliavano intorno al fuoco: facevano uscire delle nuvole lunghe, corte, larghe, gonfie, lunghe di nuovo . . . e ancora, di colpo, una fila di nuvolette a grappolo. Roba da non credere! Con 'sto gioco del fumo, 'sti cannibali stavano parlando a quei selvaggi che stavano in fondo sulla collina! Con le nuvole di fumo facevano le parole. Tanto è vero che quei Conciuba quando sono arrivati erano carichi di roba da mangiare! Hanno portato tante cose . . . che loro, questi qua, con il fumo li avevano avvertiti: "Attenti . . . che sono giorni e giorni che noialtri non "sgraniamo", non mangiamo . . . portateci da mangiare che abbiamo una fame bestia!!"

Come sono arrivati a dieci passi, si sono buttati tutti in ginocchio davanti a me, mi davano tutta la roba da mangiare e mi dicevano: "Toccaci, soffiaci addosso anche a noi . . ."

Cosa era successo?

Una stregoneria! I nostri indiani, col fumo, li avevano avvisati: "Attenti che con noialtri c'è un santone che viene dal sole che nasce, e è il figlio della luna . . . parla alla luna . . . a-ll-a luunaaa!! . . . Attenti che quella s'incazza come una biscia se non gli date retta!"

Tra quelli c'era una dozzina di selvaggi che avevano dei testoni con dei capelli ingialliti raccolti in treccine, scuri di pelle . . . quasi rossi, e avevano degli anelli sul (al) naso . . . avevano persino della ganasce con tanti denti . . . una faccia da cattivi . . . Il loro capo è venuto davanti a me, m'ha guardato un po' i piedi e poi SPIU SPIU, m'ha sputato sui piedi!

"Oh villano di un selvaggio, cosa ti prende?"

"Mi prende che non abbiamo nessuna riverenza per te, anche se dicono che sei santo. Assomigli troppo a quei cristiani spagnoli che noialtri abbiamo incontrato a quattro mesi e mezzo di cammino da qui. Sono sbarcati, ormai fa più di un anno, da una dozzina di navi grandi, un centinaio di uomini ricoperti al completo di ferro, elmi, corazze, e hanno dei bastoni che sputano fuoco. E poi ci sono venuti addosso con dei mostri tremendi, che loro chiamano cavalli: una gran bestia, che dalla groppa le spunta un uomo . . . vivo, tutto coperto di ferro, una cosa sola con 'st'animale . . . e con gli altri soldati fanno mattanza di tutti. Sono saltati addosso alle nostre donne, le hanno fottute lì, davanti ai nostri occhi e poi le hanno portate via schiave.

Buono per te che sei contornato da tutta 'sta gente che ti difende, che se ti troviamo da solo un'altra volta, ti mangiamo vivo!" E via che se ne sono andati bestemmiando.

Poi ho scoperto che 'sti selvaggi sono di una razza speciale che si chiama Incas . . . che è la estremazione corta di incazzato!

Io lo conoscevo bene 'sto programma-spettacolo. Mi sono finto indignato: "Ah sì? Bene! Arriverò io là, in quella piana e farò denuncia al gran Almirante Governatore . . . che quello è un grand'uomo di onestà e giustizia. Sicuramente lui non conosce nulla di queste ruberie e di 'sti ammazzamenti. E quando lo saprà, vedrete . . . darà una tremenda punizione a quei macellai assassini! Allora d'accordo, domani si riparte e voialtri, tutti insieme, mi accompagnate di la dei monti in quella valle!"

Nemmeno per idea! Tutti stanno zitti seduti sul culo, la testa infilata fra le ginocchia . . . senza guardarmi in faccia, mi dicono: "No, no, no, no, noialtri non veniamo! Questi spagnoli sono troppo cattivi. Ammazzano, scannano . . . non veniamo!"

"No' mi interessa, restate qui tranquilli, tanto io ho i mie selvaggi. Cannibali, andiamo!"

Nessuno che si muova.

"Cannibali, mi accompagnate?"

I cannibali stavano seduti con una faccia da spaventati.

"Allora non volete accompagnarmi nemanco voialtri? Con tutto quello che ho fatto io?! . . . Vi ho soffiato sulle vivande da farmi scoppiare i polmoni, v'ho scacciato il maligno palpeggiandovi la crapa e le chiappe e anche i coglioni, ricucito le ferite con le budella che vi uscivano . . . e adesso, per una volta che vi domando un piacere, voialtri mi rispondete di no, non veniamo con te? Di no? Al santo?! Allora sapete cosa vi dico? Andate a dar via il culo, selvaggi del cazzo!"

E detto fatto, arrabbiato come un demonio, monto su un albero grande . . . miarrampico giusto sulla cima e mi allungo fra i rami intrecciati con il fogliame, e cerco di dormire. Non dormo.

Do una sbirciata sotto . . . c'è un qualche movimento: degli uomini e delle donne di tutte e tre le tribù . . . si sono accovacciati lì, sotto l'albero. Sento che guaiscono . . . qualcheduno, piange. Non mi importa un bel niente . . . che crepino!

"Massa di cagasotto!"—ho gridato—"Non scendo più, non vi tocco più, non vi guardo più, non vi faccio ridere più! Basta!, non vi soffio

addosso il fiato più . . . basta, finito . . .
CAGAS OTTO!
Cagasotto? Faccio alla svelta io a dargli dei
cagasotto a quelli . . . Vorrei vedere se fossi io a
Brescia o a Bergamo . . . dove sto io . . . arrivano
dei selvaggi barbari coperti di ferro a cavallo e
mi ammazzano i figli . . . mi si sbattono le mie
donne, la figlia, la moglie davanti ai miei occhi
e: "Zitto lì! . . . perché se ti rivolti spacchiamo il
culo anche a te!" Volevo vedere io, se non mi
cagavo sotto . . . Mi cagavo di sotto, di sopra, di
traverso! D'accordo, ma cosa devo fare? . . . Io
voglio tornare al mio paese! Non posso restar
tutta la vita qui . . . son già passati cinque
anni . . . e più! Io voglio tornare alle mie
valli . . . a casa mia!
La mattina all'alba sento gridare i miei compagni
che mi chiamano a tutta voce: "Johan discendi
che qui è scoppiato un disastro. Questa notte 'sti
selvaggi, dal momento che tu non li guardi più,
sono caduti in una disperazione tremenda e in
quaranta si sono ammorbati di tristezza. Scendi
ti prego, fai qualcosa, perché tu sei divenuto la
luce per loro, il fiato per loro . . . la vita!"
"Disgraziati, adesso sono Jesus Cristo? Mettetemi
sotto una campana di vetro . . . vengo fuori con
le mani allargate a benedirvi! Va bene . . .
scendo."
Giunto a terra, ritrovo un mucchio di gente
rovesciata a terra , pallida con i tremori, e io, uno
ad uno, gli soffio addosso, li palpo sulla faccia, lo
stomaco . . . ma sopra tutto, mi tocca mostrarmi
contento, con gran sorrisi . . . mollargli delle
pacche di simpatia . . . insomma fargli intendere
che non son più arrabbiato.
E non è abbastanza: davanti a quelli che son
moribondi mi tocca scatenarmi in una
pantornima d'allegrezza pagliaccesca . . . mi
butti a ballare, saltar zompando . . . e grido:
"Ballate, avanti, saltate, via andiamo . . .
PAPPARAPAPPAPUM . . . ballare, ballare!"
Tutti i moribondi che ballavano! Dopo neanche
mezz'ora eran tutti sani . . . salvo otto che eran
morti!
Ballando!
"Perdonaci, veniamo tutti con te!"
Alé! Avanti! Si parte! A la fine si parte!
Si attraversa una foresta per giorni e giorni . . .
guardando in su fra il fogliame dei rami
intrecciati, si riusciva solamente a indovinare
qualche sprazzo di cielo. Si va avanti con gran

fatica . . . rami e arbusti ci bloccano il cammino.
All'improvviso, si sente gridare: "Un mostro!!"
Io e i miei compagni, prendendo delle lance
lunghe, andiamo a vedere.
Oh, sangue di Dio! Era un cavallo! Selvatico. Era
uno stallonino magro . . . tirava calci con gli
zoccoli, mollava grande morsicate ad ognuno
che gli capitava a tiro. Bisogna catturarlo.
"Oh, gente Indios, facciamo la cattura di questo
mostro! Ma dove siete?!" Alzo la testa . . . si
erano tutti arrampicati in cima agli alberi.
"Ah, vi siete piazzati comodi per lo spettacolo!
e allora, aiutato dai miei compagni, andiamo a
distendere delle corde lunghe tutte torno-
torno, da tronco a tronco d'albero . . . in
circolo, in modo da circondare 'sta bestia. Poi
abbiamo preso una canna lunga, lui era in
mezzo a una radura, ho cominciato: "Vieni . . .
bravo . . ." si arrampicava, sbofonchiava, o
dava di zoccolo . . . tremava: "Guardate, ha
paura il mostro! Cos'è alla fine un cavallo? E'
un asino che si da un po' di importanza!
Attenzione che adesso cerco di montargli in
groppa io".
Sono montato in cima a un albero, mi sono
messo a cavalcioni d'un ramo, ho aspettato che il
cavallo mi venisse a tiro, gli sono saltato in
groppa, gli ho preso la criniera . . . e lui comincia
a scaracollare di qua, di là, spintonava . . . di
botto s'è impennato, sono volato per aria.
AHHH . . . PAA! . . . e poi: UNA CULATA!
E tutti gli Indios che ridevano gridando: "Ah . . .
il santo si è ingrippato!" Come si fa presto a
perdere una reputazione!
Meno male che c'è stato il Negro che mi ha
salvato . . . ha dato una pacca sulle chiappe al
cavallo, gli è saltato in groppa, inforcandolo,
gli ha brancato con una mano la criniera e con
l'atra la coda . . . e quello ha cominciato a
saltare, a montare in piedi, di traverso,
caracollava, ma lui, il Negro, non si muoveva . . .
era incollato. Dopo mezz'ora di questa danza,
di su, di qua, di la, 'sto cavallo aveva il fiatone.
(Rifà il *cavallo che respira col fiatone*) AH,
AH . . . Allora il Negro gli ha fatto fare quello
che voleva lui, prima un bel galoppo . . .
TRUN, TRUN, TRUN TRUN, poi il trotto,
TRUN e TRUN, poi la croce: "Incrociare le
gambe!, una davanti, una di dietro, via! . . . Fa
la riverenza . . . Fa lo zoppo . . . Seduto!" e
buona sera!

C'era un selvaggio che gridava: "Oh, bravo Negro!". Abbracciava il cavallo, non aveva più paura. "Voglio montarlo!" gridava. "Anch'io, anch'io!" gridavano tutti. Anche le donne volevano far la monta a 'sto cavallo . . . e allora abbiamo fatto la scuola di monta a tutta la tribù!

Qualche giorno appresso sentiamo una nitrita a squassa-orecchi d'un altro cavallo da non tanto lontano. Ah, ah, ah . . . era una cavalla femmina: la madre dello stallonino che era scappata dagli spagnoli e l'aveva sfornato nella foresta. Era abituata alla sella e quando siamo andati a montana non s'è neanche mossa. Solamente che di lì a poco è arrivato il padre del cavallino, un maschio tremendo: era un toro con la criniera! Dava delle zampate, delle zoccolate, aveva dei denti da leone, nessuno poteva toccarlo.

C'è stato il Negro che gli è saltato in groppa, di schiena, lo stallone gli ha dato una sgroppata che l'ha sbattuto contro un albero . . . che momenti lo spiaccica!

Allora mi è venuta in mente la doma alla bergamasca che è tremenda.

La prima cosa difficile è infilargli la cavezza, che lui, come gli vai appresso, ti morde . . . e allora si butta la cavezza, la si lega alle punte di due canne messe apposta come trappola . . . lui cammina e come vede la cavezza per terra, curioso com'è, si abbassa a guardarla: "Cos'è 'sta roba?" si domanda . . . e TRAK, i due che stanno nascosti con le canne in mano, le alzano in alto di colpo e la cavezza s'infila sul muso dello stallone fino alle orecchie. Ma a 'sto punto gli devi attaccare la corda alla cavezza per far le briglie, una a destra e l'altra a manca, non bisogna andargli di fronte perché ti morde e allora si fa finta di parlare con qualcuno che sta alla tua destra . . . e la si lega di qua . . . che lui, il cavallo . . . è curioso . . . viene ad ascoltare a sentire e allora . . . Poi si passa dall'altra parte, ma si cambia uomo con cui si parla, se no a lui, al cavallo gli viene il sospetto. (*Mima l'imbracatura del cavallo: le briglie legate alla cavezza*) Le due corde si lasciano cadere morbide in lunghezza . . . (*mima di stendere le corde fino a raggiungere i testicoli dello stallone e di annodarle ai testicoli stessi*) poi c'è il pettorale, le fai scivolare lungo il pettorale, poi scivolare sulla pancia . . . quando si arriva ai coglioni fai un

anello, gli inforchi il testicolo, senza stringere . . . poi l'altro anello, dolce anche lui, sul secondo testicolo . . . poi aspetti che lui sia giù basso con la testa, lo inforchi di colpo a groppone: (*mima di saltare in groppa al cavallo che reagisce rizzandosi con la testa e il collo così da strizzarsi da sè solo, i testicoli, con relativi nitriti disperati*) TAN . . . lui all'istante: TAK! "AHHIII!", dà di schiena: "AIIIHHIIII!!" si rizza di collo TAK!: "AHHOIII" . . . alla terza ingroppata . . . vedi 'sta bestia . . . (*mima una camminata del cavallo da parata*) Un'eleganza!

Dopo due mesi, tutti questi indiani avevano imparato a cavalcare.

E via che si riprende il cammino con la nostra cavalleria.

Andavamo attraversando fiumi, canaloni e rampicandoci su per le montagne. Ogni tanto ci si incontrava con delle tribù sparpagliate su per i bricchi e le vallate.

La mia reputazione di santo cresceva. Tutti si prostravano davanti a me. C'era della gente che mi portava ori e argenti e io gli dicevo: "Ma siete matti?! Adesso vado in giro caricato di oro e argento e tutte 'ste pietre preziose come un facchino? Tenetevele voialtri! Non voglio portare pesi!"

E tutti si prostravano davanti a me in grandi riverenze.

Poi c'è stato anche la storia di due miracoli che ho fatto . . . (*Rivolto al pubblico, quasi risentito dell'incredulità che si immagina aver suscitato*) HO FATTO DUE MIRACOLI!! (*Poi minimizza*) DUE COLPI DI CULO!!

Il primo è stato quando siamo arrivati su, in cima a un altipiano dove c'è un gran lago. Sul lago c'è un villaggio con le case a palafitte . . . con le calle, i canali e i ponti . . . una Venezia piccola, fatta di legno.

'Sti Indios-veneziani ci vengono incontro e si lamentano: "Noialtri ti vorremmo portare tutto l'oro di 'sto mondo e anche le pietre preziose ma non abbiamo niente! Abbiamo soltanto il pianto dei nostri occhi . . ."

"Cosa è successo?"

Erano due anni che non c'era più la "risciada". La "risciada" è un fenomeno che avviene da queste bande . . . sarebbe come un "getto di pesci" che escono dall'acqua. Ogni due mesi, con la luna piena . . . la luna tira, tira, tira

dentro il lago, fa uscire dei pesci come scoppiassero fuori dall'acqua e volano. Loro, 'sti Indios veneziani, escono con i cesti, i canestri e prendono tutti quei pesci che piovono dall'alto e li sistemano ad affumicare, li mettono sotto sale, li schiacciano e mangiano pesci per tutto un anno . . . che sono contenti! Ma ora erano disperati: "Tu, figlio del sol che nasce e della luna . . . parla a tua madre . . . dille di non darci 'sta punizione!"
"Non so . . . mia madre la Luna è stramba . . . La Luna è lunatica!"
Boia, cosa posso fare io? Aspetto che spunti la luna e mi piazzo lì di fronte e mi metto a parlarle: "Mamma! Ehi mamma, mi senti? . . . Sì, sono io, tuo figlio . . . figlio anche di mio padre, il sole che nasce . . . ascolta mamma, tu non puoi farmi una cosa così! I pesci devono saltar fuori dall'acqua come tutti gli anni! . . . Cosa? Quest'anno sono di riposo? E no mamma, cerca di metterti una mano sul cuore . . . 'sta povera gente non puoi lasciarla morire di fame perché quei pelandroni non hanno voglia di farsi mangiare . . . Minacciali che se non si muovono tu gli fai scoppiare il vulcano che sta sotto l'acqua!"
Poi mi rivolgo ai veneziani selvaggi e gli dico tranquillo: "Forse sarà per domani mattina. Credo d'aver convinto mia madre."
E l'indomani, di mattina presto, tutti 'sti Indios pescatori sono pronti: canestri, reti tese . . . ce n'erano di quelli che intorno alla vita si erano legati tre, quattro ceste . . . e stavano in mezzo all'acqua del lago immersi fino allo stomaco.
Dio che figura faccio se i pesci non si muovono! E qui, m'è arrivata 'sta gran botta di culo che vi dicevo!
Spunta il sole . . . e: RAM!, comincia a bollire davvero tutta l'acqua del lago. Scoppiano frotte di arborelle, coregoni, piotte, persici per l'aria! Cavedani e lavarelli sprizzano fuori dall'acqua e cadono in tutti i canestri, a mille a mille! Lucci e trote che fanno zompi fuori dall'acqua fin sui tetti delle case . . . storioni cadono dentro le barche . . . e se qualche pesce, per sbaglio, ricade in acqua: "Oh, pardon!" torna subito indietro e zompa nelle ceste! Ti saltano in bocca e se non stai attento ti si infilano anche tra le chiappe!
Non si può immaginare la festa che mi hanno fatto dopo. Mi prendevano in braccio e mi

buttavano in aria come un merluzzo, da rompermi la schiena.
La seconda fortuna proprio da vergognarsi mi è capitata quando siamo discesi giù nella piana: che disastro! Erano quattro mesi e più che non pioveva nemmeno una lacrima. S'era seccato tutto: le carrube per terra, mais per terra, le pannocchie, le bestie assetate, morte con tutte le formiche che le mangiavano . . . e anche gli uomini morivano per la sete. E c'erano 'sti poveri selvaggi in ginocchio davanti a me, che mi supplicavano: "Oh figlio del sole che nasce e della luna . . . facci un miracolo!" "Oh, basta! Adesso la luna e il sole non c'entrano con l'acqua!"—"Lo sappiamo bene, ma tu sei tanto buffone, ridanciano che puoi salvarci. Se tu sei capace di far ridere il figlio dei Dio della pioggia, il Dio padre si commuove di tante lacrime che ci inonda . . ." "Fermi! Fermi! Fermi! Non capisco niente! Cos'è 'sta storia del Dio della pioggia?" "Il Dio della pioggia è quello che fa piovere. Ha un figlio unico che non ride mai . . . Ma se tu sei capace di farlo scoppiare in una risata, il Dio della pioggia a vedere suo figlio che ride gli scoppia un magone di tale felicità che si commuove, piange, piange di gioia, piange che ci bagna tutti!" "E dove sta 'sto figlio della pioggia?" "Là!" e mi mostrano un pigottone, un fagotto, un pupazzo di pezza ripieno di paglia e di stracci, tutto ciondoloni, seduto su una sedia, con la faccia piatta: non ha gli occhi, non ha le orecchie.
"Ma come fa a ridere uno che non ha nemmeno la bocca?!" "È proprio lì il difficile . . . che così non gli riesce mai! Ma tu sei tanto pagliaccio-buffone che lo puoi far ridere . . . Dai balia, salta . . ." Ohi! Ohi! Non c'è verso, mi tocca ballare . . . fare il pagliaccio . . . mi lancio a far piroetta . . . boccacce. Tutti i selvaggi battono le mani, battono i tamburi . . . gridano . . . cantano . . . e io mi contorgo tutto a fare il buffone!
Mi rovescio buttando i piedi in aria . . . mi stravacco spicciato per terra 'rotolandomi. Tutti sbottano in una grande risata. Poi all'istante una donna grida: "Ride! Ride anche lui!"
Miracolo! Roba da non crederci: dentro la faccia vuota del fantoccio, s'era come graffiato uno strappo a taglio di traverso, uguale ad una bocca

ridente . . . e due buchini che sembravano occhi luccicanti!

"Ride! Dio de la piova, tuo figlio ride . . . Commuoviti! Piangi" TON! TON!

"Si commuove!"

TON! TON! TON! "Piange!"

PTON! PTON TON . . . TON . . . PTIN!

(*Si arresta col gesto di indicare le gocce che scendono sempre più lentamente sino a bloccarsi. Si rivolge al cielo, risentito*) "Basta così?! Son tutte qui le tue lacrime? Sei un po' stitico! Piovi! Piovi! Piangi!"

PTON PTON PTON TONTONTONTO!!!!!

Comincia a venir giù un' acqua tremenda! All'alba eravamo immersi nell'acqua fino alle ginocchia! C'erano tutti i selvaggi che ballavano e cantavano (*mima una danza a ritmo di pioggia*)

PTENPTERNPTENPTEN!

Arriva la notte e l'acqua era già arrivata fino alla vita!

"Beh, Dio adesso basta così!" PTENPTENPTEN!

"Basta!!"

PTENPETNTPEN!

"Basta!! Ci vuoi annegare?! (*Minaccioso*) Guarda che ti strozzo il figlio! . . . Basta!! Attento che vengo su e ti picchio! Basta!!"

(*Il ritmo della pioggia diminuisce, ma poi riprende timido*) PTON PTON

"Basta!!"

PTIN!

"Basta!"

PTIN!

L'acqua era arrivata fino alla gola e tutti i selvaggi con fuori solo la testa nuotavano verso di me e mi gridavano: "Figlio del sol che nasce . . . resta con noi!".—(*Mimando di nuotare*) "No, grazie, è troppo umido per il mio carattere, ci vediamo un'altra volta! (*Si allontana sempre mimando di nuotare con foga*) Devo arrivare a Cacioche!"

Siamo ripartiti e 'sti selvaggi della pioggia ci son venuti appresso.

Abbiamo attraversato un fiume, un altro fiume . . . ci troviamo all'improvviso in una bufera tremenda . . . c'erano cavalli dappertutto . . . in un fiume grande c'erano sessanta cavalli che si rotolavano nella tempesta. Non so da dove venissero ma stavano annegando! Abbiamo preso tutte le corde che avevamo appresso, abbiamo fatto un lancio . . . le abbiamo lanciate imbragando i cavalli e, uno a uno li abbiamo tirati a terra. Così siamo riusciti a salvare tutti i sessanta cavalli. Adesso avevamo sessantatré bei cavalli . . . Gli Indios andavano cavalcando tutto il giorno . . . una festa!

Soltanto un anno prima non sapevano neanche cosa fossero i cavalli, credevano fossero mostri e adesso era come se fossero nati insieme! Montavano a cavallo di dritto: "Eehaaheeh!, senza la sella: "Ahaa!", e poi si rivoltavano: "Eheeplom!", e andavano rovesciati all'indietro. Ho visto uno che andava tranquillo in equilibrio sulla culatta del cavallo. Poi è arrivato un cavallo con tre Indios sul groppone . . . in piedi . . . al gran trotto si è affiancato un altro cavallo con tre scalmanati, anche loro in piedi gridando: "Facciamo scambio di cavallo?" Passa di qua, passa di là, passa di qua, passa di là! Poi ho visto una cosa mai vista al mondo: un Indios su un cavallo che andava dietro un altro cavallo, quando è arrivato appresso all'altro cavallo, lui, l'Indios a cavallo ha dato una scarcagnata coi talloni, il suo cavallo è saltato in groppa all'altro cavallo: un cavallo a cavallo di un cavallo, con l'indios a cavallo!

In quei giorni, io di sicuro ero un po' svirgolo . . . dovevamo puntare a oriente e non so com'è, ci siamo incamminati a rovescio di direzione . . . così che all'improvviso ci siamo trovati di faccia all'altro mare. Noialtri si cercava il mare Atlantico, abbiamo incontrato il Pacifico! Sacramento! C'è toccato tornare indietro. Quattro mesi di cammino per niente! . . . Ma tanto non avevamo niente da fare!

Dopo altri quattro mesi siamo arrivati a una collina . . . e su questa collina meravigliosa ho sentito un odore che io conoscevo bene: zolfo! Sono andato a sfrugugliare, c'era un filone di zolfo bello, intero, lungo . . . L'ho tirato fuori (l'ho estratto), poi l'ho nascosto. Appresso ho preparato della carbonella, poi ho cercato del magnesio, dentro una grotta l'ho trovato . . . c'era anche del salnitro: "Faccio del fuochi d'artificio, faccio canne!"

Mentre gli Indios dormivano tranquilli e beati, ho tagliato le canne, poi le ho forate, ho messo dentro la polvere nera, salnitro e zolfo, poi il magnesio, poi ho intrecciato le micce . . . e gli ho dato fuoco (*mima esplosioni fragorose*): PTIN PTAN PHIIIIIIIIIIIII! PAM! PAM! PAM! PAM! PAM! PAM!

(*Fa immaginare gli Indios che fuggono*) "La fine del mondo! Scoppia il mondo!" Scappavano di qua e di là!
PIM! PAM! PAM! PAM!
"Scoppiano le stelle!"
PIAM! PIAM! PIAM!
"Perdonaci luna!"
Tutti in ginocchio . . . e io ridevo, ridevo! Mi guardano: 'Oh, Johan Padan, sei stato tu a fare tutta 'sta bombarderia?' "Sì, ma non l'ho mica fatto per spaventarvi, ma per il fatto che adesso noialtri ci incontreremo con gli spagnoli a Cacioche, e tutti in coro gli faremo una gran festa! A loro piacciono i fuochi d'artificio e gli faremo dono di botti da inciucchirli ma bisogna che voialtri apprendiate tutti a fare i fuochi d'artificio."
E imparavano . . . Esagerati! Facevano fuochi d'artificio e li facevano scoppiare anche quando non era il caso. Si stava camminando: PAM! Stavo a pisciare(*mima botti e zompi a soprassalto*): PAM! Stavo a mangiare: PAM! Facevo l'amore: PAM! PAM! "Bastaaa!"
Siamo arrivati infine in cima a una catena di montagne. Di lassù si vedeva tutto un vallone largo, chiaro . . . e una città: (*allarga le braccia con gesto trionfante*) Cacioche! C'era Cacioche! La città di Cacioche! C'era il mare!, l'Atlantico, col porto . . . le navi . . . Cacioche! (*Quasi gridando impazzito*) "Finalmente Cacioche ti ho ritrovata! Guardate che città, viva, le grandi mura tutte di legno, i paloni, e guardate le case, i casoni . . . quei casoni là sono i magazzeni del fondaco . . . quell'altra è la cattedrale, vedete che ha il campanile tutto fatto di tronchi . . . Quell'altro là grande è il palazzo del Governatore . . . e poi altre case dei soldati, le guarnigioni . . .
e appena fuori dalle mura le piantagioni di cotone . . . di mais . . . di frumento . . . Guardate che grande! Bucate di là ci sono le montagne . . . le miniere di oro . . . tant'è vero che ci sono gli schiavi con le catene! Indios, Indios incatenati come schiavi.., anche quelli che portano balle di cotone . . . tutti Indios . . . anche quelli che caricano le navi . . . tutti Indios schiavi! E ce ne sono dieci, dieci Indios impiccati ! . . ."
Io sbircio con la coda dell'occhio: intorno a me gli Indios erano tutti bianchi, smorti in faccia,

c'erano le donne che tremavano, c'erano quelli che svenivano. "Non fatevi terrore, non abbiate paura che tanto non vi porto a Cacioche . . . Non vi porto dagli spagnoli. Non fate rumore. Torniamo indietro di due giorni di cammino che vi devo parlare!
Quando ci siamo ritrovati lontano da Cacioche in un vallone nascosto, ci siamo seduti bei tranquilli e tranquilli e gli ho ordinato: "I maschi da una parte, le femmine dall'altra! . . . Contatevi!" "Mille, duemila. . . . ottomila maschi!" "Le femmine?"—"Quasi settemila!" "E i vecchi? Quanti sono i vecchi?" "Più di tremila." "I bambini?" "Anche loro tremila." "E quelli più grandi?" "Quattromila." Venticinquemila . . .
"Troppi, troppi! Non possiamo andare a Cacioche . . . facciamo troppa confusione . . . siamo il doppio di tutta la popolazione che sta in 'sta città, compreso gli Indios schiavi! Vi voglio dire la verità: se io vi porto in bocca agli spagnoli, gli spagnoli vi fanno tutti schiavi, vi incatenano . . . e hanno anche ragione . . . senza offendervi . . . ma voialtri non siete uomini normali . . . per loro siete parenti di animali. Guardiamoci in faccia . . . voi non tenete religione, non avete dottrina, non tenete l'anima e non avete nemanco un Dio. Per salvarvi dal diventare schiavi dovrei farvi diventare fratelli cristiani . . . Se voialtri siete fratelli cristiani, gli spagnoli non vi possono mica toccare . . . per legge! Ma ci vuole un prete, un prete che vi faccia dottrina, un frate . . . (*In progressione come incalzato dallo sguardo implorante degli Indios*) Non posso farvi dottrina io che sono un anticristo, un bestemmiatore blasfemo . . . io non posso!, io non posso farvi dottrina! Ma non conosco neanche la dottrina! . . . (*Breve pausa. Poi determinato*) Vi faccio dottrina. Ma guai a chi non sta attento che dopo vi interrogo. Prima regola: l'anima è eterna . . . il corpo marcisce . . . dopo che muore va sottoterra e i vermi se lo mangiano . . . ma l'anima è eterna e non ci sono vermi che la possano mangiare . . . va in cielo, beata in Paradiso . . . se è stato buono il corpo in terra . . . se invece è stato crudele, l'anima sprofonda di sotto, precipita dentro . . . va nell'inferno e brucia in eterno. Amen!
Indios, v'è piaciuto? . . . Non v'è piaciuto. D'accordo, andiamo avanti."

La cosa difficile era spiegare agli Indios questa questione del peccato originale, di Adamo ed Eva . . . Io ho detto: Adamo ed Eva erano due Indios, erano nudi quando sono nati, proprio come voialtri . . . le zinne, le chiappe, la passera, le passerine, il passerino col pindorlone . . . tutto allo scoperto e si volevano bene e si abbracciavano, facevano l'amore, non gli importava del pudore e non si vergognavano . . . sul più bello è arrivato il serpentone canaglia, il serpentone che era il diavolo, con una mela in bocca che diceva: "Adamo, mangia la mela! Dolce, buone, rosse le mele! Adamo, mangia 'sta mela!" "No, a me non piace . . . dillo a Eva." "Eva, mangia la mela?" "Facciamo metà per uno, io e l'Adamo." Mangia tu che mangio io . . . salta fuori l'arcangelo Gabriele . . . Michele . . . adesso non mi ricordo più se è Raffaele . . . salta fuori con la spada in mano: "Fuori! Disgraziati! Avete mangiato la mela proibita di Dio! Via dal Paradiso!". E tutti gli Indios hanno gridato: "Quello di sicuro è uno spagnolo!".

Ma ai selvaggi non era facile fargli entrare in testa 'sto fatto del castigo per via del frutto divino. Che loro non conoscono le mele . . . non hanno piante di mele e nemmeno di pere . . . e allora ho dovuto mettere in bocca al serpentone un mango . . . un'anguria così, (*indica*) con 'sta povera bestia del serpentone con tutta la faccia stortata, che diceva: "(*parla con difficoltà quasi biascicando*) Adamo manghiailmangoangoango !". Difficile era spiegare anche questo fatto del pudore . . . ché loro prima vivevano tranquilli col passero, la passerina, andavano in giro con le chiappe, le zinne . . . tutto scoperto, che non gli importava niente . . . di colpo gli viene la vergogna! Quando? Quando salta fuori l'arcangelo Gabriele con la spada in mano che dice: "Avete mangiato il mango proibito?! Fuori dal Paradiso!" "Oh che vergogna!" (*Rapidamente si porta le mani a coprirsi il pube*). Come avevo detto "Fuori dal Paradiso!" "Oh che vergogna! Oh che pudore! Oh la passera . . . dammi per piacere una foglia di fico . . . da coprirmi!" Gli Indios non capivano 'sto fatto della foglia di fico per coprirsi . . . anche perché loro di fico, conoscevano solo quello d'India . . . pensa a 'sta foglia con tutte le

spine . . . te la ficchi tra le gambe "AHAAAA!" Invece quando ho raccontato di Gesù, figlio di Dio, dolce, gentile, con tanti capelli lunghi . . . a tutti è piaciuto questo figlio di Dìo . . . "Che bello Gesù! Così amoroso, appassionato che prendeva i bambini in braccio . . . poi perdonava tutti: "Hai un peccato tremendo? Oh che peccato . . . Te lo perdono! Tu quanti peccati hai commesso? Tre peccati, quattro peccati? Cinque peccati? Tutti perdonati!" Quando c'era uno che camminava tutto sciancato: "Ohi, va dritto!" "Grazie, miracolo Gesù!" Gli piaceva Gesù che faceva resuscitare tutti i morti . . . che faceva le feste . . . Invece, chi non gli piaceva affatto erano gli apostoli . . . agli Indios gli apostoli non piacevano proprio per niente! Tutti seriosi, tutti con le mani giunte, che camminavano uno dietro l'altro con i cerchioni d'oro in testa . . . tutti maschi, sempre maschi, solamente maschi . . . che agli Indios gli veniva un po' un sospetto . . . tanto che ho dovuto mettere in mezzo a questi apostoli, una femmina: la Maddalena.

Come gli piaceva la Maddalena!, con le zinne tonde e puntute, le chiappe, tutta nuda, coperta solamente di una grande cascata di capelli che faceva: "IHIAAAA!" (*scuote la testa e mima il sollevarsi ondeggiante dei capelli, che lasciano nuda tutta la sua figura*).

Tremendo è stato quando ho raccontato che Gesù figlio di Dio inchiodato sulla croce, con tutto il sangue che gli colava giù, che moriva, moriva, rantolava . . . la Madonna sotto la croce che piangeva . . . la Maddalena che si stracciava i capelli . . . Ascoltando questo racconto c'erano tutti gli Indios che piangevano disperati: "Muore! Muore! Il figlio di Dio, il figlio del cielo muore!" E si stracciavano anche loro i capelli, come se fosse un loro figlio che stava morendo, e si davano delle graffiate, si tiravano pugni-schiaffoni in faccia, si picchiavano sullo stomaco, piangevano, si buttavano per terra . . . Un giorno, una notte, due giorni, tre giorni, tre notti . . . "Basta!! Cos'è 'sto pianto disperato da piaghe!? Esagerati! È una storia antica, vecchia, non se ne ricorda più nessuno . . . E poi state tranquilli che dopo tre giorni che è morto, Gesù resuscita, torna in vita!"

(*Con voce di pianto sconsolato*) "Non è vero, tu ci racconti una bugia solo per consolarci, ma noi lo sappiamo che il figlio del cielo è morto, è morto!"

"Io non dico bugie . . . io sono un santone! Ma attenti che c'è stato un altro santone, Tommaso, che non credeva affatto alla resurrezione di Gesù. È andato lui di persona dove c'era la tomba da dove il figlio di Dio era appena uscito: vivo era! Aveva tutte le piaghe ancora nel costato . . . E lui, 'sto Tommaso malcredente ha avuto il becco di infilargli le dita nei buchi sanguinanti . . . gli è arrivato un fulmine: NIAAAA! (*si porta entrambe le mani sotto l'ascella apparendo come monco*) Cerchione, aureola e moncherini! Attenti!"
E tutti gli Indios che cantavano: "È vivo! Il figlio dei cieli è vivo!" e si abbracciavano e si buttavano per terra e facevano l'amore, bevevano, s'ubriacavano . . . C'erano quelli che hanno portato della polvere bianca che loro chiamano "boracero", borace vuol dire ubriaco . . . 'sta polvere bianca se la incalcavano nelle narici . . . e invece di tirar su così, (*esegue*) si infriccavano canne nel naso l'un l'altro e (*mima il soffiare dentro la canna*) PlUM! PlUM! "Anche tu! Anch'io! PlUM! PlUM! . . . Vedo Dio! . . ."
"Disgraziati! Vi drogate, bevete, saltate davanti al Signore!"
"Non si fa?!"
"Non si fa no!"
"Non si balla davanti a Dio?"
"NO!"
"Non si fa l'amore davanti a Dio?"
"NO!"
"Non si beve?"
"Beve solo il prete, gli altri stanno a guardare!"
"E non ci si spara le canne?"
"NO! !"
"Ma nemanco una cannetta?"
"NOO! !!"
"Oh, ma che religione di morte è, questa?"
"Non è religione di morte, è religione di vita, di vita! Che quando nel mio paese, nelle mie vallate c'è Gesù che risorge e c'è la santa Pasqua di resurrezione tutti cantano e ballano e sono contenti di grande felicità . . . e cantano delle canzoni dolci che ascoltarle vengono i brividi . . . Ora ve ne canto una di grande tenerezza:

Oh che bello, oh che allegria
è ancora vivo il figlio del ciel
è ancora vivo il figlio della Maria!
Maria vergine è di un gran contento

nessuno di noi ha più spavento
né dei turchi né del gran vento
né del gran vento né del cristian
né dei turchi né dei cristian

"Bello! Bello!" Tutti gli Indios che ballavano "Ancora! Ancora!"
Gliel'ho cantata un'altra volta e l'hanno imparata uguale precisa . . . la cantavano . . . Un po' troppo allegrotta (*esegue lo stesso motivo a ritmo fra la samba e il saltarello*):

"Oh che bello oh che allegria
è ancora vivo il fiol del ciel!

A questo punto ho detto: "Andiamo tutti a Cacioche! . . . Approntiamo le croci . . . No, non proprio tutti . . . solo mille. Per la prima volta andiamo in mille: ottocento maschi, duecento femmine. Voialtri invece ventiquatromila, state tutti nascosti . . . Se c'è bisogno di voialtri vi faccio dei segni e venite avanti . . . avanti coi cavalli!"
Più di cento cavalli . . . tutti andavano a cavallo . . . "Muoviamoci! Tenete le croci alte nel cielo! . . . Mi raccomando: non fate scoppiare le croci!" Che era una mania . . . non potevi dargli una croce in mano che subito loro la pittavano di tanti colori, ci mettevano le piume colorate, ci mettevano delle canne col salnitro con lo zolfo, il manganese, poi ci davano fuoco: PAM! IHAAAAAIII! PAM!
"Non si fanno scoppiare le croci!"
Siamo arrivati cantando davanti a Cacioche. Quando siamo arrivati davanti alle mura grandi di Cacioche, gli spagnoli sono spuntati affacciandosi dall'alto delle torri: "Ehi, guardate! Meraviglia! Ci sono degli Indios, Indios con le croci!, che cantano canti di chiesa! Indios cristiani!".
Dal bastione grande è uscito subito il Governatore e ha gridato: "Chi è stato?! Chi ha dato il permesso a 'sti Indios di far dottrina!". Ho fatto un passo avanti e gli ho risposto: "Io, sono stato io. Signor governatore, mi chiamo Johan Padan, e loro mi chiamano "figlio del sole che nasce e della luna" io non so se ho fatto bene o male a fargli dottrina . . .".
Lui, il Governatore guarda e s'accorge che tutti 'sti Indios cristiani che erano in ginocchio davanti ai bastioni, avevano grandi bacili, dei cesti-canestri zeppi di pezzi d'oro,

d'argento e mucchi di collane. Curioso domanda: "Ma per chi è tutto 'sto oro e tutto 'sto argento?"

"Per te. È un presente che gli Indios fanno a te, signor Governatore."

"A me?! Hai fatto bene a fargli dottrina." Poi si volta ai suoi soldati e dice: "Parlo agli spagnoli: da 'sto momento guai a chi si permette di far schiavo qualcuno di 'sti Indios che sono fratelli nostri in Cristo, sono sudditi nostri, della regina e del re di Spagna! Verranno a lavorare liberi. Sono liberi! Verranno a lavorare tutte le mattine nelle piantagioni . . . liberi . . . anche in miniera verranno . . . obbligati-liberi!"

E tutti gli Indios non capivano bene la connessione tra obbligati e liberi ma erano contenti lo stesso . . . Si sono buttati a bere, a cantare . . . a ballare.

Poi la notte, si sono stravaccati tutti per terra e all'alba, quando la campana corta a ha cominciato a suonare per chiamarli tutti al lavoro, infilarsi in miniera, nelle piantagioni . . . gli Indios erano spariti, non c'era più nemmeno l'ombra di un Indios!

E sono venuti a chiamare me.

Io dormivo ancora, m'hanno afferrato per la gola e m'hanno trascinato davanti al Governatore.

"In ginocchio!—m'han detto. E il Governatore: "Ehi, Johan Padan, furbo tu sei eh . . . hai fatto un po' di dottrina a 'sti Indios, li hai preparati . . . vieni qua a tastarci il polso a noialtri. Come hanno sentito "trabacho, lavoro, miniere" . . . tutti via, scappati. Adesso se 'sti Indios non discendono subito qua, non ritornano in ginocchio davanti a me prima che cali il sole, ti impicco sul pennone più alto! Come scende il sole tu monti sulla luna!"

Prima che il sole scendesse c'è stato il Negro, anche il Rosso e il Trentatrippe che sono corsi a chiamare tutti gli Indios che sono scesi rapidi. Tutti in un momento sono arrivati lì, in ginocchio davanti al Governatore e imploravano dicendo: "Signor Governatore, noialtri siamo pronti a diventare schiavi, ma tu devi liberare Johan Padan, il figlio del sole che nasce e della luna, il nostro Sciamano più caro!"

Il Governatore: "Guarda che dedizione hanno 'sti disgraziati! D'accordo! Voialtri siete liberi perché io ho una parola sola . . . ma lui lo impicco perché ha messo in piedi una religione tutta canti, balli . . . da ridere . . . Blasfemo . . . Impiccatelo!"

M'hanno infilato il cappio al collo e due boia hanno tirato. Mi sono sentito appeso, appeso che montavo in cielo, mi si strozzava la gola . . . ho visto rosso fuoco . . . il cielo che bruciava: "Sono all'inferno?!" No! No! Bruciava il cielo davvero! Tutti gli Indios, venticinquemila Indios che erano discesi con le fiaccole in mano . . . son montati dappertutto, sui tetti, sui bastioni, anche sulle chiese, in cima ai campanili, nelle piantagioni, anche sulle navi! Venticinquemila Indios!

Cinquantamila fiaccole!

Il cielo bruciava! C'è stato il Rosso che ha gridato al Governatore: "Attento signor Governatore . . . se tu non liberi subito Johan Padan, questi ti bruciano tutto! Ti bruciano le piantagioni, ti bruciano i capannoni con dentro tutto il raccolto, bruciano anche le chiese, la cattedrale, ti fanno un falò di tutto il palazzo, e anche delle navi! . . . Dopo ti voglio veder tornare a casa con delle navi di carbonella!"

Infuriato il capitano ha gridato: "Spariamo coi cannoni!"

"No, fermi! E anche voialtri selvaggi con le fiaccole, state fermi, ragionate: voialtri potete mandarmi a fuoco tutta la città, Caciche, quattordici anni di lavoro, ci sono un milione di maravedi dentro . . . tutto brucia . . . ma alla fine quanti di voialtri si salveranno da essere accoppati?

In quanti salterete per aria per le cannonate che vi spareremo? Mille, duemila . . . e voi siete pronti a crepare in tanti solo per salvare 'sto ladrone fottuto? Johan Padan che si fa passare per il figlio del sole che nasce e della luna, per venirvi a rubare tutto l'oro e l'argento . . ."

C'è stato il Cacicco che s'è rizzato in piedi: "Fermo! Signor Governatore, tu da quanto tempo lo conosci Johan Padan? . . . Da adesso! Io lo conosco da cinque, sei anni, e non ci ha mai rubato manco una foglia secca. Gli abbiamo donato ceste e ceste di oro e argento . . . manco l'ha toccato e ha detto: io non voglio fare il facchino! Tu signor Governatore che sei arrivato e nessuno ti aveva invitato, tu sì che sei il gran ladrone! Tu sei arrivato con tutta 'sta gente coperta di ferro e armata, ci hai rubato il nostro raccolto, le nostre terre, il lavoro delle nostre braccia, ci hai rubato gli uomini, le donne, l'oro! . . . e ci hai rubato anche la nostra lingua! Tu sei arrivato tutto baldanzoso con le piume in testa . . . Lui è arrivato nudo come noialtri. Tu sei arrivato tronfio, a cavallo di uno stallone . . . anche lui è arrivato a cavallo . . . ma di un maiale. Lui è giunto qui e ci ha resuscitato in vita gente che era già morta . . . tu metti a morte gente che sta ben in vita! Lui ci ha dato una religione fatta di canti, di allegria, di ballo, di sorriso e di felicità . . . Tu ci porti una religione triste, di malinconia, di morte. In ogni momento ci dici: "Ricordati che devi morire! Sei in vita ma ricordati che devi crepare!" E noialtri ci tocchiamo i coglioni!"

"Basta con le chiacchere!—grida il capitano—Spariamo con i cannoni!".

Gli artificieri, corrono a dar fuoco alle micce, ma le micce sono bagnate e anche le polveri sono fradice di umidità . . . Il capitano grida: "Ma chi è che ha pisciato dentro le bocche dei cannoni 'stanotte?! Fuori i cavalli! Montate i cavalli! I cavalieri pronti sulle loro bestie! Pronti che facciamo la carica contro gli Indios!"

Ma i cavalli, anche tirati con le corde, non vogliono uscire, si rizzavano tirando zoccolate, si rotolano per terra, e scoreggiano anche . . . dalle narici!

"Cosa hanno fatto a 'sti cavalli?" urla il Governatore. (*Fa immaginare un soldato che gli risponde*) "Signor Governatore, ho visto 'stanotte degli Indios che riempivano delle canne lunghe di polvere bianca . . . poi le infilavano dentro le narici dei cavalli, nei buchi del naso e ci soffiavano dentro: PIUM!, li pompavano . . . Ai cavalli piace!" risponde un soldato.

All'improvviso: PA! PA! PA!, fuochi d'artificio arrivano in mezzo alle gambe degli spagnoli, che saltano di qua e di là, corrono.

"Fermi! Fermi soldati! Guardate c'è una cavalleria che viene incontro ad aiutarci! Di chi è 'sta cavalleria? . . . Cento cavalli! ! INDIOS?! INDIOS A CAVALLO COME I CRISTIANI?! . . . Non c'è più religione!"

Tutti i soldati in ginocchio gridano: "Non ammazzateci! Dateci salva la vita! Non ammazzateci! Perdonateci!"

"Un po' di dignità, andiamo spagnoli, davanti a 'sti forestieri di Indios! (*Agli Indios*) Avanti,

legateli tutti, legate gli spagnoli uno a u[n] portiamoli sulle navi! Scaricate tutti i can[n] via! (*Agli spagnoli*) A voialtri spagnoli diam[o] salva la vita a tutti, anzi vi facciamo tornare a[lle] vostre case. Aspettiamo tre giorni e tre notti pe[r] vedere come va il tempo . . . Se il tempo è buono vi facciamo tornare alle vostre isole. Contenti? Bene, montate tutti sulle vostre navi!" La prima giornata è passata . . . la luna normale. Al secondo, normale ancora. Alla terza notte monta una luna grande, chiara nel cielo . . . e tutto intorno delle nuvolette tonde tonde. "Ehi spagnoli, potete partire! Buon viaggio! Via con le vele! Tira il fiocco! Vai con la randa!" C'è stato il Governatore che è spuntato fuori dal cassero e ha gridato: "Ehi, Johan Padan, imbecille! Grave errore hai fatto a lasciarci in vita! Dovevi ammazzarci tutti perché adesso arriveremo all'isola grande di Santo Domingo e come arriveremo là, carichiamo altri cannoni, armiamo altre navi in arrivo dalla Spagna e quando avremo tante navi e tanti cannoni torneremo qui di nuovo sulle vostre coste, vi spariamo cannonate per settimane intere, vi accoppiamo tutti: uomini, donne, bambini, vecchi, i cani e anche le pulci dei vostri cani!" 'Signor Governatore—faccio io—c'è un'antico proverbio delle mie vallate che dice: prima di poter tornare in un luogo dove si pensava di poterci arrivare dopo essere stati in un secondo luogo a prepararsi per arrivarci nel primo . . . dove si voleva arrivare . . . bisogna arrivare al secondo luogo dove di pensava di arrivare a prepararsi per poi poter tornare nel primo!" Le navi andavano, andavano, si allontanavano, stavano per sparire all'orizzonte, e io ho detto alla luna: "Madre! Dagli un bello scoppiettone!" PUAM! Un fulmine grande, un gran baleno, per un attimo s'è visto chiarco, poi il mare è diventato nero . . . altro lampo di luce . . . in fondo, si scorgono le navi degli spagnoli piccole, piccole e intorno a 'ste navi piccole delle trombettine di mare. Ancora dei lampi a squasso! Appresso tuoni che scoppiavano come cannoni, poi onde, onde sempre più grandi che quando sono arrivate alla marina, erano diventate alte come montagne! e dentro 'ste onde grandi c'erano pezzi di navi fracassate e frammezzo, marinai annegati, soldati annegati, capitani annegati, e c'era pure

vice-Governatore . . . c'era
. . . Tutti . . . erano tornati
come otri sgonfiate.
. . . rni e giorni per vedere
. . . spuntare qualche nave
. . . momento che nessuno era
. . . nto Domingo non potevano
. . . indietro. Noialtri abbiamo spianato la
. . . a, la città di Cacioche l'abbiamo spianata,
abbiamo piantato alberi che sono, dopo cinque
anni . . . diventati una foresta. Abbiamo
aspettato undici anni ma gli spagnoli non
spuntavano! Una mattina abbiamo visto il
mare pieno di vele . . . le bandiere erano quelle
di Castiglia e di Leon. Erano spagnoli. C'era
anche la bandiera grande di Panfilo Navael, un
grande comandante, un famoso capitano
glorioso. Quando è disceso alla marina noialtri
Indios eravamo spariti, non c'era nessuno di
noialtri. Sono scesi dalle loro barche grandi, e
poi barconi che portavano anche cavalli e
osservando le carte che avevano in mano,
dicevano: "Di sicuro qui c'è un errore. Qui
doveva esserci Cacioche, ma di 'sta città, in
questo luogo, non ci sta manco un palone! . . .
Andiamo a vedere se Cacioche è da un'altra
parte!" E noialtri nascosti abbiamo visto 'sta
armata grande infilarsi intera nella foresta.
Quando sono stati a metà . . . Quando si dice:
"Se le disgrazie devono capitare, capitano!"
Tutta 'sta armata non arriva in mezzo alla foresta,
che c'è un fuocherello che brucia lì, (indica a
sinistra) poi ce un altro fuochino che brucia là,
(indica da un 'altra parte) poi un fuocone, due
fuochi, tre fuochi, cinque fuochi . . . loro, scappa
di qua per andar di là . . . "Oh, sgomberiamo
dalla foresta! Ci brucia tutti! Fuori! Scappiamo
fuori! AHIAAAIIIAA! "Tutti bruciati! Un'armata
tutta intera al rogo nella foresta . . . Ma guarda
che disgrazia! Dopo due anni arriva il figlio di
Panfilo Navares, Michel Vaschez Navares, più
furbo, più intelligente del padre, si guarda
intorno e dice: "Non mi piace! Non ci sono
Indios che ci vengono incontro com'è
normale . . . Cacioche è sparita . . . Guardate . . .
nella foresta ci sono ossa bruciate . . . non sono
così coglione di attraversare 'sto bosco trappola,
io vado per il vallone!"
Si dirige con l'armata intera verso la montagna
dove c'è il taglio largo del vallone. Man mano
che ci entrano lo slargo si restringe, si restringe e

diventa una taglio profondo . . . una fessura
fonda, strozzata, stretta, e poi gli tocca
camminare tutto di traverso così . . . . . . (mima
una camminata tutta di fianco) che per i cavalli
camminare in 'sta maniera è difficile! Di colpo si
sente il gorgoglio ribollente dell'acqua che
discende . . . un fiume tremendo con onde che
scoppiano che stravolgono ogni elemento (come
fosse l'acqua che parla): "Attenti alla fiumana . . .
occhio che precipito, tiratevi in là, permesso!"
Sono annegati tutti . . . di profilo! Tra padre e
figlio, una famiglia disgraziata così!
È sbarcato anche Ernando de Sòto, il più grande
conquistatore della Spagna. Ernando de Sòto è
arrivato con novecento uomini e duecento
cavalli . . . più importante di Cortez era, con
novecento uomini è arrivato, cannoni che non
finivano . . . e ha incontrato gli Indios.
C'era un cronista che diceva: "Arrivano 'sti
Indios, sono dei demoni! Sono mille, sparano
fuochi d'artificio . . . appaiono all'improvviso..,
ne arrivano altri duecento . . . scompaiono.., poi
ne arrivano cento . . . spuntano dalla terra come
serpenti velenosi . . . brucia la prateria, un fiume
che sbotta all'improvviso . . . una trappola ogni
giorno!" Dopo quattro mesi sono tornati alla
marina tutti. Boia che disastro! Di novecento
uomini e duecento cavalli erano rimasti in
trenta . . . e ventotto erano cavalli!
Allora c'è stato Pedro Menderes de Vies, è
arrivato lui, un capitano con un armata, è
entrato nella piana . . . è sparito! Poi è arrivato
un altro Erige Marco le Cronigador: è entrato
con un'armata. Sparito! Poi è arrivato Luis
Cansel Bavaraos: è entrato, sparito!
Alla fine arriva un'armata che non finiva più
comandata da uno che si chiamava Tristan de
Luna . . . A uno che si chiama Tristano, cosa può
capitare? . . . È sparito! A 'sto punto il re Carlos il
Quinteros V, ha proclamato: "Basta! 'Sta Florida
m'ha rotto i coglioni! Dichiaro queste terre
Floride, terre inespugnabil.! Che vuol dire che se
uno spagnolo cristiano ci mette piede senza
l'ordine mio . . . anche se torna indietro vivo,
dopo lo impicco io, con le mie mani!".
Da quel giorno spagnoli non se ne sono più
visti.
Ha provato qualche francese un po'
sospettoso. . . . ha scoperto delle ossa bruciate . . .
"Pardon!" ha fatto fagotto.
Sono passati quarant'anni, quaranta anni dal

giorno che sono arrivato abbracciato al porco nella tempesta . . . sono diventato vecchio, bianco di capelli, bianco di pelo, ma sono felice, sono contento, sono sano . . . sono innamorato, ho mogli, figli che mi amano . . . ho tanti figli e figlie e tanti nipoti che non tengo nemanco più il conto. Ci sono bambini dappertutto . . . ne incontro qualcuno che nemmeno riconosco: "Chi sei tu? Mio figlio? Oh, guarda! Piacere! Dammi un bacino!"

Non conosco nemmeno i miei nipoti che mi chiamano "Padre! Padre!" . . . tutti mi chiamano "Padre!" anzi "Santo Padre"!

Mi vogliono bene, hanno amore per me, considerazione, non c'è mai terrore, mai paura . . . Se c'è una questione, vengono sempre da me, un disputa-problema, un consiglio . . . sempre io ci penso . . . Rispettato, amato, felice: un re!

L'unica cosa che mi fa nostalgia è l'odore fresco dei vento delle mie vallate, non so da dove arrivi, ma lo sento . . . arriva nel naso, mi svirzola, sento il profumo di quando cuoce il capriolo . . . mi sento lo scoppiettar del mosto dentro le osterie, mi sento il bollire del vino nelle botti . . . il cantar delle donne, il ridere . . . i canti d'amore . . . Oh, i canti d'amore . . . Anche i canti di chiesa mi fanno nostalgia.

Ci sono quei momenti che mi prende uno scoppia-magone che mi si strozza il cuore, il gargarozzo mi scoppia, il cuore mi batte . . . vado correndo disperato nell'amaca . . . stravaccato nell'amaca mi abbraccio la rete . . . due figliole mi vengono appresso . . . mi dondolano . . . ninnano l'amaca . . . mi dondolano piano, piano . . . io chiudo gli occhi e loro mi cantano la canzone del mio paese che io gli ho insegnato . . . proprio con le stesse parole, con lo stesso idioma del mio dialetto . . .

"Oh che bello, oh che allegria,
è ancora vivo il figlio del ciel.
è ancora vivo il figlio della Maria!
Maria vergine è in un gran contento
Nessuno di noi ha più spavento
né dei turchi né del gran vento
né dei gran vento né del cristian!
Né dei turchi né dei cristian".